DEAD CERTAINTY

DEAD CERTAINTY

Glenis Wilson

This first world edition published 2015
in Great Britain and the USA by
SEVERN HOUSE PUBLISHERS LTD of
19 Cedar Road, Sutton, Surrey, England, SM2 5DA.
Trade paperback edition first published 2015 in Great
Britain and the USA by SEVERN HOUSE PUBLISHERS LTD.

Wilson, Glenis author.
Dead certainty. – (Harry Radcliffe series)
1. Horse racing–Fiction. 2. Family secrets–Fiction.
3. Biography–Authorship–Fiction. 4. Suspense fiction.
I. Title II. Series
823.9'2-dc23

ISBN-13: 978-0-7278-8486-2 (cased)
ISBN-13: 978-1-84751-590-2 (trade paper)
ISBN-13: 978-1-78010-640-3 (e-book)

Typeset by Palimpsest Book Production Ltd.,
Falkirk, Stirlingshire, Scotland.

To the one where the honour lies

ACKNOWLEDGEMENTS

Mr Nick Sayers at Hodder & Stoughton. His belief in me and the manuscripts kept me going.

Kate Lyall-Grant and all at Severn House Publishers.

Mr David Grossman, my literary agent.

David Meykell, clerk of the course, Leicester Racecourse, for allowing me to 'do' a murder on his racecourse.

Roderick Duncan, clerk of the course, Southwell Racecourse.

Jean Hedley, clerk of the course, Nottingham Racecourse.

Mark McGrath, former manager, Best Western North Shore Hotel and Golf Course, Skegness.

Bill Hutchinson, present manager, and all the lovely staff at the above hotel with special thanks to Gavin Disney, Dan, Nikki and Katie for all their help.

Sarah at Sarah's Flowershop.

All the library staff at Bingham, Radcliffe-on-Trent and Nottingham Central, with special thanks to Steve and to Rosie for her expertise on computers.

David and Anne Brown, printers and friends for bailing me out – twice – and finding just where chapters twelve and thirteen had disappeared to!

Lois from Crime Readers Group, a savvy lady who gave me confidence at the start.

The police at Skegness and the staff at Nottingham Prison for checking facts.

Management at The Dirty Duck at Woolsthorpe.

Kirsty at The Unicorn Hotel at Gunthorpe.

Vickie Litchfield at The Royal Oak, Radcliffe-on-Trent.

And for all the people who have helped me in whatever way during the course of writing the 'Harry' novels, may I say a very big thank you and have a great read.

'The legacy of heroes is the memory of a great name and the inheritance of a great example.'

Benjamin Disraeli

To the one who has gone before, the great master of horseracing novels, Dick Francis, thank you for all those wonderful reads. I offer my sincere gratitude and humbly follow in your footsteps.

Glenis Wilson

ONE

I can remember the brushwood jump rising, wickedly high, in front of us.

I can remember my uprush of exhilaration as Gold Sovereign soared sweetly up and over.

I can remember seeing, briefly, a horse lying on the grass on the far side of the jump, legs thrashing wildly as he sought to regain his feet.

I can remember Gold Sovereign twisting in mid-air as she tried, unsuccessfully, to avoid landing on top of him.

I can't remember any more.

There must *be* more because now here I am in this hard, high bed facing a blank wall. No long sweep of green turf bathed in golden sunshine stretching away out in front, just a cold, insipid, white wall.

'And that's all you remember?' The white-coated doctor by the side of the bed peered at me over his rimless glasses and scribbled something indecipherable on to his clipboard.

I nodded. And regretted it. Any movement sent out screams of protest around my body. I breathed shallowly and waited for the pain to subside. Deep breaths were out. On its own, that told me I'd got cracked ribs at the very least. But looking down the length of bedcovers, there was a highly suspicious hump of unpleasantness which no doubt concealed a cage. It would be taking the weight off my left leg. A break, possibly, but a tentative wriggle of my toes produced no effect. What then?

I began to sweat.

TWO

Three days later I had a visitor. He was one of thousands who would have actually witnessed my accident.

'Harry, how're you doing?' It was my best friend from childhood, and, incredibly, still my best friend in adult life. He was also my boss. His concern for my welfare was truly genuine and would also, I know, be tempered by concern for my career prospects and ultimately for his own business. Mike Grantley was a much respected and successful racehorse trainer. As his retained jockey, our partnership had prospered and together we had picked some of racing's beautiful plums. Like the Cheltenham Gold Cup.

'You were totally out of it when I came before – twice, actually.'

'Eh?' I didn't recall any visits.

He grinned, more of a grimace really. 'Morphined-up, you were. In a totally better place.'

'Yeah, guess I should have stayed there.'

'What's this then, Harry? Iron man succumbing to self-pity?'

'Three days ago, Mike, I didn't know the verdict.'

His expression turned grave. 'And now you do.' A flat statement.

'Now I do.'

'Too soon, Harry, far too soon. Oh, I don't doubt the doc's a top man but he's used to patching up your average Joe Soap. And that's something you're not.' He wagged a finger at me. Abruptly he changed the subject. 'Anything I can do in the outside world?'

'Pay my telephone bill. That came before I set off for Huntingdon. Can't risk being cut off.'

He nodded. Neither of us needed to mention the reason why. 'Mobile?'

'May not be allowed in here.'

'Ah.'

'Could you just check any telephone messages that might have come through?'

'Consider it done. If there's anything urgent . . . I'll act as proxy, shall I?'

Our eyes met. The message bypassed words but was very clearly transmitted.

'Thanks.' My voice sounded husky but with a suddenly choked-up throat it was the best I could do. A man needed a good friend at times, and never more so than when he was on the canvas. 'And could you check Leo's OK? His cat flap's permanently open and he's frequently away . . . on hunting forages for days . . .'

'Food or females?'

I grinned faintly. 'Both.'

'That cat's got ninety-nine, he'll survive.'

'Yeah, I know, but . . .'

'Stop sweating, of course I'll see him right, might even let him lie on my lap. Supposed to be excellent for stress reduction, aren't they, cats?'

'You, stressed? Give over.'

Mike was the most flow-with-it-all man I'd ever met. I let my gaze travel upwards from my just-above-mattress eye level. Dressed in casual brown slacks, his shirt loosely tucked in at the waist, open-necked, no tie. His face honest, tanned and kind. He had a thick thatch of light sandy hair cut short and blue eyes that twinkled ninety per cent of his waking life. A man you would instinctively trust. He ran a mixed racing yard on the Nottinghamshire/Leicestershire border. Right now, it was in-form and doing very nicely. Up to now I'd been an active part of it and happy to be so.

Mike was a good man to have on your side. The only irritating thing about him was the fact he was almost always right. Throw him a challenge and he enjoyed overcoming it immensely. It was one of his main strengths as a trainer. No amount of setbacks riled him. And in horseracing, setbacks were par for the course. He was renowned for saying, 'Whatever the problem, there's always a solution. For a really difficult problem you just have to dig down a lot harder for a lot longer – or go sideways.'

And how I wished he could be right.

Normally, any crisis, his or mine, was bulldozed with vigour. Like the time his mother sank financially – she was too proud to tell him – and the bailiffs turned up. On Mike's part, a massive overdraft, result instant relief for Mamma.

In my case when Annabel decided she'd had enough of being my wife and gofer (I didn't blame her one bit), and took off with another chap, one with a title to boot, Mike was immediately in there, arm around my shoulders. 'All part of life, Harry. Go hide in your den till the blood stops flowing then come on out to play again.' He'd been dead right then, and I'd endorsed it absolutely.

Now, once again, when I got out of this hospital I'd be taking his advice and heading straight for my own home, or as he described it, my den.

The cottage was a crumbling pile in Nottinghamshire, south of the River Trent. It was truly a peaceful place of safety, my sanctuary in a crazy world. And now Annabel had departed – at least she'd left the cat – one of solitude.

I'd been born there thirty-four years ago, the son of a bricklayer and a cook. I was an only child. My father was killed in a freak gunshot accident whilst out acting as a beater for Sir Percy Minehold, the local landowner. My mother had been distraught. As a couple, theirs had been a wonderfully loving relationship, the kind most people want out of life and don't get.

In her distress, she'd turned to my Uncle George, Dad's only brother. It was a natural reaction. Uncle George and Aunt Rachel only lived a few miles away. George offered solace and sympathy – he was suffering too – and they'd propped each other up.

At sixteen, my head and eyes full of a vision of being the next Willie Carson, my emotional input had been the best I could give, but the state Mother was in, it wasn't nearly enough. I buried my own misery away deep inside. And got on with life. Life at that point was, otherwise, full of hope.

My mother needed someone close at hand, a mature male shoulder upon which to weep it all out. Uncle George comforted himself and her very well, a little too well. My half-sister, Silvie, was born less than a year later.

I dragged my thoughts back to the present and concentrated on what Mike was saying.

'I'm not allowed to be stressed then?' His eyes twinkled kindly at me.

'No, I reckon not. You don't stress, you just bulldoze yourself out of trouble.'

'They've just hiked up the price of fuel. Costs a fortune to fill a bulldozer now. Cheaper if I stress like the rest of humanity.'

I smiled, not widely, but it was expected. He was doing his best to raise my spirits although it would take a forklift right now. I wasn't going to ride again – a gut-wrenching prognosis. But I didn't tell him. Not yet. No sense in both of us lying on the canvas together.

Mike's bulldozer wasn't going to alter anything for me this time.

I hadn't bounced when I hit the turf three days ago and it was for damn sure I wasn't going to bounce back up into the saddle. The doctor's unsentimental, brutally frank diagnosis had been straight facts: cracked clavicle and cracked ribs – I could have told him that myself – severe external bruising, almost certain nerve damage and a shattered patella. I wasn't going to be riding again.

As I'd watched the doctor walk away, it flitted briefly across my mind that my timing in life was seriously out of synchronicity. Had this accident happened two years ago, Annabel would still be with me. But it hadn't and she wasn't. Right now she was a long way away across the ocean on holiday with my lucky successor enjoying the sun and the sights of Malta.

Predictably, outside my ward window, it was stair-rodding down.

Today, what a surprise, it was still pouring with rain.

Mike reached down beyond the dreaded humped bedcovers and retrieved some newspapers from where he'd dropped them on arrival. 'Thought you'd like to keep up with the competition.' They were copies of the *Racing Post*. 'I mean,' he glanced down at my right hand, 'nothing wrong with your fingers and thumb, right? No excuse for not working then.' And he slid a reporter's notepad and a couple of biros alongside the newspapers.

I wrote, with hair-tugging, lip-biting agony, a weekly column about the vagaries of horseracing for one of the big newspapers. Not my favourite pastime, but one which brought in useful additional coffers to add to my tax returns. At the rate my financial commitments flowed out, a corresponding incoming flow was vital.

'I know I'm not your boss when it comes to your wordsmith activities, but since I'm acting as proxy for everything else at the minute, I thought I'd do my job and keep you doing yours. Well, the one you can do with your feet up as opposed to your boots down in the stirrup irons.'

'You're too kind.'

'Aren't I just.' He grinned. 'So don't get too ecstatic and decide you'll write for a living instead of riding. I've a string of horses back at the stable that need exercise, you know.'

'I know.' Maybe I wouldn't tell him there'd be no more riding. Kinder, perhaps, to let the horrible realization creep up on him gently.

'And,' I hardly dared form the question, 'how's Gold Sovereign?'

'Eating up,' Mike said gently, '. . . and going out on the gallops.'

I nodded, relief flooding me that she'd got away without serious injury.

'So,' he slid back his chair, 'stop tying up a bed. Somebody really ill needs it.' He stood up. 'I'd better go – let you get back to ogling the pretty nurses. If you remember anything else that needs doing on the outside, just email or text me.'

I grimaced.

'Eh? Oh, sorry, out of line . . .' He looked chastened. 'Surprising how you get to rely on this modern world's technology.'

'If I need anything important, I'll ring on a prehistoric landline.'

His face lightened. 'That's it. When you've decided, let me know what colour grapes you fancy – red, black . . . green . . .'

I grabbed for one of the pens and aimed a throw at him.

He made it to the door, went through, closed it. Then opened it again and stuck his head round. He had an odd, uncertain look of concern on his face. He stared at me for a long moment. 'Don't drop your hands.'

I grabbed for the pen and he disappeared quickly. I could hear his footsteps going smartly away down the corridor.

Don't drop your hands – a trainer's instructions to a jockey about to ride a race. Basically, translated, it meant don't stop trying before you reach the finishing post – ride it out, give it all you've got.

I certainly intended to.

THREE

'd had a hard morning. As a jockey, I was well used to early starts – they were hard-wired in a way of life. But at least I'd usually had a previous night of total crash-out, deep restorative sleep. This engendered by a day spent in the open air filled with unremitting, relentless physical activity. I did nothing physical in here.

Why is simply lying in bed so tiring? And it isn't the sort of tiredness that begets sleep. The cease.ss. ty-four hours activity of the hospital ensures you're on to a loser in the sweet-dreams stakes. If you do manage to snaffle some shut-eye through total exhaustion in the pre-dawn hours, the ridiculously early start to their day completely does for it.

I'd succumbed to all the indignities inflicted upon me by the diligent nurses, from blood pressure and temperature checks, blood sample taking, needles filled with painkiller inserted into my battered rump through to the dreaded bedpan and catheter bag changes . . . you have to be strong to withstand being hospitalized.

Right now I'd lay money on Leo being stronger than me.

Dutifully, because Mike meant so well, I'd scanned the racing pages and attempted a few scribbled lines in the pristine notepad, but superlative script it wasn't.

Finally, frustrated and fed-up – not with food, I couldn't face the sustenance as served up under the guise of meals – I'd flung down the newspapers and notepad and closed my eyes.

I think I must have drifted off, far from harsh reality and my hospital bed, into welcome oblivion because I was dreaming. A beautiful dream that floated me away to happier times.

Annabel was beside me, stroking my face, honeyed words murmuring something low and soothing. Her perfume played seductive games with my olfactory nerves, replaying memories of our exquisite lovemaking, teasing, tempting.

For the first time since coming off Gold Sovereign I felt drowsily happy and content. Annabel was leaning close to me, kissing me tenderly . . . But my name was being gently called . . . and I stirred, reluctant to awaken and leave the dream behind. My eyelids flickered but the dream was still ongoing. I drifted lightly between sleep and wakefulness.

It was Annabel who whispered my name and I half-opened my eyes and looked up into her lovely face. Maybe they'd given me a hefty dose of painkiller and I was having a great trip.

'Harry . . .?' Her lips brushed my own.

Tentatively, I passed the tip of my tongue over my bottom lip. I could taste the slightly oily sweetness of lipstick. Slowly, very slowly, I risked it and fully opened both eyes. This was no trip, no unsubstantial, ephemeral dream. For a moment I found it difficult to breathe, my heart pounding like a farrier's hammer.

'It's not you, is it? I'm hallucinating, yes? Annabel's in Malta.'

'How did you know that?' The voice was Annabel's, undoubtedly.

I lay and stared at her, the woman who held my heart and always would. It was almost worth the fall, the injuries, the grotesque level of pain just to have her sitting beside me – holding my hand because, incredibly, she was.

'But you're in Malta . . .' I repeated stupidly, '. . . with Sir Jeffrey.'

'Aeroplanes make a nonsense of distance.' She smiled at me.

'You've come back especially to see me?' I could barely believe it.

'Just because we're no longer living together as husband and wife doesn't mean I don't care about you.'

'No?'

'No.' She shook her head gently. 'Of course I still care about you, about what happens to you.'

'Doesn't he object . . . to you coming, I mean?'

'He would prefer me to be there with him, but he cares about my emotional state. He knows I'd be as edgy as a cat stroked the wrong way if I didn't satisfy myself you're out of any possible danger. If you can cope . . .' Her voice tailed away and I knew she'd been talking to the doctor.

I wasn't ready to talk about the outcome of my fall. I changed the subject. 'Mike's got the cottage keys – he'll let you have them. Take a taxi, charge it to me. Can't guarantee Leo will be there to keep you company, though.'

'Dear Leo. I miss him, too.'

A tiny word, *too*, but it carried enormous impact.

I swallowed hard trying to hold in the emotion and the betraying hot prickle behind my eyelids. I must be in a pretty lowered state. For goodness sake, what was it Mike had called me – iron man? What a laugh. I suddenly felt very vulnerable.

Annabel, intuitively reading my reaction, bent over her shoulder bag resting on her knee and produced a bag of grapes. 'Green, seedless, they OK?' She knew they would be; she'd remembered my fondness for green grapes.

'Don't tell Mike you've brought me some.'

She frowned. 'Why ever not?'

I smiled. 'His idea of a joke.'

She placed the paper bag on the narrow table across the bed. Then collected up the scattered pages of the racing newspapers, folded them tidily and put them beside the fruit. She picked up the notepad, noted the pathetic few lines of script I'd dredged up.

'Stop beating yourself up,' she said firmly. 'How on earth do you expect to do any worthwhile work in your present state?'

'How do you know I was beating myself up?'

'Because I know you.'

Our eyes met.

'Time enough to think about work when you're well again.'

I inclined my head in acquiescence.

'What about Silvie? Does she know about your accident?'

I shook my head. 'And that's the way it's going to stay.'

She stared at me. 'Do you think that's fair?'

'Fair or not, it's the way I want to play it.'

Annabel sighed. 'She's not a child. I mean, how long is it now before her eighteenth? Three months? Less?'

I nodded. 'About that.'

'She's a lot stronger than you give her credit for, you know.'

'I'm here to be strong for her.'

'I know you are, Harry.' Annabel reached for my hand and squeezed it. 'And you do know you can always count on me where Silvie's concerned, don't you? It hasn't altered my involvement because you and I aren't together. Any help Silvie needs, I'm only too willing to give it.'

This time I felt the tears fill my eyes before I had time to stop them. Annabel noticed but said nothing, just squeezed my hand again. We sat silently for a few moments. My thoughts were all of Silvie in the nursing home.

'There but for the grace of God, go we,' Annabel said in a low voice.

Her words focused my thoughts back to Silvie's birth. I'd qualified from the British Racing School in Newmarket just two months before and was deferring taking up a job promise from a northern trainer because of my mother's situation.

We had no other relations, barring Uncle George – who was paying a heavy price for his 'comforting' and barred from any communication whatsoever with my mother. He was now living with Aunt Rachel in marital hell.

My mother needed my help, but thinking back, as a sixteen-year-old youth that help must have been pretty minimal. I'd rung for a taxi to get us to the maternity wing of the Queen's Hospital at Nottingham, seen her safely into the nurses' care and then sat it out – alongside the prospective fathers – until the baby was born, which wasn't long. The labour had been over very quickly, an easy birth; everything should have gone on from there perhaps not with rejoicing but with relief that normal life could now resume again.

Except that the doctor had called me in afterwards to speak to him.

Silvie was severely disabled and had Rett Syndrome – no one's fault, just a very short straw she'd drawn in life.

'Harry? You OK? You're miles away.'

'Sorry, just reliving a bit of the past.'

'Hmmm, I see.'

And she probably did. Annabel was a practising psychotherapist in Melton Mowbray. She was very good at unscrambling people's minds, and had a reputation for results. Her diary was always full, mostly from word-of-mouth recommendations. A sure measure of the success she'd made of her life. Apart from her one big mistake – marrying me.

'How did you know I was on holiday in Malta?'

'Sir Jeffrey is hardly your average unknown tourist.'

'True,' she murmured, adding without rancour, 'as your friends in the newspaper world no doubt passed on.'

'I'm not stalking, Annabel, but I still feel somehow . . . responsible.'

Her laughter bubbled up, clear and bell-like. 'Harry, darling, I'm a card-carrying member of the grown-ups. I don't need a minder.'

'I'm still your husband – well, on paper.'

'You had responsibility thrust upon you at an early age and it's a habit. I won't say a comfortable one, perhaps it's not. But until you dig yourself out and change your thoughts, it will still be a habit.'

I thought about a plaque on her consulting room wall that read: 'What you think dictates how you feel.' But responsibility felt right; I *was* comfortable with it.

'What else have you found out, about me, I mean?'

'Is there something?'

She pursed her lips and hesitated.

'Annabel?'

'You're such a practical hands-on type of man, I'm not sure how you'll react.'

'You're not ill, are you?'

'No, no, nothing of the sort – well, quite the reverse, really.'

'Eh?'

'I've just completed a training course.'

'Oh, yes? What sort of a course?'

She gave a quirky little smile. 'Spiritual healing.'

I gaped at her in disbelief and repeated, 'Spiritual . . . healing?'

'It's taken me two years.'

'You mean, "laying-on of hands", that kind of thing?'

'Yes and no. I don't usually place my hands on people, except briefly at the beginning and end of a healing, and then only lightly on their shoulders. And I always ask permission first. They may not want you to touch them.'

'And . . .' I was floundering, '. . . does this, er, healing, work then, without actually laying your hands on?'

She smiled with satisfaction. 'It most certainly does.'

'Right.' I gazed at her, nodding slowly. 'And am I right in thinking you want to give *me* some of this . . . spiritual healing?'

'The fall didn't injure your mental dexterity, did it?'

'No, thank God. But you haven't given me an answer.'

'Entirely up to you.'

'You're offering?'

'Yes.'

'I don't know,' I said slowly. The whole concept felt like a big question mark I couldn't get a grip on.

'Dear Harry,' she smiled sweetly, 'please don't sweat, there's no need. Forget I mentioned it.'

'But I can't do that.'

Right now I couldn't do anything to help myself. I didn't feel in control of my own body. And the helplessness wasn't pleasant. For a brief agonizing moment, I felt what surely Silvie must feel every day of her life, totally dependent upon the care of the nurses in the hospice. How the hell did she stand it? It made me want to cut my own throat. But rationality kicked in. Of course, Silvie couldn't know; she had never known what it felt like to earn her own living, choose a place to live, to look after herself in any way . . . to even walk.

There's a saying: 'What you've never had, you never miss.' Pray God that held true for dear Silvie.

I looked up and met Annabel's eyes and saw the genuine concern in them. What had I to lose? Nothing. What had I to gain? I swallowed any lingering inhibitions.

'I don't object to your hands touching my shoulders at the beginning and the end . . .' I began to smile. 'Or, come to think of it, anywhere else . . .'

Annabel gave a gurgle of laughter. 'Think it over, there's no pressure.'

'I have thought. I'm up for it. I'm up for anything that gives me a bit more of a fighting chance to get well.'

'OK. But first I have to see the ward manager and ask permission.'

'Ethics?'

'Hmm, and good manners and, much more importantly, according to the code of conduct I'm bound by.'

'Serious stuff, then?'

She nodded, wiggled her fingers and said, 'I'll be back in a few minutes. Don't do a runner.'

When she'd left I glanced at the clock. It was five past ten. I had a few minutes now to think about the idea of being on the receiving end of a healing. Did it mean I needed faith to make it work? I'd been brought up C of E, naturally following in my parents' footsteps. They'd been married in church, had me baptized at a tender age, we'd occasionally attended Sunday Evensong as a family, Father had had his funeral at our local church. And, nearly eighteen years ago, Mother and I had had Silvie christened there, too. But as I lay in bed, I asked myself the big question: did I believe in God? Did I have a strong faith?

And I knew the answer was no, I did not have a strong faith. A faith of sorts, yes. Maybe up to eighteen years ago I might have said strong but when Mother gave birth to that innocent baby girl and we realized with horror the extent of her affliction, something within me diminished, was tested and found wanting. If that was so, how on earth could I receive spiritual healing?

In the first place, I'd be a hypocrite and secondly, it wouldn't work. Despite her playing it down, Annabel was keen to give it a go I could tell. It was her new project, maybe she even saw it as a vocation. Obviously she was fully committed to it. She'd invested a precious two years of her life in training. Telling her I'd had a change of heart and mind would be anything but easy but I had to do it.

I eased into a more comfortable position and closed my eyes.

It was a tea trolley rattling along on its rounds that roused me from a deep, peaceful sleep. I yawned and glanced across at the

clock. It read nearly ten past eleven. Reality flooded me. Annabel.
Where was Annabel? Maybe I'd dreamt the whole thing. She
certainly wasn't here. Disappointment, deep and enervating, told
me how much I still cared for her. I'd kidded myself successfully
for a long time I was over her. Now I knew I wasn't.

A green overall-clad lady bustled in with the tea trolley and
effectively burst my self-pitying bubble. I remembered my
mother's words: 'There's always someone worse off than yourself.' After Silvie's birth it had become her daily mantra. At the
time I'd thought they'd have to be going some to be worse than
Silvie, but it seemed to give my mother strength and, even more
importantly, hope, so I'd gone along with it. And gradually over
the years I'd come to realize the truth of her words.

'Milk, no sugar, right, me duck?'

'Spot on.'

She poured tea out into a plastic beaker with a flat spout – all
I could manage lying at this angle – and pressed it into my
hand. As she whisked away through the door one of the nurses
came in.

'Had a good nap?' She fussed with the clipboard hanging
over the end of my bed.

I took a chance. 'What happened to my visitor?' If she said
what visitor I'd know for sure it had been a dream.

'Your wife, Mrs Radcliffe? Well, she gave you a spiritual
healing and then because you were still asleep, she decided
she'd fly off.'

'Oh.' Too late now to say I'd changed my mind and that the
healing wouldn't work. And what did the nurse mean by fly
off? My spirits plummeted. Could Annabel have actually flown
back to Malta and Jeffrey?

The nurse straightened the already pristine sheet and said,
'Drink your tea whilst it's still hot.' She was halfway through
the door when she turned and grinned at me. 'By the way, Mrs
Radcliffe said, "tell him I'm thinking of him".'

I nodded, somewhat comforted. 'Thanks.'

'Oh, yes,' her grin widened, 'your wife also sends her love
and says she'll be in to see you again tomorrow morning.'

FOUR

The journey home didn't take long – twenty minutes or so at Mike's rapid rate of driving – it just seemed a long way to me. For the last five weeks I'd seen little else but four bland walls; now the lushly green countryside and bluest of skies dazzled my eyes and stretched ahead endlessly. My starved senses absorbed the intense vibrant quality with delight. I'd forgotten how beautiful colours could be. It was like relearning basics.

Whereas at an early stage in the hospital I'd been utterly helpless and feeling defeated, now I felt I'd been given a fresh chance at life. Maybe not the life I would have willingly chosen but one I could accept with gratitude – for the moment. A damn sight better than my self-pitying vision of cutting my own throat.

The worst thing was, of course, my inability to ride a horse. And following on from that, my loss of potential earnings.

'I've got you a few essentials in, y'know, bread and cereal, milk, two or three different cheeses.' Mike flashed me a quick smile. 'Got to get you muscled up.'

'You're a mate,' I said, and meant it. He'd remembered my predilection for cheese, something in my racing days I'd had to eat sparingly.

'And I want you to eat it, OK? Don't give all the Danish Blue to Leo. He's like a fluffy bolster on legs. Good job he's not human. What a con cat.'

'He can obviously see through the chain-mail exterior to your soft centre.'

'Huh!'

Reaching the cottage, he swung the Range Rover in at the open gateway and drew up on the gravel drive as close as possible, I noticed, to the front door. A considerate man, Mike.

With two crutches I made a hack job of walking the half-dozen steps and ended up leaning against the windowsill while he unlocked the door. I hitched myself over the step and turned to face him. 'As far as you go, Mike.'

'What?'

'This is where I take over.'

Concern crinkled his face. 'Now wait a bit . . .'

'No, no.' I shook my head. 'Like you said, the essentials are in place. It's up to me now.'

He pursed his lips. 'So, you're going to do it the hard way, are you?'

'Yup.'

'I might have bloody known it.'

I smiled at him. 'On your way, Mike – and thanks. A big thanks.'

Slowly he returned my smile. 'Wait till I call it in.'

We were both laughing as I shut the door.

Nothing had altered whilst I'd been incarcerated; the almost palpable peace and tranquillity that I so appreciated about this cottage folded itself about me. I breathed out a long breath of contentment simply for the blessing of being back, albeit without Annabel.

Awkwardly, I manoeuvred myself across to the Rayburn on the far wall. Mike, ever practical, had ensured it was working which meant in the immediate a hot cup of tea and, later, water for a swill down. Not a bath; my left leg was encased in plaster almost to mid-thigh and was not to be wetted.

A light clatter behind me had me turning round sharply; just in time I caught hold of the hand rail along the front of the Rayburn and steadied myself. A full-throated *miaow*, a floor to shoulder jump and Leo was in one of his favourite positions, rubbing his head against my cheek.

'Didn't take you long to suss I'm back.' I stroked his broad head. 'You pleased to see me, Leo?' He settled into a deep purr that I could feel reverberating through his whole body.

Mike hadn't been exaggerating when he'd said the cat was a walking fluffy bolster. He weighed a great deal more than before my accident. 'My downfall was your gain, old son,' I told him, dropping a teabag into my favourite mug and pouring on the boiling water. He was down on floor level and at the fridge door before I was. He knew the next stage was pouring out the milk.

I filled a dish and put it on the quarry floor. 'Cheers.' I hunkered down on a kitchen chair and sipped the scalding tea appreciatively. It certainly beat the half-cold hospital version.

Later, very slowly, Leo and I made the rounds of the cottage, seeing everything from the piano to the paintings with new eyes. The joy of being home was in itself healing. Mike had done a good job of keeping a watchful gaze on the old place. The lawns had been cut very recently and the interior was dust free. It had even lost the slightly musty smell with which it had sometimes greeted me in the past when I'd been away for a few days racing. The sash window in my bedroom window was partly pushed up and I leaned across the narrow windowsill and breathed in the sweetness of the garden.

I tried to ignore the little voice inside my head which asked the question: 'How on earth are you going to find the money to keep on running this place?' Whatever work I did now would have to be a compromise. Until the plaster came off and the soft tissue had healed, the nature of my work was an unknown. For now, all I had and all I could do was write my newspaper column. But that wasn't going to float the boat. Undoubtedly I'd have to cast around for something else as well. What that would be, I hadn't the slightest idea.

But tonight I wasn't going to waste my long awaited return in a hair-pulling session. No, tonight I was going to be decadent and thoroughly enjoy my homecoming.

Leo had me suddenly oohing and aahing as, claws extended, he grappled up to my shoulder level so he could share in looking out over the garden. He was still purring. I felt like purring, too. And then his body stiffened, the purrs stopped abruptly and stiff whiskers twitched and tickled against my cheek. He gave a tiny, almost inaudible growl. I heard it, though, because he was jammed up tight against my left ear.

I scanned the garden. Immediately below was the back of the conservatory that ran along the whole of the rear aspect of the cottage. A saucy magpie had alighted on the grass and begun strutting along the edge of the lawn. Not a lover of this obnoxious cannibal killer, I gently lowered the cat down over the windowsill as far as I could reach and he leapt the remaining

four feet on to the conservatory roof. 'Go get him, Tiger,' I said
softly.

Right then the telephone beside my bed rang. I dropped
heavily on to the end of the bed, slid along and picked up the
phone.

'Welcome home,' Annabel said. 'How are you both?'

'Both?'

'Leo as well, of course.'

'Of course. We're both mightily pleased I'm back.'

'Best place in the world, home.'

'You're so right. Thanks for giving us a ring. Leo can't chat
right now – he's taking his guard cat duties very seriously and
stalking a predatory magpie.' Her laughter tinkled in my ear. I
ventured a question. 'Where are you?'

'Just closing the consulting room in Melton. Then I'm heading
home, too.'

'Right.' I tried not to think about where Annabel lived now.
A Grade II listed building down a quarter-mile drive between
the stately Poplars. Plus all the trimmings – plus Jeffrey.

'How did you know I was going to be let out today?'

'Mike kindly volunteered the news.'

Mike is an optimist. He's always held the opinion that, given
time, Annabel's pre-occupation with Sir Jeffrey would be bound
to come to an end. Like I said, he's an optimist.

But tonight I felt a bit optimistic myself. 'Any chance of a
healing? Please say if you're tired or have something else lined
up.' I waited and with my free hand crossed two fingers.

'No, nothing on, just a solitary supper; Jeffrey's away in
London.' I felt a rise of excitement. 'But do you think it wise?
Hospital visits are one thing, but an evening visit . . .'

I knew I'd pushed her comfort barrier too far. 'You're absolutely right. Not the done thing, eh?'

'Not that Jeffrey would object, of course.'

Of course he wouldn't. I'd never come across a more milk
and water character. Which is why Annabel was with him and
not me. Life with Sir Jeffrey was safe, secure and, I imagined,
also unutterably boring, the exact opposite to our life together.

'You could send me some absent healing.' I was getting to
know the jargon.

'Yes,' she said uncertainly, 'but I'd prefer to see you because there *is* something else.' I waited, letting the stretching silence act in my favour. 'Look,' she made up her mind, 'Mike sent me an email earlier this afternoon. He asked if I'd call on him as soon as. Apparently, he has some news he wants me to give you.'

'Really?'

'Hmmm.'

'What is it about?'

'I'd prefer to speak to him face to face before I mention anything.'

I let it go. 'So when would you like to come over? Tomorrow?'

'Oh, yes, he stressed it was quite urgent.'

'Nothing to do with Silvie, I take it?'

'No, not at all,' Annabel said firmly. 'If there had been any telephone messages from the nursing home, he would have let you know immediately.'

'Good. As soon as I can get mobile, I'll be going to see her.'

'If you need transport, Harry, I'd be only too happy.'

'Yes, I know you would, my love. I appreciate the offer. But you've got your work . . .'

'I can make time, rejig appointments, you've only to say.'

'Thanks, it's very sweet of you. Perhaps we could, at the end of the week, to suit you, obviously.'

'Surely. Look, I'll call on Mike at the end of morning stables tomorrow, see what little gem he's got for you and then drive over to the cottage. Do a healing, maybe have a spot of lunch. I'll bring the food with me. What do you think?'

'I think that's an offer I can't refuse.'

She laughed. Back on the firm ground of a safe daytime visit she had relaxed and was apparently looking forward to it. 'I'll bring the furry feline something nice, too – probably fishy and very smelly.'

'Charming.' I laughed. 'See you.'

I awoke early the next morning. I'd purposely not drawn the curtains and with the window partly open, the cool breeze fanned its way across the garden and into my room bringing with it the delicate perfume of the flowers. What a pleasure to breathe fresh air after the normally sealed Colditz-like windows at the hospital. As an outdoors person I'd found it almost intolerable. I'd slept more soundly last night than any night in the previous five weeks.

I lay in the blissful luxury of my own double bed, drowsily content. The coming day stretched invitingly in front. The high spot being, of course, Annabel's lunchtime visit. I wondered idly what urgent news Mike had for me. Anything short of a job to boost the falling bank balance wasn't worth getting out of bed for. I was to look back on this particular thought in the coming weeks and wish I had had the gift of second sight. It would have urged me to stay right there, safe, secure and certainly not bored. But I didn't possess second sight.

There was a scuffling and a thump and a dear, familiar ginger cat appeared on the narrow windowsill. He let out a bellow that would have awoken my neighbours, had I had any close ones, before padding across the room.

'And good morning to you, Leo.' He gave me a baleful stare and let out another strident cry. 'Oh, I see, I've got it. You want me to get out of this comfortable bed and get your breakfast, right?' He didn't bother to comment but marched to the door, threw an impatient glance over his shoulder to check I really was getting up and then exited, tail straight up in the air like a flag-bearer in the army.

Down in the kitchen I noticed as I placed two dishes on the quarries – milk and food – that on one side his white whiskers bore a suspicious red-brown stain. Had the magpie met his end? Only Leo knew that. I left him to it and with great difficulty took a scalding mug of tea upstairs to the bathroom. I washed all the parts of me I could reach and prayed for the day I could get rid of my plaster and luxuriate in a bath and shower. But my mood was still buoyantly high from getting home.

Last night we'd spent an idle evening, first watching a particularly good film on DVD followed later by listening to a CD of Mozart. Me lying back in an armchair with a couple of glasses of beer and a selection of nuts, and Leo stretched out on the softest cushion he could find on the settee. A beautiful, peaceful evening that I'd really appreciated – one of the many to come, I'd hoped.

I was glad afterwards that I'd taken the time to appreciate it.

At twelve thirty Annabel's Audi scrunched in over the gravel and I opened the door to greet her. She dived into the boot and emerged with a picnic basket. 'Goodies,' she called. Not the only ones, I thought. Dressed in cream linen slacks, a deep honey-coloured silk shirt with a flimsy tan scarf knotted loosely around her throat, she looked good enough to eat herself. Her long butter-blonde hair was caught up in a casual twirl on top of her head precariously kept in place by a tortoiseshell clip. I felt a most inappropriate stirring accompanied by the urge to release the clip and let the blonde hair fall free. Perhaps Annabel's misgivings about visiting last night had been justified.

'What an excuse for a man,' I said. 'I can't even offer to carry your basket, ma'am.' We stood and smiled at each other. Well, Annabel smiled – mine was more a wide grin. I was ridiculously pleased to see her.

'I thought we'd do a healing before we eat, is that OK?'

'Fine.'

She walked across the kitchen, deposited the food basket on the pantry floor and closed the door. 'It'll be cold in there till we're ready.'

'I've laid the table for lunch in the conservatory. Can we do the healing there? I've shifted a couple of chairs out of the way.'

'Lovely.'

I followed her through to the double glass doors that led out into the conservatory.

'Sit down, Harry,' she patted the back of the dining chair I'd placed in the centre of the room, 'get comfortable. I need to prepare.'

'Right.' Dutifully I sat down and Annabel stood behind me. She had explained to me all about healing whilst I'd been in hospital, and what procedure she followed. I understood that she had an essential sequence to follow before she could begin: grounding, attuning, asking permission and also for protection for us both. It had been an eye-opener to me when I realized what was involved. Basically it was energy healing, she'd explained. Everything, including human beings, is made up of energy and illness was a block in the flow of energy in the physical body. But it also involved the more subtle ones, the emotional, mental and spiritual.

'Take yourself to a beautiful place, a beach, by a river . . . somewhere you feel at peace and happy,' Annabel murmured and placed her hands lightly on my shoulders.

I waited for the now familiar warmth and tingling. Within seconds, the tingling began. At first I felt it around the top of my nose, spreading down through my lower lip, and the palms of my hands before running down my legs. The tingling increased in power and brought a slight discomfort around my knee joint. I could feel the energy running out through the soles of my feet back to the ground. A very deep calm flowed simultaneously through my mind and body and I relaxed into the feeling of peace. As Annabel worked down at all the various joints, I opened my eyes fractionally when she reached my knee. She didn't touch me at all but held her palm a little way in front of my kneecap. The tingling increased tremendously all around the joint. Annabel herself remained motionless with a deep stillness about her, but I noticed that her hand seemed to be rocking back and forth gently in front of the joint.

When she came to see me in the hospital for the second time, I'd tried to put her off, explaining that although I'd fallen asleep the previous day, I'd changed my mind about having healing. Very gently she teased it out of me why that was. Then she'd given me a full explanation of what healing actually was and what it could potentially do. She'd been to see the ward manager to ask permission before she went ahead – and also to ask a crucial question.

'I needed to make sure you had had the bones set, Harry. No way would I have given you a healing if they weren't set.' When I'd asked why, she'd replied, 'Spiritual healing is very powerful energy. It is quite capable of beginning to fuse bones. I needed to make sure yours were already aligned and set in the correct position. If they hadn't been, the healing could have resulted in an inappropriate fusing.'

I'd looked at her in astonishment. 'That powerful, yes?' She'd nodded.

Thereafter I'd readily accepted a healing from her on each of the three further occasions she'd been to visit me. I'd always felt very much better after each session, much calmer, more positive and – a welcome plus factor I'd not expected to feel – a definite increase in my energy levels.

On a mental level, it had me back on track – my depression had totally gone.

I became aware of Annabel putting slight pressure on the top of both my feet. Thanks to her explanation, I knew she was now almost finished and was grounding me – I could have otherwise been left feeling spaced-out. A nice feeling but not conducive to everyday practical living.

She moved around behind me and placed her hands upon my shoulders. I took a deep breath and reluctantly opened my eyes.

'How do you feel?' she asked softly.

'Marvellous,' I told her and it was true. I did.

'Ready to eat?'

'I certainly am.'

'Stay here. I'll carry the food through.'

I moved across to a plump, soft-cushioned cane chair and relaxed back. Until the plaster came off and I could start my exercise routine, there was nothing I could do physically. But by having spiritual healing, I felt I was most definitely already contributing towards my recovery.

It was a very empowering feeling.

FIVE

The goodies carried through on a tray by Annabel were all she'd promised and more. She cracked open a thermos food flask and poured us each a generous bowl of clear vegetable soup, then topped them with tangy croutons. On side plates she'd placed open sandwiches of smoked salmon, and standing to attention in a separate container were a battalion of celery and carrot crudités, together with a creamy dip.

Looking at the expression on my face, she laughed. 'I thought you could stand a bit of spoiling.'

'Am I arguing?'

'Don't you dare.'

'Does Jeffrey get this treatment all the time?'

She dipped a spoon into her soup. 'No. Occasionally, perhaps.'

I paused with my own spoon ready for a second dip. 'This isn't shop-bought. It's delicious. Thank you.'

She smiled at me. 'Glad you like it.'

I put my spoon down and stared at her across the table. 'Why?'

'I like cooking.'

'You know I don't mean that.'

She blushed.

'You wouldn't be feeling sorry for me by any chance . . . would you?'

Always truthful, her blush deepened. 'A little, perhaps. I can't bear seeing you suffer and you've been through an awful lot of pain.'

'I can take pain – have to. The possibility of it goes with the job.'

'I'm aware of *that*,' she said in a low voice, and I was perturbed to hear the edge of bitterness in her voice.

'Sorry, of course you are.'

It was the very reason she'd upped and left me.

'OK.' She stopped sipping the soup. 'Yes, I am feeling a bit sad for you, well, if I'm levelling, and I am . . .' She lifted her gaze and met my eyes. 'I'm feeling sorry for us both.'

The long seconds stretched as we stared at each other. There was no doubt what she meant. Two years too late.

I deliberately broke the tension. 'Annabel, I shall do my damnedest to get back in the saddle again.'

She nodded slowly. 'I expected you to.'

'But,' I ploughed on, 'should it not be possible, I can only accept the final verdict.' She nodded once more and we both continued our meal.

'I went to see Mike before I came today.'

'Oh, yes, I'd forgotten you were going after morning stables. What's he got to say?'

'Well, it's relevant to your last remark.'

'Oh?'

'Have you read yesterday's *Racing Post*?'

I made a face. 'Have to ring the newsagents and renew my order now I'm back. It represents writing work, not my favourite occupation.'

'Hmm.' She stacked the empty soup bowls and nudged a plate of smoked salmon towards me. We started in on the next course with enjoyment – it was delicious. 'Mike gave me a copy to bring over in case you hadn't got one.'

I took a further bite of the wholemeal sandwich and waited, aware of tension in her voice.

She placed the newspaper on the table. It had been opened and folded to a particular page. 'He thinks it could be worth following up. It would certainly fill in the time factor until you've finished with all the hospital physio treatment.'

'You mean, until I know for sure what the final verdict is.'

'Well, yes.' Her eyes, always expressive, were troubled.

'Annabel, don't sweat,' were also her words to me in hospital. 'What the result turns out to be has to be accepted.'

'I know.'

'You really flew over from Malta to see if the healing would work the oracle, didn't you?' I said gently.

'I . . . I hoped it might.'

My heart swelled with love for her. Despite all her personal feelings of antipathy regarding my work and the fact that it had driven a crow bar between us, she had still hoped she might repair me so I could get back on a horse again, with all the attendant risks. 'You're a woman in a million, Annabel.' I laid my hand on top of hers. 'God, I just hope Jeffrey realizes it, whilst you're with him.'

'I intend to stay with him, Harry. He's a good man.'

'Yes, I didn't mean that quite how it came out. I meant I hope he appreciates what a fantastic person you are.'

A scratching of claws on glass drew our attention. The atmosphere lightened immediately. Leo was standing on his hind legs outside the conservatory giving faint, faraway miaows at a volume we didn't appreciate until Annabel had jumped up and let him in.

'Darling Leo.' She bent and scooped him up, cuddling him close and soft-talking him.

I knew I was in a bad way right then because I wasn't just jealous of Sir Jeffrey, I was even jealous of the bloody cat.

Annabel bore him away to the kitchen to sample 'something fishy and very smelly' and I reached across the table for the *Racing Post*. I don't know what I was expecting but what I saw didn't figure in my imagination. Amongst all the newsy items was an article. Mike had drawn red lines top and bottom to catch my attention.

It set out the intention of one of jump racing's top lady trainers, Elspeth Maudsley, to retire from racing after forty-five years under the headline 'Right Time to Retire'.

Originally she had been assistant trainer to her then husband, Victor Maudsley. It had proved a paying partnership. Their stable had produced a gratifying number of runners over the years. After an acrimonious divorce that made headlines in most newspapers at the time, Elspeth had taken out a trainer's licence in her own name and had carried on the business. Her strike rate of winners was again impressive.

'In everyone's life there is a right time to do certain things,' she was quoted, 'and it's time for me to say goodbye to training.' She went on to emphasize that her interest in horse racing was undimmed and she looked forward to seeing her own horses racing, albeit in the hands of another trainer. She'd quipped at the end of the interview, 'A much younger one than myself.' It didn't actually give her age, a lady's privilege to keep schtum, but she must have been mid-to-late seventies.

I'd ridden for her loads of times in the last twenty years. She was a fair-minded, tough lady who expected – and received – respect.

I'd been drawn in and read the article with interest, exactly the reaction the journalist who had written it had been after. But interest apart, why had Mike wanted me to read it? Why send it via Annabel and tell her it was urgent? I could work out the first question easily – Annabel equalled the surety of my reading the intended article – but why the need for urgency? I was pondering on the second when the girl herself, angling a loaded tray, came through the glass doors into the conservatory, preceded, predictably, by a self-satisfied Leo. He leapt up to a padded window seat and proceeded to wash himself meticulously, even behind the ears, which always made me smile.

She placed the tray on top of the newspaper, seemingly assuming that I had, in fact, read it. On the tray were a cafetière, jug of milk and pot of honey plus two mugs – one of them my favourite.

'I didn't think you'd say no to some coffee.'

'You're right.'

She flashed a quick smile, depressed the cafetière and poured out the fresh coffee. The strong aroma filled the conservatory.

'You don't get this service in hospital, you know.'

'That so?' She added a generous spoonful of honey to each mug. I was immediately transported back to the first time I'd invited her here to the cottage. It was early in our courtship and she'd been intrigued as to why I'd laid a tray of coffee and placed a pot of honey on it.

'For energy,' I'd explained as we'd sipped in delicious, exciting closeness.

'Don't get any ideas, Harry. You're rushing your fences.'

I'd laughed outright at her misinterpretation. 'I do hate to disappoint you, but what I said, I meant. At six o'clock in the morning before you disappear into a stable on an empty stomach, a coffee laced with honey keeps you going for about three hours, till you get to eat breakfast.'

It had converted her there and then. She never drank it any other way afterwards.

Annabel handed me my mug and clinked it delicately with her own. 'Here's to your rapid recovery, Harry.'

'Amen to that.'

For a few peaceful minutes it seemed like the last two years had never happened. But I was acutely aware of living in the moment and of appreciating her company to the full. Not for a second did I want to take her for granted.

'What did you think, about Elspeth Maudsley retiring?'

'People do at that age; trainers are no different.'

'Hmmm.'

I drained the last of my coffee. 'OK, come on, Annabel, what did Mike want me to think?'

'What do famous people do, when they are about to retire?' she hedged.

'I dunno. Sell up, go to the Bahamas, write their autobiography . . .'

'You got it.'

'All three?'

'No, of course not, well . . . I'm not sure about the first two, but certainly the last.'

I looked hard at her. 'Please, tell me I haven't got it. An autobiography is, by its definition, something the person in question writes.'

'You know you've got it. Not everyone *can* write a book.'

'I certainly can't.'

'Oh, come now, you write for the newspaper.'

'Not the same thing.'

'It is. They're both non-fiction.'

'But I can't write a book.'

'It's still words on paper.'

We stared at each other.

'Mike sent the paper over with you so you could try and persuade me?'

'Yes.'

'But, I mean . . .' I floundered. 'What put the idea into his head? It doesn't say anything in the article about an autobiography.'

'Apparently Elspeth was speaking to him about the possibility of you doing the writing for her.'

'We're not talking about me being a charity case, are we?'

'Oh don't be silly, Harry.' Annabel stood up and began gathering together the coffee things. 'You said yourself you won't know the verdict about your riding for several months possibly. And you do *need* some work. It would tide you over, admit it.'

'I think you're crackers, you and Mike – no, all three of you, Elspeth as well. I've never done anything like it before. I don't even know if I can.'

'Get started – and find out.'

I struggled to my feet, shaking my head.

'If you don't,' she wagged a finger at me, 'someone else will. Mike told me Elspeth said she'd give you a week to think it over.' She reached up and gave me a quick peck on the cheek. 'Anyway, I must get back to work. I've enjoyed our lunch.'

I was immediately contrite. 'I have too. Thank you for the food, and thank you for coming, Annabel.'

She smiled and gave me another quick, chaste kiss. 'One week, Harry.'

SIX

I let the newspaper lie on the conservatory table until late in the evening. I'd had a scrappy sort of supper, fed the cat and, with no excuse to procrastinate any further, forced myself to pick up the paper. I went into the sitting room and flung myself down with frustration on to the settee.

I read the article again, and then a second and third time. Annabel and Mike wanted me to do the writing – I wanted to about as much as I wanted a second shattered kneecap. Yes, I needed a job, some income and I couldn't earn money from my chosen profession, not now, maybe not ever. Did I even have a choice? There was nothing else on offer. I tossed the paper on to the floor in disgust. Was this what my life had come to?

I stared morosely at the blank television screen and ran through some meagre options: live on savings until they ran out – which, of course, they would do; hope like hell for a miracle so I could get back to riding horses again; sell the cottage – or go and see Elspeth Maudsley and talk about the bloody book.

I had a week.

I struggled upstairs to bed and slept on them.

Unicorn Racing Stables, where Elspeth held court, were about twenty-odd miles from my cottage. On hearing my voice on the telephone that morning, she had immediately said, 'Stay where you are. I'll send one of the lads over to pick you up.'

Now, Darren, covered in pink pimples contrasting sharply with his carroty-red crew cut, drove me through the main gates with impressive pillars topped by stone unicorns and barrelled down the long drive to the stable yard at the bottom.

Elspeth was just coming out of the tack room. A sturdily built woman, taller than average with shrewd blue eyes that bored into you, she had a presence that was almost tangible and commanded instant respect.

'Ha, Harry.' She thrust out a hand and pumped my own. 'Sorry about the fall. Any idea how long you'll be grounded?'

'Not as yet, no.'

'Months, then?' she persisted as we walked over to the house. I nodded. 'Probably.'

'Plenty of time to ghost write my book, then.' She said it with a certain satisfaction.

'Look, Elspeth,' I began, 'we need to talk about it first.'

She stopped in front of the oak front door and unlocked it, ushering me inside.

'Harry, if you weren't going to do the job, you wouldn't be here, would you?' Those shrewd eyes lasered into mine. 'So, let's stop beggering about and get down to what you really want to know. Which is, how much will you be paid?' Her directness didn't exactly have me draw in breath – I knew her as a formidable lady who didn't tolerate fools. All the same it took away my psychological bargaining power.

She took me into the kitchen and proceeded to pour out the already perked coffee. For sweetening, I noticed with a small stab of ridiculously superior pride, she only used brown sugar. Following her down the hall, she waved me to a seat in her office. She plumped down into a black leather swivel chair behind a cluttered desk.

As our discussion wound on, it became clear she was giving me no chance of getting ahead of her. Her decisions on all aspects of the production of the biography had been made and no way were they open to negotiation.

'So,' she leaned back in the swivel chair and let it rock her gently to and fro, 'you know what's on the table, what do you want to do?'

We both knew I didn't have the luxury of turning the offer down – and it was a pretty fair one, much more than I'd expected.

'I've written a column for the newspapers, so yes, OK, I *can* string words together, but honestly that's as far as my writing talent extends. I've never attempted a book before. Are you quite sure you want me to do the work?'

'Oh, yes, absolutely sure.'

'And if I fall off whilst I'm attempting it?'

'You won't.'

'I might.'

'Then I'll leg you back up on to your computer again.' She was smiling, not a warm, comfortable smile, but a complacent self-satisfied one. She knew perfectly well I'd have a bash at it – with nothing else in sight to rely on it was a walkover. I'd give it a good go. The outcome was an unknown.

'One snag, Elspeth. As you can see, I'm not able to drive . . .'

A hand flipped dismissively. 'You can start on my first box file of cuttings, photographs, interviews I gave, etc. I've been seriously preparing the paperwork, since I decided retirement was my best plan. The cuttings are all as they appeared in the press but I'd just chucked them altogether in a great cardboard box.' She laughed. 'One the television came in years and years ago.'

My heart, already down on the polished floorboards, burrowed down below the foundations. It was going to be a bloody nightmare.

Elspeth saw my expression and guffawed. 'Don't look as though you're tied to a railway track. It's not that bad. Like I said, I seriously sorted it all out, about three years ago. That was when I approached a publisher and floated it past him. He snapped at the chance.' She guffawed some more. ''Course, I did hint there'd be some juicy little bits. Anyway, I put every-thing relevant into box files, one for each year since I married Victor and took out an assistant trainer's licence. So,' she broke off and fixed me with a hard look, 'stop worrying – I'm not. It'll be a doddle.'

Whilst I didn't agree with her, I could see it probably wasn't going to be half as bad as I'd expected. 'I'll need to bring my tape recorder over and take you through your early days, child-hood, schooldays, teens . . . family history, all that background material.'

'Make a start on the first of the files, tell me what day you want to do the interview and I'll send Darren over for you.'

She had it all thought through. I capitulated; there wasn't a lot else I could do. We settled for Thursday, three days hence. It would give me time to go through some early stuff and hack out a list of questions I'd need to ask her.

I'd already decided I would visit Silvie on Friday, and nothing on God's earth was going to stop me. If Annabel was tied up I'd just have to take a taxi.

Elspeth handed me the earliest file and what looked like an ancient shoebox. 'Family photos,' she said succinctly. 'Don't lose them.'

'I won't,' I promised.

We were on the point of leaving her office – she'd already stretched out her hand towards the doorknob – when the door was thrust wide open into our faces. We both stepped back quickly.

A man barged in, face darkly flushed and looking for a jaw on which to land his fist. It was Marriot, Elspeth's son. 'You can't be bloody serious!' He swung his head in his mother's direction first, then in mine. He reminded me of an enraged bull. All that was needed was for him to furiously paw the ground.

'All this crap about your *autobiography* . . .' He sneered at her. 'You're going to actually let . . . him . . .' he jabbed a stiff forefinger in my direction, '. . . rifle through all our private papers. Are you quite mad?'

'Relax, Marriot, it's already been out in print courtesy of the newspapers. All I'm doing is setting it out in a book. The journalists made their living out of writing up my life, now I'm going to take a fat cheque off the publisher.'

The flush faded a little, he unclenched both fists. 'Well, make sure it is only the stuff already out in the public arena. I demand you let me read the manuscript before it leaves this house. You hear me, Mother?'

Elspeth's eyes were chips of blue ice. 'I can hear you, but don't forget,' she raised her voice and practically spat the words at him, 'this is my house and I'll damn well do as I please on my own patch.'

The last of the dull pink left Marriot's face, leaving it deathly white. Fighting for control, he marched out of the office, down the hall and we heard the heavy front door crash behind him. I was embarrassed that I'd been witness to the unpleasant scene but Elspeth drew a deep, ragged breath and gained control of herself.

'Ignore him, he's always had a short fuse, gets it from Victor, it's in the blood, genes, whatever.' She walked to the door and swung it open. 'Darren will drive you back. Give me a ring if you can't get here on Thursday, otherwise I'll expect you around nine o'clock, OK?' I inclined my head and she put out her right hand. 'No backing out now,' she warned. 'Shake on it.'

Reluctantly I grasped her hand. 'Thursday.'

'Where to, Guv'nor?'

I'd struggled to climb into the car, belted up, placed the box file in the passenger foot well and perched the precious shoebox of photographs on my knee. 'Back to my place, thanks.'

'Right.' Darren shot a quick glance sideways at the box. 'Anything breakable?' he added uncertainly.

I thought of the way Darren habitually drove and grinned. 'No, only Mrs Maudsley's heart if I damage them.'

He took off in true form, heading for the gates. I wasn't concentrating on the driving – my thoughts were revolving around the job ahead, and I'd taken one of the photographs from the shoebox and was trying to guess at the family line-up.

I could make this as easy as possible or get bogged down with data and struggle. Genealogy wasn't my thing.

Countless thousands logged on to try and trace their ancestors but I found life in the present took me all my time to process and gave me all the problems I was able to cope with. My ancestors – and their then difficulties – were definitely in the past. Any trials and hardships they had faced were over and since there was nothing I could do in the twenty-first century that would help or change any of their sufferings, it didn't make any sense to go backwards. Life was always in the present. Right now my present was throwing up enough difficulties.

By now, we were about halfway home travelling downhill on a stretch of road I'd always enjoyed driving along.

I lifted my gaze from the old photograph in my hands and let the soft green light soothe my ragged nerves. The resistance I'd felt to seeing Elspeth and beginning the biography had used up more nervous energy than riding a full card of afternoon races. I felt shattered.

The high banks on either side of the quiet lane were tree-lined and the foliage extended way above and out meeting the trees' branches on the opposite side. The effect was a dim green tunnel of peace, quintessentially English. I drank in this fugue of respite, grateful to have the initial meeting over with and looking forward to getting home, stretching out my plastered leg and downing a mug of tea.

Darren, by my side, was delightedly giving the blue Nissan full throttle, hugging the gentle bends with the aplomb of Lewis Hamilton. I returned to my perusal of the contents of the shoebox and let him enjoy his power trip.

At the bottom of the hill the road curved sharply to the left. He gave lip service to a tiny touch on the brake then spun the wheel following the grass verge right round.

Subconsciously, I suppose, I was waiting for him to pick up speed again and when he didn't, I raised my gaze from the photograph – a split second before he let out a loud curse. Flooring clutch and brake, he yanked the wheel to the right. The car slewed sideways. The photographs flew from my lap and sprayed all over the interior. I grabbed for the door handle, missed, was flung forward against the dashboard and clouted my forehead with a mighty crack.

In front of us, positioned across the narrow lane, was a massive horsebox, effectively blocking any movement in either direction.

The Nissan's near-side front wing hit the horsebox broadside on with a horrible rending of screaming metal.

We were bounced away, the car fully out of control. With two wheels off the ground we did a juddering twist and seemed to hang sideways in mid-air. It happened fast. No time to think, no time to act. Just a gut-jerking knowledge we were about to get hurt – or worse.

The car flipped over, slammed back down on to the unfor-giving tarmac and rolled. We were strapped inside and we rolled with it. For the first time, I appreciated my plaster cast. It acted like a prop and prevented a lot of movement, anchoring me on the passenger side. Despite both air-bags inflating, Darren, with no cast, wasn't so lucky. His legs were jerked upward and sideways and I heard a bone snap. He gave a thin high scream.

The Nissan rolled once more and stopped. Groggily, automatically, I checked my own arms, legs and collarbone and gave a tentative wriggle of my spine and pelvis. No stabbing pain, no numbness. I licked a run of blood from a cut lip, grimacing at the metallic iron taste. Gingerly, I explored the side of my temple and found an egg shaped lump already forming. There'd be bruising and muscular strain making themselves felt later but I'd been lucky, damned lucky.

Turning as far as I could, I reached out to Darren. My hand met a warm, sticky mess. I felt the blood trickling wetly down my wrist. Struggling to inch myself round, I could see he had hit his head. The impact had knocked him unconscious – a mercy in the circumstances. However, the worst of the blood was pouring from a ripped ear lobe. It looked much worse than it was, thank God.

I looked down to where his leg had been forced sideways and groaned. It was at a crazy angle. There was little I could do, pinned by the inflated air-bags and my plaster cast. We both needed help.

I wriggled in the limited space feeling for my trouser pocket and eventually managed to get my index finger and the second one round the leather case containing my mobile phone. If I didn't look sharp some other vehicle would be coming down the hill and round the corner.

Looking up, I saw with something approaching panic that the car's perambulations had thrown us so far back down the lane towards the junction that we would stand no chance of being avoided. We were invisible to any oncoming vehicle. The first thing they would know of our plight would be when they crashed into the Nissan. My hands were slippery, covered in sweat, as I struggled to get the phone free of my pocket. Without stopping to think, I dialled Mike's number. Please, God, he wouldn't still be out on the gallops. He wasn't.

'Where exactly are you?' His tone was brisk. 'Right, I'm there. I'll contact the police. Hang on.'

My hand holding the mobile dropped in my lap. With a strange detached interest I looked down. Shock, I thought, observing it from what seemed like a long way off. My hand was trembling violently.

Muzzily, I looked to my left. I frowned, trying to make sense of it. The lane ran away between the hedges unimpeded. There was no sign of the massive horsebox that had caused our accident. It had simply disappeared. There wasn't a vehicle in sight.

The lane was completely empty.

SEVEN

'This is getting to be a habit.' Mike shook his head a little without taking his eyes off the dual carriageway where he was doing the maximum seventy miles an hour. 'And it's not one I want to cultivate.'

'What habit would this be?'

'Bringing you back from hospital.'

I tentatively touched the bandage encircling my forehead and hastily dropped my hand. 'For once, I'd have to agree.'

'I mean, it's not as though they serve decent grub and it's such a waste of diesel.'

'At least I'm heading in the right direction – home – not still stuck up in a ward on the third floor like Darren.'

Mike stopped bantering, changed down and took a left off the A52. He slid a quick sideways glance at me, his manner serious now, unlike his normal light-hearted self. 'Was it deliberate?'

'Without proof, you can't say, but yes, I reckon it was.'

His lips tightened. 'A bitch of a thing to happen.'

'I'm damn sorry Darren got caught in the crossfire. One thing having a go at me, unforgivable someone else getting hurt.'

'So, who's in the frame?'

'One for sure – Marriot Maudsley.'

'Elspeth's son? Oh, come on, Harry, what gave you that idea?'

'He was hellishly angry up at Unicorn Stables. But to take it to those extremes . . .' I shook my head slowly. 'We could both have been killed. If it *was* him, there must be something very damaging in the family archives he doesn't want me to uncover and make public.'

'Financially, y'mean?'

'Could be,' I nodded, 'or possibly something very dark.'

'Only one way to find out.'

'Honour my handshake with Elspeth . . . and dig deep.'

'You got it.'

'Rather be riding racehorses.'

'With that on?' He inclined his head towards the plaster cast around my left leg.

I sighed. 'Point taken.'

He jabbed his left forefinger hard into my right biceps. 'Harry, you *will* ride again.'

'Hmmm . . . the jury's still out on that.'

'In the meantime, where do you go from here?'

'Home!' I said it explosively, with great gut feeling. 'I've seen enough of the inside of hospitals.'

'I meant workwise.'

'Sure,' I took a deep breath and calmed down, 'sure, I know you did. The first job will be to scrutinize the contents of that cardboard box Elspeth entrusted to me. And talking of which, what the devil happened to all the stuff, photos, papers, et cetera? I seem to remember I had the box on my knee but when Darren hit the brakes the whole bloody lot sprayed everywhere.'

'I can answer you that. Obviously they won't be in the same right order but they're all back in there. And the box is sitting on your desk at the cottage.'

As a mate, Mike was the best. 'That's a pint I owe you down at The Horseshoes.'

'Oh, yes, I'll call that in.'

And when he'd dropped me at the cottage door, declined coffee or tea saying he'd got evening stables to supervise, I let myself in and found Elspeth's precious box exactly where he'd

said it would be. There was no chance of missing it. My desk
has a tooled green leather top and the box was sitting on it –
bang in the centre.

I struggled through to the kitchen, brewed up and took my
mug and my plastered leg back into the study.

I sat down in the comfy battered armchair and prepared to
put the box on my knee, but at the last moment, it was usurped
by a most indignant ginger cat demanding my attention. Leo
thrust the top of his furry head firmly under my chin and began
purring loudly. His claws sheathed and unsheathed themselves
in their pads as they kneaded into my right thigh – one thigh.
His back legs skittered about on the impervious hard plaster on
my left one. I slid an arm under his bum and gave him a bit of
purchase.

I'm a cat and a dog lover but I'd dispute the dog lover brigade
who claim you only receive love and loyalty from the canines.
Leo was unwavering in his wholehearted loving welcomes and
you could have put money on them.

He never does anything by halves, throwing himself fully
into the moment. Right now he was saying very clearly how
much he loved me and was glad to have me back at Harlequin
Cottage. I reached around him with my free hand and retrieved
my tea from the oak side table. The box and its contents could
go hang for a few minutes whilst our mutual admiration society
was re-established.

In the end it was my mobile phone ringing which called a
halt to our indulgence. Leo, having worn out his pads, was
preparing to doss down but found himself dispossessed of my
knee whilst I fumbled in a trouser pocket for the insistent phone.

'Ah, that you, Harry? You back home yet from that goddamn
hospital?' It was Elspeth Maudsley.

'Hello, Elspeth, yes, just back.'

'Doing all right?'

'Mending.'

'Good. I'm just a little concerned, Harry . . .'

I pre-empted her next words. 'No need to be. Your property's
here, safe and sound. Apparently, Mike Grantley searched
the interior of the Nissan after the crash and picked up all the
papers.'

'What about the photographs? Are they still intact?' There was an edge of tension in her voice.

'Er, yes, yes, I understand they are. 'Course, I haven't had chance yet to go through the box. But it's on the desk. I'm hoping to do so later.'

'Oh, good, I'm sure they will be. You understand that photographs are precious, especially if they are the only ones from way back.' Relief had softened her voice.

'Of course.'

'Well, I'll leave you to settle in. Are you coming over as arranged Thursday? Or shall we say the following Thursday?'

'Oh, the following one. I really need time to go through your papers. I've lost almost a couple of days because of the accident.'

'Yes, sure you have. OK, then. See you a week on Thursday.'

A second later there was a double click and she rang off. I sat for a moment before checking out the number. She had rung me from the landline at Unicorn Stables. However, someone had been listening in on an extension. They had tried to time their replacing of the receiver in tandem but hadn't quite managed it.

I'd have put my shirt on it being Marriot Maudsley. And if I was right, that meant he knew I was back in circulation and resident again at the cottage. It could be I was way off beam casting him in the role of villain but somehow I didn't think so. It added up to an unwanted feeling of vulnerability, something I'm not familiar with. I'd always been in charge of my body – and its many emotions – until now. But with only one leg working, swift defensive action – if needed – was a no-no. Not a happy thought.

'There are times, Leo, my lad,' I said, scooping him back up into my lap, 'when I really wish you were a dog. A bloody big breed of dog, something rather like a Rottweiler.' Leo's tail lashed twice – he clearly wasn't amused – but he allowed himself to be stroked and placated, and moments later was curled up on my knee, purring throatily.

My fridge was full of fresh vegetables and salad plus the freezer was concealing delicious delights but my appetite would have registered nil on the Richter scale this evening. Instead, I went through everything in the cardboard box, reading all the newspaper clippings, but in this first of Elspeth's boxes, there weren't that many.

Childhood and teenage triumphs were recorded: at a gymkhana, astride a fat chestnut pony, wearing a red rosette, aged eleven, being picked to play the lead in a school production when only thirteen, a brilliant school report at fifteen. Miseries, too, were laid bare: failing the eleven-plus exam and being turned down for a place at RADA were two of the major disappointments.

We are supposed to be formed by our childhood experiences and digging into someone's early life was certainly giving me insights into Elspeth's character as a grown woman. It was at this point that I changed my mind about the business of writing the biography. It had changed from hideous, unavoidable graft into something else. Something not exactly riveting but certainly intriguing and interesting enough to stir my imagination and make me think perhaps, after all, I could make a fair job of it.

Although the clippings and papers were a manageable amount, the photographs outdid them by about three to one. I began to understand that edge of tension in Elspeth's voice after I'd laid all of them out on the carpet in date order starting with a totally nude baby laying tummy down on a fluffy blanket – Elspeth herself at two months old. What must her parents have conjectured would be the future of their precious little girl? I doubted it would have been as a hugely successful racehorse trainer. Were they actually still alive? It was possible, just. I didn't know, just as I didn't know anything else about the family history. Not yet.

I placed this first photograph face down in the box and the date on the back stood out boldly in red ink: 1936. I had to give it to her. She had certainly made it relatively easy for me to go through all her stuff. Each photograph had the appropriate date clearly written in red on the reverse. Undoubtedly, she would have filed them in the correct order when she handed over the cardboard box to me. However, since the accident had spewed them to the four corners of the Nissan, they were completely, hopelessly jumbled up. No matter. I painstakingly set about going through the pile, carefully considering the photograph in relation to the family tree before laying it face down on top of the preceding ones inside the box.

Another surprise help was the details of each picture had also been written alongside the date. A tiny potted family archive in itself. I needed a viable starting point and I intended going through each of the photographs tonight filing them chronologically. Tomorrow I'd log on to my computer and come up with a family tree. I'd print off a hard copy and take it with me to Elspeth's next Thursday, get her say so and approval of the accuracy.

As I laid each photograph back in the box, I made a note of it on the ruled pad I normally kept for drafting out copy of the newspaper column. By the time I'd worked through the dozens and dozens of photos, I'd listed out all those that I considered family members with a separate list of friends and acquaintances. It was neither tedious nor boring; instead it had absorbed me completely. So much so that only after placing the last one in the box was I aware of a whiskery, ginger face inches from my own where I was sprawled out on the carpet. Two deep green eyes were gazing intently into my own. Leo supplemented the telepathic message he was transmitting with a loud, bass miaow.

I screwed my head round and took a look at my watch. 'Bloody hell!' No wonder Leo was giving me the evil eye, well, eyes. It was close on midnight. Outside, through the window, the sky appeared black, pretty well devoid of stars. He bellowed again, louder. The volume was astounding considering he was only a cat, albeit a very large one. 'You're quite right,' I agreed with him, 'it is *way* past your suppertime.'

I slid the lid on to the box and, reaching up, put it on the chair cushion being the nearest flat surface. Then I set about peeling myself up off the carpet using my crutch as a lever. It took some doing and I was cursing the idea of getting down there in the first place but Leo wasn't bothered. He wove in and out around my ankles, tail banner high giving encouraging little mews, happy now his objective was in sight. I eventually staggered through to the kitchen and poured out a generous ration of cat food.

'Only the dry stuff tonight, lad. It's too late to indulge you

with anything more tempting.' But Leo didn't appear too troubled. Food was food and he was hungry. Whilst he ate I brewed
tea and when he'd finished I did my duty as doorman and
opened the back door of the cottage. Leo has a cat flap but now
and again he likes the VIP treatment – tonight was one of those
occasions. I suppose he thought being kept waiting four hours
for his meal warranted a gesture on my part.

I left him to his nocturnal sojourn and took my tea up to
bed.

I *think* I locked the kitchen door, but with hindsight, maybe
I didn't.

EIGHT

I t had reached a maximum of twenty-two degrees during the
day, and even now was well above the comfort zone for
sleeping. My bedroom was stifling. I threw open the window
and left the door wide. It was a night for stripping off completely
and lying on top of the sheet, not under it. I did just that.
Relishing the relief of stretching out my legs, I sat propped up
against pillows and supped tea.

I still had little idea about the complexities of Elspeth's family
tree but, come morning, I'd log on to the computer, Branston
– so called for the obvious pickle I frequently found myself in
when using it – and get to technical grips with all the visual
information I'd sorted out.

Being in hospital certainly shielded you from outside concerns
and slowed down the pace, but life came whacking back at you,
seemingly with double the momentum, the moment you were
home. Darren, of course, would still be in that shielded cocoon.

A wave of unwarranted guilt swept me. Undoubtedly it was
because of me he was stuck in a hospital bed. The guilt swirled
and subsided. Stupid to think I could have pre-empted or altered
the situation. All the same, I'd ask Mike if there were any
chance of a ride for the young lad, even if it was only in a
bumper. The kid needed some encouragement. A stable lad's

life is a bloody tough one, I know. I'd been one – the perks were few.

I put down the empty mug and switched off the bedside lamp. To the left of it, the red neon on the radio alarm flicked from 12.18 a.m. to 12.19 a.m. At least there hadn't been a power cut whilst I'd been stuck in hospital so the contents of the freezer should still be edible. Drowsily, I slid down, my head cushioned on the goose-down pillow.

At this point, normally, I crashed out and left the world to go its own way but tonight – no chance. One thirty a.m., and still sweating from the humidity, I hauled myself off the bed into the bathroom and cold water sponged my whole body, minus the left leg. God, that felt better. I returned to my room more than ready to fall asleep. But sod's law was operating and I was still awake at gone three o'clock.

Work was usually an exhausting routine, but always at the end of the day I fell straight into the arms of sleep and notched up a welcome seven hours. Since the first crippling accident I'd managed maybe four, perhaps half-a-dozen good nights. The thought made me want to get out of bed right now and go and muck-out a line of stables at Mike's. Even as the ridiculous thought filled my mind, I sighed at my own absurdity, thumped the pillow and closed my eyes.

And then I heard it – the unmistakable click of the latch being lifted on the kitchen door. Somebody had entered the cottage.

My eyes flew open, then I froze, physically and mentally. At three o'clock in the morning one didn't have visitors – especially visitors who arrived unannounced. Closing my eyes to cut out any visual stimuli, I focused intently on listening for the next sound from downstairs. It could be your common or garden burglar, striped jumper, black mask, swag bag over one shoulder . . . It *could*, but I didn't believe it.

Aggressive attempts on my person were becoming too numerous to be coincidences. Whoever had got inside the cottage, and at this point I berated myself for not checking the lock last night, was not here to pay a civilized social call. Far from it, I imagined.

If I'd been fully fit, both legs working, I'd have been down the stairs three at a time by now, protecting hearth and home, but I was acutely conscious of my vulnerable state. The result of a confrontation right now was the likelihood of even further disabilities to add to my battered body. Assuming, of course, that I was lucky enough to still be alive when my assailant left.

Straining my ears, I must have waited three or four minutes. To me, it seemed like hours, but no further sound disturbed the silence. Maybe it had just been Leo coming back in through his cat flap. And as the time trickled by my red alert diminished. The thought crossed my mind: I'm getting jumpy in my old age. I should hammer the negative trait firmly into the ground. I let my eyelids close and willed myself to relax and let go.

I could hear the distant sound of water begin pattering. It was soothing. Rain? Not forecast. It increased to a gentle *slop, slop* that was very soporific. My imagination drifted into a dreamlike state where I felt I was lying in the bottom of a softly padded boat rocking gently to and fro on the water. It was a lovely feeling. I could even smell the engine fuel. Oh, yes, going on a beautiful trip down the river. At last, sleep here I come.

The next second a tremendous crash reverberated through the cottage accompanied by an ear-splitting squall from an irate cat plus a bellowing of choice expletives worthy of a sailor.

Leg or no leg, I was out of bed and hopping frantically along the landing to the head of the stairs. An overpowering smell of petrol fumes funnelled up the staircase. My heart was hammering its way out of my ribcage and I flung myself down, barely touching the treads, and landed in a bruised heap in the hall. It was pitch dark but I dared not switch on the light. The air was heavy with the stink of petrol: one spark would be all it took to set off a raging inferno.

An angry spitting and growling came from somewhere to the right.

'Leo!' I yelled and crawled across the hall, keeping my nose just a fraction above the floorboards, and into the kitchen. Something heavy and metal clouted my plastered leg. It was a petrol can. Obviously empty, it skittered away, clanking, across the hard quarry tiles.

The intruder had exited through the kitchen door, leaving it wide open and allowing in a beam of moonlight. My eyes were adjusting to night vision and the minimal help of the moonlight enabled me to see across the kitchen. Leo had backed himself into the narrow gap between the sink unit and the Rayburn. His eyes, enormous, vividly green and wild, glared out at me. He growled fiercely interspersed by spits and swears.

'It's only me, you old fool, come on out.' I crawled across the cold quarries and put out a hand to him. 'You're all right.' But he was not to be placated and lashed out with a wide spread paw spiked with four grappling irons. A nanosecond before they connected with my bare flesh, I jerked out of reach. Whoever had entered the cottage had obviously given him a good fright at the least, possibly injured him. Until he calmed down, though, nobody would get anywhere near him. Not without being severely mauled. He'd reverted to the behaviour of his ancestors, feral and fearsome.

I inched away and stuck my head over the doorstep. The freshness of the air was a blessing. I hadn't been aware of my shallow breathing until now and I gulped in grateful draughts of the precious stuff. Leo, being low-slung, would fare better. He needed a lot less to keep his ticker ticking.

As my head cleared with the influx of oxygen, I cautiously lifted my nose from two inches above the stone step until I could comfortably bend my head to both sides and have a full visual check of the driveway and garden outside.

The moonlight pooled along the gravel leaving dark charcoal shadows on both sides along by the hedge. The five-barred farm gate between my drive and the country lane outside was swinging open. Again, I waited, perhaps ten minutes this time, before levering myself upright and feeling around in the hall behind me for my crutch. I hobbled outside, the gravel playing hell with my balance, and went as far as the gate.

I slipped through, keeping tightly to the side of the hedge, and glanced up and down the lane. The moonlight illuminated it somewhat and my night vision was working overtime by now. No vehicle sat parked up, nothing moved. Unless my would-be arsonist had darted from the doorway round the back of the cottage, he'd made a quick get-away. I retraced my steps, closing the big gate firmly behind me.

Once inside the cottage, I grabbed my powerful torch from
the kitchen cupboard and played the beam around the room. The
offending petrol can I pitched out over the step and stood it
upright in the garden, replacing the cap I'd found that had
been lying on the doormat. Moving through each of the downstairs rooms, I flung open all the windows, the front door and
opened wide the conservatory doors to the back garden. It was
black as pitch out there and I didn't fancy scuffling and
fumbling my way between shrubs and bushes trying to find
someone who was by now probably approaching the county
boundary.

I still didn't dare switch on any lights but Leo seemed to
have calmed down and was emboldened perhaps by the torch-
light to belly-creep, very slowly, towards me. Sitting down
awkwardly on the kitchen floor, I patted my good knee.

'Come on, old lad. It's all right. Let's have a look at you.'
He climbed painfully and slowly on to my lap. I stroked him
very gently, soothing away his fears and murmuring encouragement. All four paws and legs seemed to be OK but as my
questing hand travelled the length of his body checking for
tender spots, he stiffened and swore loudly as my hand reached
his rump.

'OK, old lad, OK. You're hurting there, aren't you?' I played
my fingertips gently down both hips and then along his tail. It
felt most peculiar, floppy, way out of line. It was a bridge too
far for Leo. He spun round and sank his teeth into the fleshy
part of my palm. Now I was swearing in tandem. If a bite from
a domestic cat hurt this much, I wouldn't fancy a mauling from
a tiger! Clawing himself off my knee, he took refuge back in
the gap by the Rayburn. His ferocious emerald gaze dared me
to try it again. No way was I going to. Not till I'd downed a
whisky.

Whatever was wrong, a dislocation or maybe even a broken
tail, it wasn't life threatening but it needed attention pronto.
Leo was going to have to submit to being carted off to the vets
to be looked at. A battle of some proportion was about to begin.
I'd rather have been taking my chances of injury riding in the
Grand National.

*   *   *

The emergency vets was way over at Dunkirk, the other side of Nottingham, and by the time the return taxi dropped Leo and me back at the cottage there didn't seem to be that much of the night left. Settling a now dopey and docile cat into his basket, I offered him a saucer of milk from which he condescended to take half-a-dozen laps. His tail, which the vet had diagnosed not as a fracture, thankfully, but a dislocation, was wrapped firmly in half a yard of white bandage. If it had been a fracture, Leo would most likely have had to undergo an amputation – instant Manx. And that would have been a tragedy. Leo's tail was impressive: long, extremely furry and very expressive. We should both have missed its presence. But my relief at the diagnosis did nothing to damp down my simmering anger at the hoodlum who had violated my privacy and caused the cat pain. I left Leo nodding off beside the warm stove and, suddenly aware how shattered I felt, decided to give the stairs a miss. In the lounge there were loads of decently squishy cushions on the three-seater. Added to this the cottage was vulnerable if not actually begging to be turned over – all the doors and windows wide open.

I collapsed gratefully on to the settee, adjusted two or three cushions behind my head and lay back to await the dawn. This time I fell asleep instantly, one thought dominating my mind: whoever had harmed Leo, I intended to track down the bastard. And when I did . . .

NINE

At an indecently early hour I telephoned Annabel on her landline. A sleepy, upper-crust, and grumpy man's voice answered. It was Sir Jeffrey.

'Sorry, I really hope I didn't wake you.'

'You did.'

'I do apologise, I wanted to speak to—'

'Annabel.'

'Er, yes.'

'Hold on.'

There was an unmistakable rustle of bedclothes. I winced
and gritted my teeth. Lucky, lucky sod. A picture of them both
snuggled up intimately in bed burned itself into my mind.
Annabel never wore nightdresses; she always slept naked. Just
the thought of her was arousing me even before she spoke.

'Yes?'

'It's me, Annabel.'

'Hello, Harry. You need me?'

By God, what an understatement. I gripped the receiver hard
and managed to say, 'I'd like your help.'

'Are you in trouble?'

'No, no, not me. Leo, actually.'

'Oh, the darling, what's wrong?'

'He could do with some healing.'

Her voice changed, warmed and softened as women's do
when children and animals are involved. The maternal nurturing
instinct kicking in, probably. It was a very feminine sound,
loving, caring. I swallowed hard.

'We've just got back from the emergency vet over at Dunkirk
and, well . . .'

'He's feeling sorry for himself?'

'Yes.'

'What happened to him?'

'Some bastard got into the cottage during the night. He
dislocated Leo's tail.'

Annabel gave a tiny moan of anguish. 'Oh, no!'

Jeffrey's voice chipped in. 'Darling, what is it? What's upsetting you?'

What he meant was *who's* upsetting you, although he knew
damn well it was me. In his place I'd be feeling the same. What
he *really* meant was get the hell away from her. But Jeffrey
was much too well-bred and polite to lower himself and show
his emotions. What did she see in him? Did he show any passion
towards her when they made love?

I fought down my jealousy.

'Some distant healing would be wonderful if you could send
Leo some.' With Sir Jeffrey lying beside her I dared not ask
her to come over to the cottage. But it didn't stop me really
wanting her to.

'Of course I will. Is he in much pain?'

'No, the vet gave him a jab but I suppose he will be when it wears off.'

'Yes,' she said very softly. 'Don't worry, Harry, leave it with me.'

'Thanks, Annabel, I really appreciate it.' And I meant it. I knew the power behind the healing. I'd been on the receiving end myself.

Replacing the receiver, I looked up the number of an acquaintance who had heroically opted for a career in the fire service. Even as we were speaking his pager powered into action and a second or two later I was holding a dead mobile. But at least we'd swapped the necessary information. On my part, describing the state of the kitchen awash with petrol and on his, the action required to get rid of the noxious fluid. Amazingly, once the fumes dispersed through open doors and windows, which they had, it was childishly simple – simply swill it away.

Obediently, I filled a bucket with soapy suds and grabbed the yard brush. It could have doubled for a sitcom. Trying to brush the petrol over the doorstep with a strong arm action should have had the brush head doing sterling work but since I had one leg in a 'do not get it wet, Mr Radcliffe' plaster, I was hopping about like a flea on speed.

High up on the worktop well out of the battle zone, Leo, in a tranquillized doze in his cosy bed, lay smugly superior watching the entertaining proceedings.

As I line danced and pirouetted and sent a river of water slopping out of the kitchen door, he yawned widely and settled down for a nap. After the night I'd had, I could have done with some shut-eye myself.

Instead, I swabbed and swilled as anger welled up inside at the blatant arrogance of the unknown man – or woman – who had come within a few seconds of firing my home. My precious home, my place of peace and safety. Huh! So safe, both Leo and I could have fried.

I seized a corner of the sopping doormat and hurled it with force out the back door. Its working days were over. Thank God the kitchen floor was still in its original state. Red quarries withstood a load of abuse. Had the floor been wooden, as my fireman adviser had told me down the phone, it would have had to be ripped up and replaced. Wood was absorbent. It would have been a possible inferno only awaiting a lighted cigarette to be injudiciously dropped.

Finally, satisfied the floor was petrol-free, I scrubbed down the wall tiles of any possible petrol splashes. By now the anger in me was roaring and I burned it off in savage physical effort. The result was the tiles ended up gleaming – never before had they been so clean.

I stood surveying the restored kitchen – two hours it had taken me – and I felt the anger die away, leaving me drained. It was indeed a negative emotion. I dropped the cleaning cloth into the bucket. A coffee shot was needed.

I carried Leo, complete with basket, into the conservatory then went back for my mug of strong coffee. We were both sprawled out there a few minutes later when I heard a familiar, loved voice.

'Just look at the pair of you, not safe to be left.' And Annabel walked in. 'How's my gorgeous boy, then?'

My eyes widened in amazed anticipation and I gazed up at this angel who had just materialized, but she swept past me and homed in on a positively smirking ginger cat. He gave a welcoming yowl and rubbed his head against her breast as she cooed and hugged him tight. Lucky sod. What with Sir Jeffrey and now Leo getting all the loving attention, I was definitely surplus. I dropped my gaze to give them some privacy and took a swig of coffee. But at the same time, part of me lit up inside and rejoiced she was here. As far as I was concerned this was where she should be.

'So, what happened?' Annabel transferred her attention to me. A slight frown furrowed the fine brows and the look in her eye said 'no bullshit'. I didn't even try to pull wool. 'So,' she sighed gustily, 'some lunatic tried to torch the cottage.'

I tilted my head. 'That's a fair assumption.'

'And if he'd succeeded, you'd be in the morgue now.'

'Only me; they don't take cat corpses.'

She clutched Leo closer to her. I noticed he wasn't objecting.

Annabel growled with annoyance. It was one of the endearing little habits she had that I found particularly attractive. She could also purr. But that was pre-Sir Jeffrey, of course. The reason I knew was because she'd reserved it exclusively for times spent in our double bed. Annabel was most definitely a feline female. And I loved her.

I wondered if she ever purred for sir.

'Who have you upset? Even a lunatic doesn't put himself to the trouble of spending money buying a can of petrol and lugging it round here without some provocation. Whoever it was intended to finish you off.' Her frown had deepened into grooves across her forehead. She was obviously worried, and I didn't like it.

'At this moment, Annabel, I don't know who or indeed why. But I intend to find out. Please don't worry; I don't want you getting upset. Whoever the bastard is, what he does to me is one thing but when it affects you . . . And I'm not having it. He's not going to win, full stop. So be a good girl and don't let it get to you, OK?'

'Too late, Harry, it's already got to me. Your well-being has always been my Achilles heel . . .' Her voice tailed away. A change of subject was definitely needed.

'What did you tell Jeffrey? I know he wasn't impressed by my ringing so early.'

She shrugged. 'You needed me for Leo. Anyway, he shot off down to London straight after breakfast.'

'Ah, breakfast. I knew there was something I'd forgotten.'

'Haven't you eaten?'

'No, too busy doing the hokey-cokey with a bucketful of suds and the yard brush.'

'Right.' Determinedly, she set Leo down in his basket.

'Whoa there, girl.' I struggled to my feet. 'You're not going to run around after me.'

'We're bloody lucky that you're still actually here, so shut up and sit down.'

She swept out, headed for the kitchen. Leo and I exchanged wise looks. You don't argue with Annabel in that mood.

I sat.

An hour later I was reluctantly waving her off in the Range Rover. Leo missed the goodbyes; he was fast asleep, having received a soothing healing from his mistress.

She leaned through the open window. 'Let me know how he gets on. Don't forget, if you need me, ring on my mobile.'

'Will do.'

Fully fed with a delicious ham omelette under my belt, I went through to my office. I kept reminding myself nobody was holding a loaded gun to her head forcing her to go to Melton Mowbray and Jeffrey. She was going because *she* wanted to. And that was the end of it. I was very grateful to still have her caring loyalty. I had to respect her choice and let her go. I tried to aim a kick at an inoffensive chair leg but hadn't allowed for wearing a plaster cast.

Time to get down to some serious work. Work for which I would get paid. Work that would float my boat, until . . .? Until!

I picked up Elspeth's shoebox of cuttings and photographs and buried myself in the data starting from Elspeth's birth and followed her through babyhood and infancy. I needed to get an emotional feel for the environment she had been born into and lived in during her early years – a pretty privileged one, materially. Not only that, she seemed to have been a very welcome and dearly loved infant. The foundations for her future, notwithstanding whatever was to come later in her life, were deep and solidly laid. Her basic self-esteem and confidence would have been firmly established, a launch pad for leading the kind of life she would enjoy and thrive in, and again, the more I learned about the Maudsley family and Elspeth herself, the more absorbed I became.

My notebook seemed to fill almost by itself as my pencil raced across the pages noting the early situations and circumstances forming the young child's character and personality. And interwoven within were all the people adding to the mix. I began to really understand why there was a national obsession with finding out about your family tree – all the ancestors coming back to life – to entertain, to shock. But the really enthralling bits, I knew, were yet to be revealed in her adult life. I was just building the skeletal shape. All the juicy fleshy bits would come later and, judging from Marriot's reaction to his mother's decision to bare all, some pieces of the jigsaw could prove to be very enlightening – even dangerous.

I stopped writing. The horsebox blocking the road had been dangerous, the petrol swilling about on the kitchen floor had been dangerous – what next? Just what was waiting to be discovered in Elspeth's biography? Undoubtedly it would be something explosive. It had produced an explosive reaction already. And I was the man who was soon to discover and take the lid off this particular gunpowder keg.

My mobile sprang to life and belted out the theme from *The Great Escape*. It was Mike.

'Fancy a pub lunch?'

'Sure.'

'Pick you up in twenty minutes, OK?'

'Fine.'

I switched off the phone and went through to the kitchen, poured a glass of mineral water and downed it. The clock read twelve-thirty. I'd been immersed in the biography for nearly four hours.

Checking on Leo, I found him still sleepy and comfortable. He stretched out a front leg and flexed the grappling hooks he used for claws. A pink cave, edged by sharp, ivory spikes, opened up as he yawned widely. Then he withdrew his leg, and tucking it neatly underneath his body, closed his eyes and went back to sleep. His 'do not disturb' sign was firmly in place. Thank God for Annabel and her healing touch. I assumed the vet's painkiller injection must have worn off by now but it was obvious he wasn't in pain. Sleep would be the best thing for him right now. He didn't need me and my going out would ensure total quiet, allowing him uninterrupted quality slumber.

'What d'you fancy?' Mike flipped the menu over the table. 'And it's my shout.'

'Give over. I'm not a pauper yet.'

We were ensconced in the bar at the Dirty Duck. It's one of our habitual watering holes – the food and drink are excellent and it's a hard to beat location. Belvoir Castle is a stone's throw down the lane and running along by the side of the pub was the Grantham Canal.

Mike had monopolized the conversation from the moment he'd swung out of the cottage drive headed for Woolsthorpe.

One of the yearlings he'd bought the previous year, a bay colt, Harlequin Boy, had outstripped his hopes and, having won a maiden race, was entered for a listed.

He was filled with positive enthusiasm, convinced it would certainly come in the frame. 'You never know, could even win, get some black type,' he'd said, grinning wickedly. The high spirits were infectious and we were both relaxed and looking forward to a good meal. His positive outlook was one of the things I most liked about Mike – a refusal to be brought down by life's knocks.

We'd ordered pork and sat sipping gratifyingly chilled beer surrounded by the most staggering collection of brasses – all so highly polished and gleaming they dazzled the eye. Someone must experience a lot of job satisfaction, after expending a load of elbow grease, to produce such a magnificent display day after day. I'd never been in the Dirty Duck when they'd needed a buff up.

Mike took a gulp of cold beer. 'So, how are things going with the biography? You and Elspeth coming to blows, yet?'

'Not with Elspeth, but very nearly, remember, with the son and heir.'

'Ha, Marriot.'

'That's the one. 'Course, that was before the horsebox incident. I haven't seen him since. However, things have gone on from there . . .'

'They have? Like, how?'

'Like some oik trying to set fire to the cottage in the early hours this morning.' His jaw dropped. 'He didn't get to strike the match though; Leo was acting guard cat.' I laughed at his expression and filled him in.

'Good grief! Poor old Leo.'

'I note your sympathy doesn't extend to asking about the state of my lungs after breathing in petrol fumes.'

'You're as tough as a pair of miner's pit boots.'

'I didn't get any sympathy from Annabel, either. She came dashing over to give him a hands-on healing.'

'A delectable female, Annabel.'

'Am I arguing?'

'No, but it's Leo I feel sorry for.'

'Yes, so do I.' I'd stopped laughing. 'And I intend to find out who did it. Because I'm damn sure they aren't going to stop. Too many coincidences, Mike.'

'Yes,' he nodded, 'if you can call them coincidences. But they're not, though. Have you reported it?'

'To the police?'

'Yes.'

'What can they do? They aren't being paid to babysit me, or Leo, are they? No, I'm just going to have to be a bit more careful. A lot more careful.'

'If you need any sort of help, back-up . . .'

'Thanks. I'll hold you to that. One day I might have to. Against my better judgement, of course.'

'Oh, of course, fully understood.' He downed the last of his beer just as two beautifully presented steaming plates of loin of pork were placed before us. We unwrapped shiny cutlery from inside napkins and didn't allow outside events to dull our appetites.

'By, that went down well.' Mike leaned back against the padded bench seat and reached for a glass of iced water. I was a forkful or two behind him but nodded agreement. It was good food; the Dirty Duck had its reputation to uphold.

The outer glass door of the pub opened and a ragged line of men drifted in on a stream of laughter and chat. They were obviously a party of fishermen judging by their conversation. If they were looking for a cooked meal as opposed to simply a liquid lunch they were going to have a bit of a wait. All the tables were taken. The pub was filled to its customary capacity.

I finished my meal and set down the knife and fork. 'Perhaps we shouldn't linger.'

Mike agreed. 'We'll have a few minutes sat outside by the canal, shall we?'

'Why not? Watch the water, eh.'

We stood up, preparing to leave. Our movement must have caught the eye of one of the men who had just come in. He hesitated, his manner diffident, then straightening his shoulders he walked down between the tables towards us.

I looked up at his approach. I couldn't place the man immediately but I definitely knew him.

'Well then, Harry.' He held out a hand. 'How're you going on?'

TEN

I t took me a few moments to place him, eighteen years is a
long time – people change, grow older or, in his case, old.
He'd changed a lot. Much thinner and his hair was no longer
black but completely grey. Probably caused by all the nagging
I'd no doubt he'd received on a daily basis from Rachel. Deep
creases lined his face competing with a network of wrinkles
that covered his cheeks and forehead. He'd not had an easy ride
since we'd last met.

'Uncle George.' I held out my right hand and grasped his.
'Good to see you.'

He stared hard at me, nodding slowly. 'And it's good to see
you, son. I'm sorry about your loss. Elizabeth was a lovely
woman.'

My mother had died from pancreatic cancer three years ago.
I'd wondered if Uncle George might make the funeral but he
hadn't.

Mike would have attended had he not been abroad racing.
So, it had just been Annabel and me, plus the vicar. I'd decided
it wasn't right to subject Silvie to the ordeal. The slightest stress
had a devastating effect upon her health. Mother's death had
been a merciful release and I wouldn't wish her back to suffer.

'Let me buy you a drink . . . and one for Mr Grantley.'

I flashed a quick glance at Mike. If he wanted a quick exit,
I'd have to fall in with his decision. I hoped not. I really wanted
to talk to Uncle George, fill in a few of the blanks from the past.

'Thanks, make mine a lime juice, though.' Mike smiled. 'I'm
designated driver.'

'A beer would be fine for me,' I said. 'But how about we
take the drinks outside? We can't really talk in here.'

'Right. Got it. You two find a seat and I'll bring the drinks
out.' He headed for the bar.

We wandered outside into the sunshine and sat by the canal
bank.

'Bit of a turn-up after all this time, eh, Harry?'

'Tell you the truth, I nearly didn't recognize him. By God, he's aged.'

'He recognized me – and we've never met.'

'Well, if you will keep having your photo splattered all over the papers . . . Leicester's front runner in the successful trainer's stakes . . .'

Mike hooted with laughter. 'Only when the papers are short of copy. A photo fills in a lot of column inches.'

The pub door opened and we watched Uncle George pick his way across to us balancing a tray of drinks.

'Let me know when you want to get off, Mike. You've got afternoon stables – I haven't.' He must have picked up the self-pity in my voice.

'No, but then,' he grinned slyly, 'I haven't got Elspeth's biography sitting on my desk waiting to be written.'

'Ouch! That's it, stick the knife in a bit more.'

'Any time, mate.'

'Here we are, lads.' Uncle George puffed his way up the bank. 'Help yourselves.'

'Cheers, George.' Mike took the lime juice.

'Yes, thanks, Uncle George.'

'Pleasure.'

'What's brought you to the Dirty Duck, then? Never seen you here before.'

'No, don't get out much really, well, only with the fishing club. That's who I've come with today. We've been to a venue up north, quite a bit farther away than our normal fishing spots. We had lunch at a pub just this side of York. Coming down the A1, the other chaps fancied a beer break before we headed for home. So . . .' He took a pull from his pint tankard. 'By gum, this is good stuff an' all.' He smacked his lips. 'Any road, I wasn't going to put a spoke in the wheel and disagree. Not when it delays getting home.' He looked sideways at me as he said it. I picked up the lead.

'Still difficult?'

'She never lets up.' He shook his head sadly. 'I'm not being disloyal, son, y'understand. Rachel's the first to tell anybody daft enough to listen. Keeps dredgin' it up. Well, it's been nigh

on eighteen years.' He shook his head again. 'At least she lets
me out to go fishing. Reckons only men are stupid enough to
sit on a riverbank watchin' water. Thinks it's safe, y'see, no
women to chat up. As if I'd *want to* . . .' He slurped some more
of the excellent beer.

Mike and I were silent. Mike was probably thinking the same
thing as I was as we looked at the wrinkled, grey-haired man:
any woman would surely run a mile.

A flotilla of Mallard ducks paddled slickly down the canal.
Preened to perfection, their colours were bright and glistening
in the sunlight.

'No cares. Have they?' Uncle George waved his tankard
towards them. His voice held a sour note.

'Oh, I don't know.' Mike pursed his lips. 'A lot of the duck-
lings get pulled under and eaten by pike. Then there're foxes,
poachers, and of course, got to admit it, I don't say no to a nice
bit of roast duck myself.'

Uncle George smiled briefly. 'Aye, son, you're quite right.
We've all got to take our chances an' all.'

Mike's little sally had lifted Uncle George's mood and I was
grateful. I was feeling sorry for the old man. He didn't seem
to have much happiness in his life.

'Well, now we've met up again, we'll keep in touch. P'raps
you and Aunt Rachel might like to come over to my cottage
for supper sometime.'

His eyes widened apprehensively. 'Oh, no. She'd never agree.
It'd only fan the flames a bit more. It's a nice thought and
thanks but,' he sucked in his lips, 'I'll not tell her I've met you.
It'd do more harm than good.'

'OK. I'm sure you know best.'

Neither of us mentioned Silvie, the reason behind his marital
hell.

For a while the three of us sat and supped the chilled drinks,
feeling the sunshine warm on our faces, watching the sunlight
glinting on the water. It was peaceful and relaxing, the perfect
antidote to my hassled and sleepless night.

Until Uncle George said, 'So, how is the poor lass? She'll
be eighteen soon, won't she?'

I'd just taken a long pull of beer. Swallowing it too quickly,

I choked a little. Silvie was a subject I never usually discussed. Except, perhaps, on rare occasions with Annabel, but that was all. It was the way I dealt with the horror and sadness of it. Horror, yes, because every time I visited her it was like seeing her when she'd been born. A ghastly shock compounded with the grim knowledge that she would never get better, would always be in the same totally dependent state for the rest of her life. And it was odds on it would be a short one.

Now, facing the man who was her father, I felt backed into a corner by his questions.

'Look, I really think this is sacrosanct family stuff.' Mike rose to his feet. 'I'll go for a bit of a walk. Eh?'

'You don't need to.'

'Yes, Harry, I do.'

He was trying to make it easier for me to open up in front of Uncle George. I appreciated it. And being on our own would help; I could see the sense in it. But from wanting to talk to Uncle George, I was now seriously getting cold feet.

Mike flipped a hand and walked off down the towpath beside the canal. There was plenty of it. It extended about as far as Grantham.

'Now, Harry. What have you to tell me?' Uncle George fixed his gaze on my face.

'Really, I can't condense eighteen years, all the ups and downs, mostly downs, into a few minutes chat . . .'

'All I'm asking, son, is how is Silvie?'

'Well, the answer to that is she's in exactly the same state medically as she was when she was born.'

'There's no hope, then? Of any possible improvement, I mean.'

'None at all, I'm afraid. Her overall health is very fragile most of the time.'

'Poor, poor lass.' Uncle George shook his head sadly. I saw the glint of tears. I patted his shoulder.

'I think it's worse for us. Silvie isn't aware of how she is, her condition, so it isn't the same. She's never known anything different. She's surrounded by loving care, that's the main thing. And I do think her days are relatively happy – well, as far as I can tell.'

'Do you go to see her sometimes?'

'Oh, yes, I go fairly frequently. Well, I did before I got a smashed up kneecap a few weeks back.'

'Kneecap, eh? Didn't like to ask. Not the best injury a jockey can have, is it?'

'No, it's not. They, the hospital, had to wire it round. They'll pull the wire out when the bones have knitted together.'

'I expect you've a lot of supporting tissue, muscles, ligaments, that sort of thing that's going to take time healing.'

'You're not wrong.'

'And the verdict at the end of all your physio and stuff, have they said?'

'Can't commit themselves, can they? But they've warned me, my racing days are probably over.' I tipped my glass and drank the last of the beer.

'Does he know?' Uncle George jerked his head towards the figure of Mike returning.

'Best he doesn't just now. Not until he has to.'

'I see.'

He probably did. Spelling it out that Mike was my employer wasn't needed. Nor the fact that most likely, in a short while, he wouldn't be.

Mike was nearly back.

'Uncle George,' I said urgently, 'I'd like to talk some more about . . . you know, the past. And about Silvie's future. Could I meet you somewhere without Aunt Rachel knowing?'

'Give me your number, Harry. I'll call you when there's a chance of making it, OK?'

'Sure.' I dug into my wallet and pulled out a card. 'Anytime. If I'm not in, there's an answerphone at the cottage. Or leave a message on my mobile.'

'Right.' He pocketed it just as Mike rejoined us.

'All OK?' He checked his wristwatch. 'Afraid I'll have to make tracks.'

Uncle George stood up and shook hands. 'Very nice to have met you, Mr Grantley.'

'Now, the name's Mike, yes?'

Uncle George smiled. 'Yes. And I hope to meet you again.'

'Bound to, I'd say. It's a small world.'

*   *   *

Mike dropped me off at the cottage on his way back to the stables. He zoomed off to attend to his horses and I remembered I'd a sick cat to attend to.

Leo looked to be in exactly the same position as when I'd left him at lunchtime – curled up, cosy and comfortable in his basket. But the cat tray needed changing. A dead giveaway.

'Looking for sympathy, mate?' He opened his mouth in a soundless mew and stretched luxuriously. His bandage was still securely in place, thank goodness. He'd obviously made no attempt to tug it off.

'What would you fancy – some fresh chicken or a tin of rabbit, hmm?'

He launched himself from the recesses of his bed and wound in and out between my legs. He was even purring.

'I can see you'll soon be back to normal. I'll be sure and let your mistress know. She'll be pleased, too.'

I chopped up some fresh chicken into little pieces and changed his drinking water. 'There you go. Now I'm off to do some work.'

I left him chewing happily and went into the office to telephone Elspeth. She answered on the second ring.

'Hi. Need to take delivery of the next shoebox, Elspeth. And I've a score of questions that need answers. OK?'

It was OK. Would I like to be ready at eight thirty in the morning? I would? She'd send a car.

ELEVEN

A much-battered Metro arrived on time the following morning driven by one of Darren's sidekicks, John. Looking at some of the dents, I wondered how wise it was to be travelling with him, but beggars, especially one with a plastered leg, can't be choosers. And at least he'd got here by eight thirty. Elspeth was efficient; I'd never doubted it – she was an extremely successful businesswoman. Her staff would all have to toe the line – including me.

I pondered on this for a moment as I climbed in. She could have had her pick of ghost writers to do the job, yet she'd chosen me. Must have thought I was up to it even if I didn't. But that was then. Now, I was beginning to think I could actually make a fair fist of it.

Yesterday's afternoon of hard graft followed by burning the midnight oil had helped to change my opinion. The biography was forming up pretty well. I'd run off a hard copy of her family tree back to her grandparents. It consolidated my notes and formed a focus. If Elspeth approved my hard work, we were flying.

John was a lad of few words, plenty of grunts but little conversation. We travelled in silence but it was an easy one. I ventured a question.

'How's Darren progressing?'

John gave a big sniff. 'Dunno.'

The famous stable lads' sniff. It covered all situations and conveyed nothing. One thing John and Darren had in common, though, was the desire to get from A to B in the swiftest time possible. I gave up on the chat and watched the countryside flash past. We were approaching Harby rapidly and it crossed my mind I could very well be stepping into the lion's den should Marriot be at home. After all, it was his patch and I was the interloper. But I didn't have long to dwell on the danger. The journey was over in twenty minutes and we belted in through the entrance gates at Unicorn Stables. John slammed both feet down.

'Can't drive you back, mate. Goin' racin'.'

'Fair enough. What course?'

The sniff again. 'Redcar.'

'Right, have a good day, and thanks.'

I walked up to the big house and rapped on the oak front door. Seconds later it swung open and Elspeth motioned me inside.

'Didn't expect a result this fast. Thought you said you wanted some more time.'

'Well, it's gone rather well. But I'm stuck now because I need to progress through the next phase of your life history.'

She showed me to her office. The shoe boxes were neatly

piled on a corner of the huge desk. I produced the printed out family tree and spread it on the desk top.

'If you could just check I've not made a cock-up that'd be a big help.'

She put on a pair of glasses and pored over the paper. Nodding now and again, she ran a finger down the male line.

'Yes . . . yes, and Marriot's name last . . . Yes, Harry, it's all correct.'

'Great, we're definitely in business. Do you want to read my notes so far? Or perhaps you'd rather wait and read them say, halfway through, or even right at the end?'

'The halfway stage, I think. If there are things that I don't like or simply don't want you to, shall we say, broadcast, you can alter them at that point.'

'Yes, sounds fair enough.'

'Now,' she removed the glasses and fixed me with a direct stare, 'what are these scores of questions that need answers?'

I fished in my backpack and took out a handset recorder. 'If you've no objections, I'd like to switch on the tape so that it records all our conversation. That way, I don't have to scribble down notes as we go along and I can give all my attention to what you're saying. Maybe ask some more questions in addition to the ones I've listed down, should your answers prompt them.'

She nodded compliantly. 'I suggest then that before we start we have coffee and sit in the lounge in comfort. You can plug the recorder into a power point in there if you need to.'

'Actually, it runs on batteries so location isn't a problem.'

She inclined her head. 'Come along then. I've left a tray already laid in the kitchen. Just needs the coffee pouring. Whilst I'm doing that, make yourself comfortable in the lounge, sort out your questions or whatever and I'll bring coffee through, all right?'

'Thanks, Elspeth. Sounds fine to me.'

By the time she returned complete with tray – and jar of honey! – I'd spread out the sheets of questions on the settee and made sure the tape recorder was all ready to go.

'Any idea how Darren's progressing, by the way?'

'Due out of hospital shortly. 'Course, he can't come back

here in the lads' hostel; it's not suitable. I think he's going home to mum until he's mobile again and fit to ride.'

'Pity it happened. I feel bad about that, he was doing me a favour driving me back and look where it's landed him.'

'You shouldn't. Wasn't your fault, was it? He was simply carrying out my orders.'

'No, but if he had been doing his normal job and hadn't been driving he wouldn't be in hospital now.'

Elspeth shrugged her shoulders dismissively. 'Can't let you have John to get you back today. Still, Stan can act as taxi – that is, if you don't mind travelling in a horsebox.'

'No objection at all. I'm just glad of a lift home.'

'Stan's the box driver and he's taking just the one horse to Nottingham races for the three thirty this afternoon.'

I nodded. 'Fine, I'm not worried what time I get home.' And I wasn't. Leo seemed on the mend. He was very resilient. Beneath the bandage that was still in place, he must have been healing rapidly. Sleep was by far the fastest way back to health and animals were intuitively aware of the need. They were far cleverer than humans. Leo spent ninety per cent of his time fast asleep. The other ten per cent was split between trips to his dinner bowl and litter tray.

Elspeth leaned back and sipped the scalding coffee. 'Fire away with your questions.'

I placed the voice-activated recorder on the low table just in front of us.

'I suppose these are all my childhood and upbringing ones, are they?'

I nodded, then added 'yes' aloud for the benefit of the tape. 'What I'd like is for you to not only answer the direct question but, if you could, imagine yourself back as a child and try to remember what emotions you felt. I really want to get inside your skin, as it were, to bring you to life for all your readers.

'The more emotions you can recall at specific times, and also the events that were happening then, will help enormously. Facts and figures are fine, they're very necessary for the structure, but what we're after is the big "R".'

Elspeth took another sip of her drink and raised both eyebrows questioningly.

'Readability,' I said. 'The very best way in this book, because it's *your* biography, is to engage the readers' emotions in tandem, so they identify with the same feelings, the sights you saw, smells, touches, experiences, thrills and, most importantly, any whacking great disappointments. We need to get reader sympathy with you, Elspeth. Hook them in so they find themselves rooting for you. Do you follow?'

'Oh, yes, Harry, indeed I do. I need to have all the men back as little boys fighting to carry my books to school. Plus, all the women as young girls crying with me because I've put on so much weight over the summer holidays, probably because of all the ice cream' – she snorted with laughter at the memory – 'and I can't get into my brand new school skirt for the autumn term.' She smiled slyly. '*That's* the effect you're after, isn't it?'

'Exactly. We want the readers on your side. Think you can do it?'

'You just throw me the question, I'll catch it.'

And catch it she did. I was amazed how much she could remember from the time she was about four.

On her fourth birthday her parents had arranged a party in the garden for their only daughter. A dozen handpicked 'suitable' children had received invitations and the tea was going with a bang in every sense of the word – they'd thoughtfully provided crackers and balloons.

However, when Elspeth's mother had brought out individual dishes of ice cream crowned with a drizzle of honey and chocolate sauce, it had served as a rallying call to the local wasp population. In the furore that followed, as the children batted and flapped away hysterically at the vicious yellow and black invaders, several of the little guests, including Elspeth herself, had gone from spooning in 'yummy mouthfuls' – her words – to being stabbed by fierce burning needles.

'One of the wasps actually landed on my spoon just as I'd raised it to my lips. I'd opened my mouth to lick the ice cream and the devilish thing stung my tongue. The pain was frightful! It made my eyes water and my lips swell up. I just screamed and screamed.'

I sat nodding, unwilling to interrupt the flow of memory, and the tape purred away on the table recording every word.

'My parents had to take me to hospital because my tongue swelled so much. Anti-histamine job needed. And it hurt for days after. Do you know, I haven't thought about that for over seventy years and here you are drawing out all my past.'

'I'll bet a whole lot of your readers will identify with getting stung by a wasp. Whatever age you are, it's very painful.'

She threw her head back and laughed. 'And I've just remembered, we had a wind-up gramophone playing. You know, the sort where you had to place the needle in the groove at the start?' I nodded. 'My father had just put on a record, and it was playing "The Teddy Bears Picnic".' She hummed the first few bars and I found myself joining in; it was contagious, like yawning.

'Isn't it amazing what you have stored inside your head.'

'Just keep it coming, Elspeth.'

For the next two hours we beavered away and I got some excellent copy. The job was turning out to be much easier than I'd ever anticipated.

'I have to stop you now, Harry. Things to do.' Elspeth rose to her feet.

'Of course.' I dragged myself from the comfortable settee and began putting all my stuff away in the backpack. 'Can I take, say, a couple of the other shoeboxes back with me?'

'Help yourself – just don't lose them is all I ask.'

'Scouts' honour.'

Out in the stable yard, Stan was loading the horsebox with racing equipment, sweat scraper, bandages, cooler, horse passport. He spotted me coming.

'Hi, want a lift back to Radcliffe-on-Trent? Elspeth said you might.'

'I'd appreciate one, thanks.'

'No probs. Just have to finish loading up Bloody Sal.'

'Eh?'

'She's the only horse racing today – Scarlet Salvia.'

'Aah.' I grinned. Nicknames for the glamorous horseflesh helped to run stables, rather like policemen using black humour to help them cope with demanding situations.

'Can you manage the cab steps?' he queried with a doubtful look on his face.

'No chance,' I said airily.

'Oh.'

'So it'll have to be the side ramp.'

'Right.' He carried on stowing equipment.

I leaned against the horsebox and breathed in all the intoxicating smells associated with being around horses. OK, some of the smells are pretty pungent but God, it felt good. I'd not realized how much I'd missed my racing life. What I'd do if the patella and ligaments didn't heal as they should and I was permanently grounded . . . I forced my attention away from the depressing image. It didn't do to bring in the negatives.

Down the yard, one of the lads – Stan called him Pete – led out a bright bay from one of the stables. The horse flexed its neck, ears pricked, taking everything in. It had a lovely swinging action as, swishing its tail, it walked towards the horsebox.

'Looking good.' I nodded in the horse's direction.

'Yeah, the lads have a bit on.'

'Pity I can't.'

He laughed. 'You know and I know there's no such thing as a dead certainty with racehorses, even when it looks nailed on. The only dead certainty in life is death.'

'I'll make sure I remember that.'

There was no point offering any help in loading the horse: in my present condition I was a total liability. Not a nice feeling.

Finally Stan had everything stowed to his liking and gave me a hand to scramble aboard. Pete, the stable lad, was sitting inside the cab. In the aisle at the back of the cab there was a lads' seat facing the horses. Unfortunately, the aisle was narrow and had little leg room. I opted to stand and braced myself at the corner for safety. I couldn't see much through the little side windows but I wasn't the one driving. Stan was an experienced box driver and drove very smoothly. Nottingham was a local course and the journey was twenty-five miles max. My cottage was perhaps eighteen miles; we'd be there in half an hour.

'All OK back there?' Stan called through from the cab hatch.

'Fine, thanks,' I shouted back.

The horsebox lurched forward a little and moved off slowly. Scarlet Salvia seemed unaffected by the movement of the wheels turning beneath her hooves.

I thought over the personal moments Elspeth had shared with me. They would bring the writing to life as I edited them into the script. But although she had opened up quite willingly this morning, I'd gained the impression that the memories she'd shared had been ones she didn't mind disclosing.

I was pretty sure that the ones from her teenage years and onwards would be severely pruned back to what she wanted me to know – not the full story at all. But, hey, it was her biography and she was paying the piper – me. So, as long as there was sufficient material, and it was interesting enough for me to weave it into a page-turning read, who was I to argue or demand to be told secrets. And I knew there would be secrets. Marriot's reaction had confirmed that.

'Coming down Harby hill now, mate,' Stan's voice informed me. 'Brace yourself in case I have to slam on.'

'Gotcha.' It was the same spot coming up at the bottom of the hill where Darren and I had crashed broadside into the horsebox. I braced. This time, however, there was nothing in the road to cause an accident and we sailed on without incident.

'Joining the A52 soon,' Stan updated me a few minutes later. 'Sharp left turn, OK?'

'Thanks.' It was considerate of him to prepare me and I leaned into the manoeuvre and then felt the horsebox pick up speed. We were travelling down the Bingham bypass, headed for the Saxondale roundabout. I knew from experience there was likely to be a nose-to-tail job and a wait, possibly a sudden braking. I felt the gears change down as we hit congested traffic. Even so, he had to brake suddenly, and accompanied this by a few rich suggestions directed at whoever had just cut him up, but being prepared, I managed to stay upright.

The box turned left and I returned the favour to Stan. 'In a couple of miles, Stan, there's a left turn, just before you get to the Radcliffe-on-Trent bypass. Leads to the cottage.'

'Ta.'

'Will you be coming back after the race?'

'Yeah, well, about an hour or so, when Bloody Sal's been washed down.'

I thought about it. Stan would park in the special horsebox

park. So would all the other boxes. I was fairly sure the horsebox that caused Darren's accident was a local one. It didn't make any sense to have had it shipped in from a long way away. There hadn't been time; it had been organized pretty smartly. Was it possible that box might be at Nottingham today? Yes, it was quite likely. Only one way to find out.

'D'you mind if I come to the races with you, Stan?'

'Well,' he hesitated, 'I don't suppose Elspeth would mind . . .'

'Don't worry about Mrs Maudsley. I'll clear it with her.'

'OK, then, scrap going home for now, yes?'

'Yes. Thanks. There's something I want to check on at the course.'

'Anything I can do?'

'Might be. Tell you when we get there; it's difficult talking through a wall.'

He laughed. 'Right.'

TWELVE

We made good time getting to Colwick, where the course was situated, but all the same it was a relief to get out of the box and down the ramp. Leaning on the crutches lost its appeal after a while.

Stan and the lad, Pete, needed to take the equipment and the horse over to the stables to await being led to the saddling boxes edging the pre-parade ring. I was back to being a liability right now.

'OK, what was it you needed help with?' Stan tossed me the question but his eyes and attention were elsewhere. He scanned his watch to check on the time. On racecourses it was all about timing. He needed to declare the horse well before the race; too late and Scarlet Salvia wouldn't be allowed to run. I quickly told him about the horsebox I was trying to find. He screwed up his face and shook his head.

'Haven't a clue, mate. That colour box is common as muck. I mean . . .' He flicked the back of his hand towards a sizeable gathering of boxes already parked up and the intermittent convoy on their way in.

'Point taken. I'll just hang around here in case I spot it.'

Stan nodded, obviously anxious to be getting on with the job of unloading the horse. 'Give you a lift back, yes?'

'Thanks a lot, yes, please.'

I stuck my crutches in place and hobbled away to find a better vantage spot to monitor the incoming ragged line of boxes bumping unevenly over the grass. A great many had their trainer's name written across the back which could have proved a massive help except, in the seconds before the crash, the only sight I'd had of the box was sideways on. I wouldn't know if it had a name printed across the rear or not.

Thinking hard, I relived that pre-crash split-second. The side facing me had been the offside. I adjusted my position so that I could view the incoming boxes from that angle. It was unfortunate that the box was painted in the most commonly used colour. But as I considered that, it occurred to me it was no coincidence. The box had probably been selected for exactly that reason – anonymity. Although the Nissan had sustained damage, it had bounced off, rolled over, bounced again; the massive box had probably got away quite lightly. Even so, unless it had been immediately repaired and re-sprayed, it would still bear the evidence of impact.

But there was no way I could hobble around checking all the boxes. For one thing, I stuck out as an oddity with my left leg plastered, and for another that very fact prevented my progress. It reduced my mobility to a maddening and frustrating degree. It wasn't doing my recovery any favours and just lugging the weight around was exhausting.

I looked across to the right of the box park. The stable lads' canteen beckoned. It was an oasis providing sustenance for the ever-ravenous crew of lads. Even more importantly, for me, it was somewhere to sit down whilst I kept up surveillance for the damaged vehicle. And best of all, I didn't need a racecourse pass to get in.

I struggled my way across and opened the door. Directly in front was a service counter but I diverted right and found a vacant table by the window. After a few minutes, I was getting

dispirited by the sheer amount of vehicles painted cream.
Needles and haystacks came to mind.

The canteen door opened and a man came in. He glanced
around, noticed me – noticed me noticing him – and hesitated.

'Carl,' I said, 'how're you going on?'

He walked over. 'Harry.'

'Sit down, take the weight off.' I pushed a chair away from
the table with the rubber ferrule of my crutch. It drew his gaze
down from my face to the plastered leg.

'Heard you'd copped it at the same fence.'

'Yeah, came down on top of you, Carl.'

'Wouldn't know, I was out cold – concussion and a dislocated
collarbone.'

'So how come you're here, at a flat meeting?'

'Helping out the guv'nor.'

'Still with Fred Sampson, then?'

He nodded. 'And you? You're not here helping anybody, not
with that.' He nodded towards my plastered leg.

I made a quick decision and decided to risk it. Carl wasn't
a friend of mine. An acquaintance yes, a jump jockey I saw in
weighing rooms and at racecourses, but not a friend. However,
he was mobile and I wasn't.

'I'm looking for a specific horsebox, a cream one. One that
I'm sure was deliberately planted to cause an accident to the
car I was travelling in.'

He stiffened. 'You what?'

'Hmm. Except I got away lightly. Unfortunately Darren, who
was driving, got injured. He's still in hospital.'

'So what makes you think the box will be here, today?'

'I don't know that it will, just working on a hunch that it's
a local based one. Could be wrong . . .'

'Did you see who it belonged to?'

'No.'

'So, how're you going to recognize it?'

'I figure it will have a bit of damage down the offside.'

'Could have been re-sprayed by now.'

'Yes, it could, but somehow I don't think so.'

He shrugged and stood up. 'Anyway, I've not seen a box like
that. I'm getting some grub.'

'Do me a favour.' I fished out a fiver from my wallet. 'Could you get me some as well, maybe a mug of tea, too?'

He took the note. 'I'm having a grilled bacon sandwich – you want the same?'

'Sure, that'll be fine.'

Over at the counter they were doing a brisk trade. Carl attached himself to the queue and I resumed my checking through the window. There were plenty of boxes to check, an endless line driving past, but none fitted. I was getting more disheartened with every box that rolled by.

Carl came back to the table with mugs of tea and mammoth sandwiches that gave off a gorgeous aroma of cooked bacon. The smell alone was enough to make you feel hungry and raise flagging spirits.

'Cheers,' I said, raising the welcome mug to my lips. 'What runners have you got, then?'

'Princess Delilah, in the three thirty.'

'That's our race, too.'

'So which is it?'

'Scarlet Salvia.'

He buried his face in his mug. 'No chance.'

'Come on, she's favourite. I mean, four to seven, nailed on I'd say.'

'Well, you'd be wrong. Hope you haven't put Harlequin Cottage on it.'

'No,' I laughed, 'no bets on, except the lads have.'

He snorted. 'Tough. Ours'll walk it.'

I didn't want to argue with him. I bit into the sumptuous sarnie and decided my last meal on this earth, if I got the chance, would have to be one of these. Pure heaven.

Whilst I slowly savoured the sandwich, Carl wolfed his hungrily, rapidly disposing of the food, washing it down with gulps of hot tea.

'Got to go.' He pushed up from the table. 'Have to help with the buckets and cooler.'

I nodded. 'See you around. Might even ride in the same race.'

He shook his head. 'Shouldn't think so, not with your injury. Need a miracle.'

'Well, thank you, Carl.'

'S'true though, ain't it?' He set down his empty mug and walked out of the canteen.

I took another bite of my lunch but somehow it didn't taste quite the same. I pushed my plate to one side and settled for the tea.

The television high on the wall showed the runners for the three thirty. Scarlet Salvia was dancing her way round the parade ring giving Pete a hard time. She looked the very epitome of how a racehorse should be, coat gleaming, neck arched, up on her toes. She'd obviously attracted a following; her SP was now backed down to two to five. If she won, there was going to be an awful lot of happy punters – especially if they'd taken an earlier price – and some woeful bookies.

Princess Delilah, in contrast, was sweating heavily, white patches spreading under her flanks making her appear almost skewbald. Her nervous energy loss must be excessive.

Out from the weighing room came the tiny, brightly clad jockeys, their silks a vivid contrast to the emerald green of the turf. The familiar summons 'Jockeys please mount' rang across the racecourse. In seconds, they'd been legged up into the saddles.

The crowd packed in around the parade ring eager to see their selection at close quarters. And probably not a single person actually longed to swap places and be sitting astride one of the horses – except me. If I didn't get a tough grip on my emotions, I was in danger of some serious self-pity. That was unacceptable; it was enervating and totally pointless. Mentally, I shook myself.

The bell rang and the horses streamed from the parade ring and out on to the course.

Princess Delilah took off, jaw angled and set, with the jockey sawing left and right trying to hold her. She had no intention of settling and covered half the distance down to the start bucking, lunging and running sideways, pulling the jockey's arms out.

Meanwhile, Scarlet Salvia was cantering smooth as cream, totally calm and with ears pricked, enjoying herself hugely. All the other horses were going down to the starting stalls in a collected fashion and, if I'd had to give an opinion, I'd have said Princess Delilah would end up as back marker. Why Carl had been so sure his horse would take the race was a mystery. The energy she'd expended before she'd even reached the start must have completely negated any chance she might have had.

I watched them all going into the stalls. Carl's horse, predictably, was still playing up and had to be blindfolded and it took the efforts of four stall-handlers to get her loaded.

There were just eight horses in the race and they left the stalls as one, lunging forward eager to be doing the job they'd been born for – racing. And racing to win.

I glanced at the lads lounging around and seated at other tables. Like myself, they appeared to think the race was sown up and would go to the favourite with Princess Delilah tailing off.

We were wrong. The race, all two minutes or so of it, was dominated by Delilah. She pulled away from the other seven runners and only in the last furlong did she begin to tire. Scarlet Salvia was leading the rest of the pack and, scenting the leader weakening, made a supreme effort and drew level upsides, but with the post coming up fast, Princess Delilah held on and won by a short head. A loud collective groan rang out around the canteen. It was clear that a good deal of the lads' weekly pay had been wagered on the favourite.

Princess Delilah would almost certainly find herself in the dope testing box but I doubted they would find anything. The horse had phenomenal stamina, of that there was no doubt.

But Elspeth was not going to be amused. She'd expected her horse to win easily – coming second was not good enough. Like the first man on the moon, everybody remembered him. But as to the second man, how many could even name him? No, Elspeth wasn't going to be pleased. I was quite relieved the interview had been held this morning and not later after the racing. I could drop off at the cottage and let Stan and Pete make the journey back to Unicorn Stables and face Her Ladyship without me.

I unlocked the cottage door, walked in and let the backpack slide from my shoulders. The peace of the cottage wrapped itself around me. Nobody had attempted to break in nor violate my home during my absence, thank God.

I made a mug of tea, checked on Leo – still sleeping – collected up my mail and backpack and went through to the office. There was just one message on the answer phone. Uncle George had telephoned whilst I was out playing silly buggers chasing a non-existent horsebox. I downed half the tea and then called him back.

'Hi, Uncle George. Just found your message.'

He seemed pleased to hear from me. 'It was good to see you the other day. How're you going on?'

'Fine, and yourself?'

'I'm OK, when I put my earplugs in.' He chuckled. 'Just kidding. It's not bad really, when she's got the lead short and tight and she can see me.'

'So, where do we meet when the lead's loose?'

'How about a halfway pub?'

'No can do, can't drive, well, not till after next week.'

'What happens then?'

'Hopefully the plaster comes off.'

'Oh, sorry, of course, stupid of me. So how about I drive over, pick you up and we go to your local?'

'Sounds fine. When?'

'It'll have to be Friday. Rachel has her hair done on Fridays, after she's had lunch with her sister.'

I thought quickly. Annabel had offered to take me over to see Silvie at the care home on Friday.

'I was going over to see Silvie this coming Friday, Uncle George. How about you join me?' The phone was silent. 'Uncle George?'

'I heard you, Harry. I'm sorry, son, but no, I'm not doing that.'

'Come on, Uncle George. You were asking after her well-being at the Dirty Duck.'

'Yes, well, that was because she's Elizabeth's child and I wanted to know.'

It was my turn to say nothing. The silence stretched. 'What exactly are you saying?'

'I'm saying you and I should meet up. Have a beer and a

chat, face to face.' His voice hardened. 'But not over a telephone, OK?'

'Right.' I found my fingers were gripping the phone harder than they needed to. 'But not this Friday. I must go and see Silvie.'

'Can't you put it off, this visit?'

'No,' I said shortly, irritated. 'No way.'

'Give me a ring next week then, eh? We'll fix a time for me to pick you up.'

'Will do. Bye, Uncle George.'

I replaced the phone and stood staring at it. The conversation bothered me. Not so much what he had said but rather what he hadn't. Maybe it would all become clear next week. And maybe I wasn't going to like what I heard.

I drank the rest of my tea in one gulp. It had gone cold.

THIRTEEN

On Friday a discreet double toot of a car horn outside on the drive had me glancing out of the cottage window. A powerful cream Jaguar had just drawn up. I didn't recognize the car but I knew the driver intimately – Annabel.

I'd hobbled down to the gate earlier and hooked it back so that she could drive straight in without having to get out. She'd thoughtfully driven up over the gravel as close as possible to the cottage. I went out, locked the door behind me and clambered in.

'Morning, Harry. Glorious day.'

'Definitely. What's with the car?'

'I thought Jeffrey's Jag would be easier for you to get into.' She smiled. 'Thanks for opening the gate. That was very considerate.' As she spoke she slid into reverse gear and backed out.

'I appreciate the lift.' I patted the dashboard. 'Some car, eh? What does Jeffrey think to you nicking it to tote me around?'

'Doesn't know,' she said cheerfully. 'He's away in Brussels. Anyway, he doesn't need transport – you do.'

'Simple as.'

'Exactly.' She flashed me one of her Julia Roberts eat-your-heart-out smiles. 'So, how's my gorgeous boy?'

I frowned, pretending I didn't know who she was talking about. 'Are you referring to me?'

'You're not my gorgeous boy.'

I sighed. 'What a shame.'

'He is all right, isn't he?'

'I've taken out an overdraft to pay for all the first-class food he's guzzling and he's sleeping for England. Satisfied?'

She smirked. 'Great.'

I suddenly twigged. 'Have you been sending Leo absent healing?'

She nodded, swung the Jag on to the A46 and barrelled along towards Newark. 'Morning and night.'

'Thanks. It's working.'

'Oh, I know it does.'

A thought crossed my mind. 'Have you ever tried it on racehorses?'

'Not so far.'

'But you could?' I persisted.

'Yes. Anything alive benefits – humans, animals, plants.'

'Amazing.'

'Not really, we're all made up of energy, the scientists have proved it, and that's what spiritual healing is, loving healing energy.'

'I'm glad you studied and qualified. It kind of suits you, complements your caring nature.'

'Oh, give over.'

'Do you send me absent healing?'

She smiled gently. 'But of course—'

We finished the sentence together: 'Morning and night.'

'Does he know?'

'Jeffrey? No, he doesn't. He's a generous man. He allows me all the personal space I need.'

'Did I?'

She gave me a quick glance. 'When we were married, do you mean?'

I twisted in my seat within the confines of my seat belt and plaster and looked directly at her. 'We're *still* married, Annabel.'

She gave a soft sigh. 'We are, aren't we.' It wasn't a question but a stated fact.

'Annabel—'

'No, Harry, don't. Don't say any more, please. I need to concentrate on driving.'

'Of course.'

I eased back into my seat. The care home was only minutes in front and I needed to steel myself for the visit. Silvie would never know the pain I felt every time I saw her. Hopefully, she would only see a smiling face, feel a loving embrace from someone who cared about her. She was my kid sister, not a person to be scared of. But God help me, I was. Scared that one day my steel shield would slip and she'd see all the shameful pent-up revulsion and grief, the rage at the injustice and, perhaps worst of all, she might see me feeling sorry for her. That would be my undoing, mine and hers. It would bring home to her something she was blissfully unaware of – that she was an object of pity.

'Harry?' Annabel was looking at me with concern. 'Is something wrong? You're covered in sweat and you've gone terribly pale.'

I let down the window and took deep, ragged breaths. 'I'm OK, really. Just my demons kicking in.'

'I could stop.'

'No, we're practically there now.'

And we were. The tall iron gates flanking the entrance to the residential home were visible at the end of the road. 'Drive on, Annabel. I'll take a pull before we go inside.'

She said nothing, simply drove the last furlong through the open gates and down the short tree-lined drive right up to the front door. On cue, it opened and one of the nurses came out on to the steps. I could have done with a couple of minutes to gather my thoughts but she was already smiling and greeting us.

'Hello Mr and Mrs Radcliffe, how nice to see you.'

My already shaky hold over my emotions shook some more.

'We're looking forward to seeing Silvie.' Annabel tactfully took the lead. 'Is it convenient?'

'Of course, she'd love to have a visit. If you wouldn't mind signing the visitors' book, I'll take you to her.'

I smiled and murmured a thank you, but the nurse had already turned around and was leading the way down the wide hallway to one of the passages running off at the far end. We followed her. Finally, stopping in front of the door I knew led to Silvie's suite, she tapped lightly and went in.

It was a beautiful room, decorated in white and gold with gold velvet curtains at the wide windows that overlooked the extensive, well-maintained gardens edged by tall lime trees. Off to one side was a splendid bedroom with en-suite lavender coloured bathroom with a pretty selection of bath essences and soaps. It was also equipped with an ugly hoist.

My kid sister was sitting, supported by a kind of harness with a headrest, in a wheelchair in front of the old-style French doors. She had heard us come in but couldn't turn her head to actually see us. One arm waggled over the side of the chair and she made a series of murmurs and gurgles. I swallowed my betraying emotions and strode across the room.

'Hi, Silvie. How's my best girl? How're you doing, sweetheart?' I wrapped my arms round her and hugged and hugged.

Physical contact, as the matron had informed me years ago, was vitally important, helping her to feel loved, integrated and part of her surrounding world. It also gave her a reassuring sense of security and peace. Silvie had gold-star care and lived a cosseted, pampered, hideously constrained life in a luxurious prison – the very best I could afford for her.

She nuzzled into my face and I kissed her gently. 'Annabel's here too – look.' I moved away to let her see.

'Hello, my precious.' Annabel enveloped her in a big hug.

Silvie gurgled with pleasure.

'I'll leave you all for now,' the nurse said, 'but I'll send in a tray of coffee, OK?'

'Lovely,' I said. 'Thanks very much.' Coffee would indeed be welcome.

I sat beside Silvie and held her hand. It seemed even frailer than the last time. With her short brown hair styled in an urchin cut and her pale porcelain skin, she could have been mistaken for a twelve-year-old.

I realized with shame it had been nearly seven weeks since I'd last visited Silvie. One week before my accident I'd driven over by myself to spend an hour with her. Any longer was too tiring and much frowned on by the nursing staff. But that was before I came off Gold Sovereign at Huntingdon. I hadn't been since.

She was looking at my leg now with puzzlement, her face creased and tense. Even in her limited state, she knew something wasn't right. I patted her hand and took it gently in mine and placed it on top of the plaster.

'It's hard, isn't it? And cold. My leg's still there, underneath, fairly soft and warm, but I hurt it. I fell off a horse, daft thing to do, wasn't it? When I come to see you next time the plaster will be all gone and my leg will be better.'

I squeezed her hand gently and smiled. Whether she understood any of it was doubtful but she enjoyed the sound of the human voice, plus the tactile aspect.

Reaching round to my back pocket, I withdrew a rolled-up pretty battered brochure that a zoo in Lincolnshire issued to their day visitors. Once, years ago, I'd visited with a previous girlfriend and kept the illustrated handout to show Silvie, thinking she might enjoy it. The girlfriend was long gone but the brochure had endured. It had proved a big hit with Silvie. Every time I visited, she expected me to show it to her. Even after all this time, it still held her attention and seemed to give her pleasure.

Now, I laid it on her knee and we pored over the pictures of brightly coloured parrots, monkeys and seals, even a big cat, a Lynx with spots and whirls on its pelt. She made little happy noises as I took her finger and traced the different creatures and explained all about them.

Annabel sat on her other side with an arm around her and joined in. We were so engrossed, the three of us, we didn't notice the nurse return with a tray of coffee and a feeder beaker of juice. Annabel and I sat and drank our coffee whilst the nurse skilfully helped Silvie.

I hadn't realized the hour had gone by but I knew the tray was a gentle reminder that as soon as we'd finished our refreshment, it was time to leave so that Silvie could rest. She tired very quickly, and indeed, casting a covert glance at her face, I could see her eyelids beginning to droop. Annabel had noticed, too. She replaced her cup on the tray.

'We have to go now, precious.' She gave her a last hug.

'Afraid so, Silvie,' I agreed, holding her face between both my palms and covering her face with soft kisses. 'But we'll come again soon, very soon.'

The nurse accompanied us to the front door. 'If you wouldn't mind signing out, please. It helps if there should be an emergency, like a fire, to know who is in the building.'

'Of course. And thank you all so much for looking after Silvie. If there's anything she needs, just give me a call.'

'Her needs are really very simple.' The nurse smiled. 'But we will let you know if there is anything.'

I thanked her again and we took our leave.

The drive back was not exactly sombre but coming face-to-face with the brutal reality of Silvie's life did sober you up. It made you grateful for your own health, even if a little impaired.

It also opened your eyes, made you realize the full scope of your own life, your own opportunities, as opposed to the restricted reality she lived in.

I thought about Uncle George declining the chance to see her. But freshly raw from the previous hour, I could see that it wasn't an experience that a stranger could cope with easily. Perhaps, like myself, he was just scared of breaking down in front of her.

'Silvie really enjoyed our visit.' Annabel finally broke the silence as she turned at the roundabout and drove on to the A52.

'Mmmm, yes, she did.'

'It's much harder on you, Harry, than it is on her. You do know that.'

'Yes, I know. Doesn't help.'

'No,' she sighed, 'I don't expect it does.'

'I'll just bury myself in work when I get back – that helps.'

'Good.'

She said no more and when we reached Harlequin Cottage, she declined my invitation to come in.

'No, I won't if you don't mind, must get back.'

'You're one in a million – you know that, don't you? How many other women would accompany their virtual ex-husband to visit his disabled half-sister? Very few.'

'She was in our lives from the very first, Harry. When I agreed to marry you, I knew my future would also include Silvie. I accepted that, and accepted willingly.'

'But we're not together, Annabel. There are no perks for you, are there? Just a lot of hurt.'

She bit her lip and looked down at the steering wheel. 'I've moved on, Harry. Jeffrey's in my life now. He makes me happy.'

'Does he?' I said softly. 'Does he make you as happy as we used to be? I would guess not. What we had was sublime. You can't top that.'

'Please, don't remind me.' Tears shimmered in her eyes and I felt like a complete heel.

'I'm sorry, sorry . . . Forgive me, Annabel. I'd cut my arm off before I'd hurt you.'

'Do you think I don't know that? There's no need to apologise, I know you're hurting very much right now. And it's bad and it's frustrating because there's nothing you can do to help her. Go in and get down to all that pile of work you need to be doing. You said it would help so go and get stuck in.'

She gave me no time to answer but whipped the Jaguar round, drove out of the gate and roared away down the lane.

I stood listening to the throaty roar of the powerful engine until I could no longer hear it. Then I went inside the cottage and closed the door.

FOURTEEN

For the next three weeks or so I did as she'd ordered and worked on Elspeth's biography. Not exclusively, though. I took time off for a couple of things.

A vet's visit with a less than cooperative Leo – who returned minus his bandage, but lashing an irate now fully healed tail against the indignities of being pinned down on the surgery examination table.

And somewhat similarly, going off myself to hospital, transported and escorted by a jubilant Mike. The plaster had been duly cut off, my kneecap freed from the ring of wire surrounding it and an X-ray had proved the knee had 'fused exceptionally well' – the orthopaedic chap's words. Apparently, I could now look forward to masses of physio at regular intervals.

'Soon be in the saddle again.' Mike patted the driving wheel happily as, minus the plaster and crutches, I climbed in with just a walking stick for the journey home.

'I'm still grounded, Mike. What matters now is the soft tissue and nerve recovery.'

'Oh, yes,' he waved his hand airily, 'a formality for the normal man, not you.'

'Thank you very much.'

I'd resisted his entreaties to celebrate in his local pub and gone straight back to the computer and the biography. It was really taking shape and I'd telephoned Elspeth and asked for the shoeboxes of information and press cuttings about her middle years as a trainer. She'd had them ferried over by the uncommunicative John and I'd ploughed on, clarifying the odd query with her over the telephone.

But all the time, part of my instinct was alert for any possible danger. It was unwarranted. The cottage remained intact; there were no further attempts to finish me off. And so far, I had not come across anything detrimental to Marriot's reputation. My antennae stopped twitching and settled down.

Until one Friday morning, the telephone rang and it was Uncle George.

'Harry? I've given up waiting for you to call me.'

'Yes, sorry about that. I've been busy on this biography. Have to be, until I have a final verdict about my racing future.'

'Ah, yes, your leg injury. Rough luck that. Is it about anybody interesting, this book?'

'Elspeth Maudsley.'

'The lady trainer who's retiring?'

'Yes,' I said, surprised. 'How did you know?'

'Rachel's sister, Lucy, y'know, who she has lunch with on Fridays? Well, seems they're both members of the same women's guild. Elspeth, apparently, told her she was getting her autobiography out soon. And Lucy reports back all the gossip to Rachel, of course.'

'Of course. It's called the sisterhood.'

'Anyway, can you manage this lunchtime? I'd really like to talk to you.'

'Well, I've got rid of my plaster so I'm more mobile.'

'Glad to hear it but I think I'll drive over and pick you up. Shall we say in about an hour?'

'Fine by me. Look forward to seeing you.'

'Just point me towards a pub, any will do.' Uncle George, true to his word, had turned up an hour later. I pointed; Uncle George drove.

The Royal Oak was in the centre of the village, about a mile from the cottage. He bought the beers and we ordered a ploughman's lunch each. Choosing one of the corner alcove tables, he sat down and took a long pull from his glass. Then he cleared his throat.

'How much do you know, Harry?'

I stared uncomprehendingly at him. 'About what?'

'Your mother's relationship with me, for a start.'

He'd floored me from the off. 'All I know is you got her through the difficult time after Father's death.'

'Yes, that's true enough. Don't forget though, your father was also my brother. I needed support too, and Elisabeth helped me more than she realized.'

'I don't really want to know the intimate details. I mean, the outcome was impossible to keep secret.'

'You're referring to Silvie?'

'Of course I am.' I gulped my beer. I was finding this conversation unexpected and awkward.

'She will be eighteen very soon now – no longer a child.'

'True enough. And thank you for setting up the trust fund. I can't deny the financial relief will be very welcome, especially now my own future is so uncertain.'

It was Uncle George's turn to stare at me. 'What are you talking about?'

'You don't have to be modest, or pretend. Mother told me. You've set up a large sum of money to be paid over to Silvie when she comes of age. It was to be used for supporting her, paying for her care and so on.'

'Elizabeth told you?'

'Yes.'

'Have you actually spoken to the solicitor, seen the paperwork then?'

'I know Mother went to see our family solicitor years and years ago. But I've never been. She just told me.'

He ran a thumb along the edge of his chin. 'This is very difficult for me, Harry . . .' He paused as two piled plates of lunch arrived.

The young girl placed the meal on the table before us, smiled and said, 'Enjoy.'

When she had gone, Uncle George resumed speaking. 'I suggest you go to see your solicitor, ask him about this document, actually take a look at it, if he will allow you to. Familiarize yourself with it – and the clauses.'

He didn't meet my eyes but started eating his meal. I slowly followed his example and tried to marshal my thoughts.

'Why do I think that wasn't what you were going to say?' I nodded in the direction of the waitress. 'Before she turned up.' He didn't answer. 'Come on, Uncle George. What aren't you telling me?'

'Look, son, just do as I ask, go to see the solicitor. I can't, and Elizabeth's gone, so it has to be you.'

'What do you want to know?' I forked in some more of the delicious Stilton. 'It doesn't make much sense. You and my mother arranged this between yourselves. I was never consulted – nor told any details. Except that when Silvie came of age, she would be financially secure. I mean, for goodness' sake, I was just a kid myself, only sixteen. I simply accepted what Mother said and I've thought no more about it for nearly eighteen years.'

'I'll admit I was going to tell you a secret, something I've not told anyone else, but I can't. I need you to do this for me first. I promise, as soon as you've seen the solicitor, we'll meet up again and I'll tell you everything . . . everything, OK?'

'Are you trying to tell me you've gone down the pan financially, is that it? There's no money left in the pot? Because if it is you're not alone. Half the country's flat broke. There's no shame in it, you know.'

He stared morosely at his plate. He wasn't going to tell me. I reminded myself he was not a young man. It wasn't fair to hassle him.

'OK.' I sighed. 'I'll make an appointment and speak to the solicitor. How's that?' I saw the tension leave his face and he relaxed.

'I'd be very grateful, son.'

'I'll sort it out with Nigel first thing Monday,' I promised reassuringly, but at the same time my heart dropped below floorboards because it now seemed Silvie would no longer be cushioned and secure. She was going to be my sole responsibility and I didn't know how I was going to bring home the bacon.

'Who's Nigel?'

'The family solicitor. He took over when his father died. He's a sound chap. Don't worry about it any more, Uncle George.'

'Thanks, I appreciate it.'

I tried a change of conversation to lighten things. 'Aunt Rachel lunching with her sister?'

'Hmm.' He nodded, having resumed eating.

'Let's hope she enjoys it and comes home in a good humour.'

'Ha.' He washed down the food with a mouthful of beer. 'Talking about Lucy, it's reminded me about the second thing I wanted to tell you about, well, ask you, really.' I raised an eyebrow. 'This lady trainer, she has a son called Marriot, yes?'

'Yes.'

'Have you met him, had any dealings with him at all?'

'Our paths have crossed.'

'A nasty piece of work. Watch your back, Harry.'

'Whoa, you'll have to explain. In what way?'

'Let's say he looks out for number one, right down the line. And if anyone poses a threat in any way he can get very, well, protective of himself.'

'Have you had first-hand experience, then?'

'In the past, yes. When I was still in business. And through his father.'

I stared at him and felt a tingle along my spine. 'Through Victor Maudsley?'

'Yes.'

'How come?'

'Golf,' he said succinctly and placed his knife and fork neatly on his plate. 'We were golfing buddies, way back.'

'Are you still?'

'Nay, son, not any more. Not since Rachel put a stop to my . . . er . . . activities.' He looked embarrassed and I didn't pursue it, but my mind was doing somersaults.

'What do you know about Marriot? What's he do? I know he's not in racing. I could ask Elspeth, but so far I haven't done.' I didn't intend to either. I didn't want her to tell Marriot I'd been asking.

'Since he married into the Simpson family he's been a director in the family brewery business. His wife's name is Chloe. There's one daughter, no sons.'

'Any children?'

Uncle George shook his head. 'Not so far. But they've only been married about three years. Marriot got around quite a bit as a young buck – was over forty when he married Chloe. Did very well for himself there.'

'And she's younger than him?'

'Quite a lot. In her late twenties, I think. The wedding was a big affair, written up in one of the glossies. Rachel pointed it out to me.'

'And where do they hang out?'

'The old ancestral pile or one wing of it, anyway. Up in Derbyshire.'

'Hmm, may find some coverage in one of Elspeth's shoeboxes.'

'Why are you so interested in Marriot?'

'I think there's something I'll discover doing this biography and in some way it's harmful to Marriot. He knows I'll find out. That's why he's scared. And whatever it is, it's got clout. I've had one or two unpleasant "accidents" since I started this book.'

'You think Marriot's behind them?'

I drained the last of my beer. 'Yes,' I said, 'I do.'

'And does Elspeth know her little lad's being a naughty boy?'

'Shouldn't think so. Mamma wouldn't stand for it. She runs the show.'

'Sounds like some sort of family secret to me, if the biography might throw it up. But what could it be?'

'That, Uncle George, is what I need to find out – before there's another "accident". I may not miss the flak next time.'

FIFTEEN

'Harry, how are you?' Nigel Broadbent, my solicitor, pumped my hand, beamed at me and gestured to a chair in his office. 'Have a seat. What can I do for you?'

Monday morning, grey, damp and depressing, matching my mood exactly. I'd been mulling over Uncle George's words since we met last Friday. None of them were in any way comforting. But the devil must be faced, and if there were no coffers to feather Silvie's nest, I needed to know.

'Thanks for seeing me. Bit short notice, I know, but I was only made aware of the problem two or three days ago.'

'And what might this problem be?' Nigel was still beaming, leaning on his forearms as he bent forward over the desk.

'It's regarding my half-sister, Silvie Radcliffe. I believe my mother had a trust fund of some sort drawn up to mature on Silvie's eighteenth birthday, in a few weeks' time. Is it possible I could see this document, please?'

Nigel's smile wavered. 'What has prompted you to ask?'

'Is there a problem?' I didn't want to play fencing games – I just needed to see for myself what was written down. And, because of how Uncle George had phrased it, what get-out clause it might contain.

'Hmmm.' Nigel sat up straight. 'The problem is you say your mother was instrumental in engaging our firm's services, yes?'

'That's correct.'

'I am aware of the sad fact of your mother's death, of course.

But your own name may not appear anywhere on this particular document. And if that is the case, there may be a problem with data protection.'

He reached for the phone and asked his secretary to locate the file and bring it in.

'I'm pretty sure my name won't figure. I was just a kid, sixteen, when Silvie was born. All I know is what my mother told me.'

'And that was?'

'A large sum of money would be paid to Silvie on her eighteenth birthday. I was assured it was paid for by her father.'

'And do you know the father's name?'

'Yes. My Uncle George, my father's elder brother.'

His eyebrows lifted just a fraction before he had them firmly under control again. 'Did this George Radcliffe tell you himself he was the father?'

'Well, no. But he is. My mother was in a terrible state after Father's death. It was an accident, you see, a shooting accident, so it was an almighty shock to her to lose him. As a couple they were very close and when he died it knocked her over. Uncle George was grieving too; they kind of propped each other up.' I made a rueful face. 'A little too well.'

'I see.' Nigel looked down at his fountain pen, rolling it back and forth between his thumb and index finger. If he was trying to save me embarrassment, it was far too long ago and too late to do that.

There was a tap on the door and a tall woman in a dark blue suit entered and placed a folder on the desk.

'Thank you, Karen.' Nigel dismissed her with a nod and reached for the document. He slid it from the folder and immersed himself in reading it through.

I sat and waited.

After a few minutes, he raised his head and eyed me. 'I'm afraid I can't agree to your request to view this, Harry.'

'But surely . . .'

He lifted a hand, silencing me. 'There's a specific clause on confidentiality, I'm afraid.'

'So what happens now?'

'Nothing.' He smiled gently. 'Be patient for a little while

longer. As soon as Silvie's birthday arrives she'll be eligible to receive the money.'

'I don't understand.' I shook my head. 'I rather thought there *was* no money.'

'Quite the contrary.' Nigel tapped the folder with his pen. We have invested the whole sum from the moment we were instructed and it has now accrued very substantially. And if Silvie wishes, after she takes possession, we can re-invest on her behalf.'

'So,' I said, slowly trying to get my head round it, 'there's no problem, no clause that would preclude her taking the money?'

'None.'

'Does it have signatures?'

'Yes.'

'How many?'

'Two.'

'My mother, presumably.' Nigel nodded. 'And . . . Silvie's father?'

'That's right.'

'Well, thanks very much for looking into it for me. You're quite sure I can't take just a quick glance?'

He stood up and held out his hand. 'Please don't worry yourself over it. Everything is in perfect order.'

We shook hands. Then on my way to the door, a thought hit me.

'Nigel, if Silvie . . . if she doesn't . . . live, to see her birthday, what happens then?'

'The money reverts to her benefactor.'

'I see,' I said slowly.

'There's no reason why she shouldn't reach eighteen, is there?'

'Her health is pretty fragile,' I admitted. It was something I always tried to push away from my mind whenever Silvie was ill, which was quite often as she was subject to respiratory infections. His face altered, the affable smile fading.

'I'm sorry, very sorry. But the money is specifically for her alone. You do understand that, don't you?'

'Of course!' I bristled. 'I wasn't interested in any of it for myself.'

'No, no,' he placated me, 'I never thought for a moment you were under a misapprehension regarding the allocation of the money.' He held the office door open for me. 'As I say, leave it to us. Whatever circumstances occur, we are here to look after your best interests, and those of Silvie's, of course.'

'Thank you, it's appreciated.'

His beaming, reassuring smile had reappeared. 'You don't have to concern yourself with anything. When Silvie's birthday arrives, we will be in touch immediately, all right?'

Anything but, I thought, but it was required of me so I nodded. 'Yes.'

Back at the cottage, I resisted a whisky, settled for a strong coffee then reached for the phone and dialled Uncle George's mobile.

'Are you OK to talk?'

'Yes, fine. I'm in the greenhouse. There are only tomato plants listening.'

'I've been to see Nigel, just got home.'

'Right.' There was barely concealed excitement in the one word.

'No, not right at all, Uncle George.'

'Oh?'

'He was cagey as could be. Said there was a confidentiality clause.'

'So you didn't find anything out at all?'

'I didn't, no. Well, that's not quite true. Apparently the amount of money is, according to him, "substantial".' A silence followed. 'You did say you'd tell me everything once I'd been to see the solicitor. I'd like us to meet.'

He sighed heavily. 'Yes, yes, I did. And I keep my word so . . . when?'

'As soon as possible – this Friday any good?'

'Yes, can't make it before.'

'Fine.'

'Same arrangements as before?'

'Fine,' I said again.

'Right then, Friday.'

I replaced the receiver. Going through to the kitchen, I made a quick bite and took it back to eat at my desk. I'd reached the part in the biography when Elspeth was beginning to make a name as a trainer. She had been bringing on Moneymagnet with the Yorkshire Cup in mind. If the horse won, it would be a boost to her reputation and stables and, hopefully, produce a rash of new prospective owners.

It isn't essential for trainers to actually attend in person but most do, especially at a prestigious meeting. The owners seem to expect it as part of the payback from all their folding stuff passing from their pockets or banks to the trainer's. So it was with a smidgeon of distrust when I came to an entry in her racing diary that detailed Moneymagnet to run at York races followed by a question mark and Victor Maudsley's name pencilled in, supposedly, to be there instead of her. What could have been more important to Elspeth that day? Not a lot of things, I'd have thought.

I put a question mark in the margin of my script at that point. It needed sorting. Everything up to that point had gone so smoothly with the writing that there was bound to be a hiccup that brought my creative output to a shuddering halt. Now the question had derailed my ongoing writing flow.

Only one thing to do: go and chat it through with Her Ladyship.

I saved my material, stretched my arms to the ceiling and rotated my neck and shoulders, then sent her an email asking for a time to see her.

I was expecting a slight delay and had gone to stick the kettle on for a mug of tea when her email shot back. It basically said, 'come now'. A horsebox was already on the way back to Unicorn Stables from Nottingham races. Stan was driving and could pick me up in fifteen minutes. Would that do?

'Yes, please,' I replied. And closed down my computer.

When the horsebox arrived ten minutes later I was already out in the lane, standing by the cottage gate. The cab door on the passenger side swung open. I climbed in and Pete hutched up, leaving me a bit of space to park myself.

'How's it going, mate?' Stan, ratting cap at a jaunty angle, grinned across at me and engaged gear.

'Pretty good. Did you get a result at Nottingham?'

'Sure did.' His grin was wide. 'Buckshee came in three lengths clear at twelve to one. Elspeth's going to be in a happy mood – it was a six-thousand race.'

'Very nice.' I nodded. And indeed the atmosphere was light and cheerful. 'She's a good trainer.'

'Yeah, shame she's decided to call it quits.'

'She's old, though, ain't she?' Pete piped up.

'Don't let her hear you say that,' Stan warned. 'Else you'll be down the road.'

'Will be any road, won't I, when she goes.'

'You'll need a reference.'

'Nah.' Pete stuck his chest out. 'Reckon I can get a stable job easy. Plenty of trainers are taking on.'

'The ignorance of youth, eh?' Stan shook his head at the lad's words. 'A lot of them will be much harder to work for.'

Pete slumped back and didn't reply.

'How did you get on when you brought Scarlet Salvia back?' I asked. 'She was expected to walk it, wasn't she?'

Stan chuckled. 'Evening stables were over and Elspeth was entertaining some owners. We got Bloody Sal stabled and fed then buggered off down the pub. Reckon Elspeth'd calmed down by next morning 'cos she didn't say much.'

I became aware that Pete was staring at me. I turned and looked directly at him. 'What?'

'I've just remembered. When Stan and I were coming back in the box with Bloody Sal, there was an accident at the Saxondale roundabout.'

'They happen,' I said, 'frequently. It's noted for it.'

'Yeah, but that's what made me forget.'

'What're you rabbiting on about?'

Pete turned to Stan. 'Well, you were driving. Just as we got to the roundabout, remember, there was a horsebox a few cars in front and it was the one. But then the accident happened and I was looking out for you, trying to help, an' I forgot all about it.'

'Get on with it.'

'I'm telling you, ain't I?' Pete yelped.

I felt a rise of excitement. 'Are you saying you saw the horsebox I was looking for?'

'That's right. It was a cream one an' it had some damage above the wheel arch.'

'Well done, Pete. You're saying it was on the approach to the roundabout – which way did it go?'

He seemed to be trying to reconstruct the scene in his mind. Then, nodding decisively, he said, 'Newark, down the A46. And I'll tell you something else – I saw the trainer's name an' all. Written on the rear it was.'

'Who?' I urged. 'What trainer was it?'

He scowled with concentration.

'Come on, lad, think.' Stan added encouragement.

'Hang on, I'm trying to, ain't I?' Then his scowl cleared, he grinned and slammed a fist into his palm. 'Got it! It was Fred Sampson.'

I felt the shock hit my solar plexus.

Fred Sampson's box had been coming back from Nottingham races. And the man helping Fred Sampson was the man I'd sat next to whilst eating bacon sandwiches in the stable lads' canteen, the person who professed to know nothing about the box or its whereabouts.

He was also the jockey I had landed on top of at Huntingdon races.

It was Carl.

SIXTEEN

My meeting with Elspeth had a surreal feel to it. I found it hard to concentrate. Thoughts crowded and jostled through my mind. One piece of jigsaw had dropped into place. It had been Carl driving the horsebox that had parked across the lane and caused the car accident that had landed Darren in hospital. Now the question was who had paid him?

Or could he have been bribed, even blackmailed into it?

I dragged my attention back to what Elspeth was saying.

'I'm impressed. You're galloping on faster than Shergar. No, really,' she nodded, 'and it seems to be good stuff. My publisher was on the phone to me yesterday enquiring how it was progressing. Told him I was giving you a free hand but we'd had a couple of meetings. Now I can ring him and update him properly.'

I nodded and let her do the talking. All I wanted to do right now was escape back to the cottage, pour a whisky and mull over the facts I'd just found out. I needed to speak to Mike as well, to get his take on it.

'So,' Elspeth paused for breath, 'what's your problem?'

I hastily adjusted my thought patterns.

'I need to clarify a race meeting. According to your racing diary for that date, it seemed you didn't attend. And it was potentially a very important race, not one you'd have missed, I should have thought. So, why did you?'

'Let me rake out my personal diary for that year. You're fortunate, I'm a magpie. I *do* save all my diaries.' She smiled at me. 'I keep them locked away in a chest in my bedroom. Some things, I'm sure you will agree, are very personal. Help yourself to more coffee and nibbles, I won't be long.' She walked gracefully from the room.

I did as I'd been bidden and refreshed my coffee mug. The 'nibbles', like everything else at Unicorn Stables, were first class. Traditional home-made biscuits, they were very moreish. Whatever she paid her housekeeper, the lady earned it. I crunched on a strawberry shortbread finger and was grateful for a few minutes alone.

Now I had a name to work from I could plan my next move. I could, of course, approach Carl face-to-face, demand an explanation. Let him know I knew. But it would not be the best move. I not only needed to know why he'd done it but just who was behind him pulling the strings – Carl was just a bit player in this production.

I wondered if it could have been Carl who had entered the cottage with the intention to set fire to it. No, he didn't know where I lived. Even as the thought went through my mind, I knew, beyond doubt, it *was* Carl. When we'd been sitting in the stable lads' canteen he'd passed a comment which at the time hadn't registered. I'd thought he was being particularly tactless in talking about my racing future. But he'd slipped up without realizing it. He'd actually called my cottage by name – Harlequin Cottage. There was no reason why he would have known that – unless he'd been given the specific address, along with an order to try out a spot of arson.

I felt anger rising in me. His actions had caused a lot of pain to Leo and, but for the cat, the cottage could have burned down. I was going to have a showdown with Carl very soon, I thought grimly.

The door opened. Elspeth entered holding a very feminine-looking diary. She sat down near me and opened the pink cover. 'Right, now, what was the date again?'

I reined in my anger and told her.

'Hmmmm, yes, I do see what prompted you to check with me. Of course, if I'd been able to, I'd definitely have been at the racecourse . . .'

'But?' I prompted, not wanting her to slide out of telling me the reason behind her decision.

'It was the year Marriot was twelve. And he was the reason I couldn't leave the house. He was very poorly, in bed. I sent Victor to the races in my stead. We were still married, you understand, at that time.'

'Right.'

She smiled and shook her head gently. 'I might be a very successful trainer' – no fake modesty about Elspeth – 'but I'm also a mother.' Giving an expressive shrug, she added, 'In a situation like that, there's no contest.'

She was showing me a different side to her I'd not seen before. Elspeth was the iron lady of racing, in a lot of people's opinion, but what she had just told me implied a soft centre. At least as far as Marriot was concerned. I had no doubt that Marriot also knew, and turned it to his own advantage when he wanted to. Her next words confirmed it.

'My weak spot, of course,' she said softly and poured herself more coffee. I noted she didn't mention her daughter, Paula.

'Do you wish Marriot were following in your footsteps? As a trainer, I mean, taking over here at Unicorn Stables?'

'You don't own your children, Harry. They have freedom when they reach adulthood. What I would like doesn't come

into it. You have to let them go. The name of the game is life.'
She might have said it in a light-hearted way, but underneath I
suspected there was a big hurt that he had turned his back on
her way of life and, because it was so intrinsically a part of
her, on Elspeth herself.

'Do you want to take any more box files back with you?'
Elspeth reverted to her normal razor-edged business self. Again,
I suspected, we were getting a little too close to home on the
subject of Marriot.

'How many have you left?'

'Oh, I don't know, probably five, maybe six, and some of
them may not contain anything relevant. They deal with the
years just before and following my divorce from Victor. Oh,
yes, and one has an awful lot of photos, cuttings from maga-
zines, that sort of thing, from when Marriot got married. You'll
just have to sift out what's not required.'

'OK.' No way would I tell her that it was probing this box
that held my closest attention. But had I . . . spoken to Uncle
George, she may have been quite right and I'd have skipped
the wedding stuff. Now, knowing a bit of the background, I
was eager to plough through the contents of this box, see what
it threw up.

'Anything else, then?' She flashed a glance at her watch.

'Hmmm, there are two or three people who figure in your
circle of friends that I'd like to speak to now that I'm mobile
again.'

I fished a short list from my pocket. 'Is it possible you could
give them a ring or drop an email confirming my credentials
in asking questions?'

'Yes, with the proviso your questions are tactful, discreet
ones and not loaded.'

'Do my best.'

She sighed. 'A good job the publisher's paying. However, he
does expect a bit of . . .' she eyed me speculatively, 'spice?'

'Exactly.'

'But I don't want other people getting hurt through any of
my, shall we say, possible indiscretions?'

'Point taken, Elspeth. I shall be discretion itself. Neither of
us wants a libel suit chucking at us.'

She chuckled. 'That's the spirit.'

Down the hall, I heard the front door bang. My heart rate stepped up its pace a little. Heavy, solid footsteps made their way towards the office door. Now, my heart rate went into overdrive. I knew who would be coming through the door at any second.

And I wasn't wrong.

The door swung open and Marriot came in. He saw me, checked his stride and glowered.

'Marriot, darling.' Elspeth held out her hand and moved towards him. 'What a nice surprise.' She inclined her face to receive a kiss. Totally wrong-footed, he turned the glower off and dutifully kissed his mother's cheek.

'I'll be off then, Elspeth. May I take the box files?'

'Certainly.' She pulled out a deep drawer in the desk and extracted five boxes.

I packed three into my backpack and stuck the other two under my arm.

'What's in those?' Marriot asked truculently.

'They cover the last twenty-five years up until now.' I covertly watched him assessing what they might contain about himself and saw the wry quirk of his mouth. Knew he'd realized they would include his early manhood, and all that implied – plus his marriage.

'Well, you don't need this one.' He snatched one of the boxes from under my arm. Predictably, it was marked with the years 2007 to 2011.

'Now, now,' Elspeth held out a hand, 'of course Harry will want it. Don't worry, darling, he's not interested in your wedding coverage. But he does need to go through it for the necessary information leading up to my retirement.' Very reluctantly, Marriot gave it back to her.

'Don't forget,' he snarled at me, 'I'm going to read it before it goes to the publisher, so watch your back.'

'I will,' I assured him truthfully. 'You can bet on that.'

He smiled nastily. 'How's your sister? Keeping well, is she?'

I caught my breath, feeling a sudden constriction in my chest.

'Yes, how is she, Harry?' In contrast, Elspeth's smile was sweet. 'She must be nearly eighteen, isn't she?'

I nodded, my throat so tight I could barely swallow.

'Your payment for the writing must be welcome now you're not able to ride. I don't suppose the nursing home comes cheap, does it?'

Mutely I shook my head, wanting only to get out of the room, the house, and escape back to the sanctuary of my cottage.

'I've asked John to run you back,' she went on, almost as though she could read my thoughts. 'And don't worry about those interviews you mentioned, I'll let them know.'

'Thanks,' I croaked, scooped up the errant box file and, resisting the urge to run, walked out.

SEVENTEEN

A furry tornado hurtled across the kitchen, landing with a solid thump on my shoulder. Instinctively I reached up for Leo's tail and steadied him.

His action prompted a thought. Had the cat jumped on Carl as, intent on arson, he'd entered the cottage that night? If so, and it was more than likely, that would explain the dislocated tail. Odds on, Carl would have grabbed him. Not to steady, but to try to pull the cat off. The nearest bare flesh would have been his face. And it would certainly have resulted in a nasty mauling, I could guarantee it. The squalls and yells of pain I'd heard were consistent with that scenario.

If I'd found out earlier that Carl was to blame, I could have had a good look at his face. But I hadn't known and I hadn't noticed.

I went through into the lounge, poured a small whisky and sat sipping it whilst doing some serious thinking. Halfway down the glass, I placed it on the coffee table and reached for my mobile.

'Mike, Harry. You eaten yet? Fancy a bite at the Unicorn? No, no way, I'm not a charity case yet. This is my shout – besides, I need to run stuff by you . . . OK? Great, meet you in half an hour.' I rang off and put the mobile back in my trouser pocket.

Reaching for my jacket and the last couple of issues of the *Racing Post*, I locked the cottage and pointed the Mazda towards Gunthorpe.

The Unicorn was a well-known watering hole. Standing right beside the River Trent at Gunthorpe, it was a favourite haunt for anglers, boating enthusiasts, walkers and the ubiquitous motorbikers. A rambling country pub-cum-restaurant, it boasted a very long conservatory running along the south-facing wall. The views from there over the river to the rise of woods on the far side were magnificent. Farther down from the pub, the narrow tarmac road petered out at the stile and start of a footpath over the fields beside Gunthorpe's impressive lock and weir.

I glanced at my watch as I entered through the back entrance, directly accessed from the generously accommodating car park. Barely seven o'clock, early yet so every chance of getting a table for two overlooking the Trent. I went to the bar, picked up a still mineral water and wandered through into the conservatory. Definitely a place to unwind and appreciate the wide spread of sky and water. Although half-full, mostly with couples, there was a good choice of tables. I chose one at the end nearest the lock and weir.

Mike would be along in his own good time; he had much to do at the stables, unlike myself. I felt an unwelcome flood of longing to be back riding horses. I doubted I'd ever come to terms with just being a writer, it didn't seem like a proper job at all. I shrugged my shoulders irritably. The jury was still out – it wasn't a sentence yet.

I spread out Saturday's issue of the *Racing Post* on to the table and flipped through to the declarations on page eighty-two. Runners for Sunday, Monday, Wednesday and Thursday were all listed, though strangely not Tuesday's. These had been written up today in Monday's copy. I placed this to one side for now. It was a bit short notice to do anything about it if I discovered tomorrow to be the day for action. I liked to think out a plan in advance rather than charge into a situation that could backfire.

As in every other walk of life, in racing there was an exclusive hotline with gossip, insider knowledge, call it what you like, that rivalled the Met's famous HOLMES for up-to-date data. Right now, I was on the outer fringe, unpleasant but true. I needed Mike's help on this.

Minutes later a hand came across the table setting down a half pint of bitter and he slid into the chair opposite me. I'd not noticed his approach being buried in the newspaper.

'Oh, hi, Mike, glad you could make it.'

'What? Miss a free dinner? Give over.' He took a big appreciative slurp of beer. 'So, how goes it?'

'Better than I'd hoped as regards the writing.'

'And otherwise?'

'I've just discovered who was driving the horsebox.'

'You have? Who was it?'

'Remember when I came off at Huntingdon on that April bank holiday Monday? Well, it was the jockey I landed on, Carl Smith.'

'Good grief! But he can't be the main man – he's just a bit player, surely. Who do you think's pulling his strings, then?'

'My money is still on Marriot. I've no proof, of course.'

'Hmmm . . . where do you go from here?'

'Funny you should ask . . .' I tapped the *Racing Post*. 'Just checking the declarations for later this week. Any ideas which racecourse Carl Smith might be at?'

Mike pulled the paper closer. 'Let's have a look.'

I sat back and sipped my mineral water, allowing him time to study the runners. Mike was silent for a few minutes before stabbing a forefinger decisively at a particular race. 'Sandfly's down to race Thursday. John Constable's his usual jockey but he had a bad fall last Saturday. John's cousin's one of my own stable lads and he was telling the others over breakfast yesterday. Fred Sampson will probably need Carl to help out.'

I grinned. 'Knew I could rely on you, Mike. Leicester it is then. Thursday.'

'Having sung for my supper, shall we order?'

'Absolutely.'

I folded up the newspaper. The subject was dropped whilst we enjoyed a sizzling steak and chips. But nearing the end of our meal it was Mike who brought up the subject again.

'OK, Harry.' He speared the last chip and replaced knife and fork on the plate. 'So what's your next step? Are you going to Leicester to face him down?'

'Yep.'

'Could turn a bit hairy, y'know.'

'I'm sure it will. However, there's going to be further moves against me – bound to be. I need to get in first. There has to be a reason behind these attacks. I want to know why.'

'How are you going to . . . er . . . *persuade* him to tell you?'

'Appeal to his basest nature.'

'You mean, offer him cash?'

'You must admit it usually works.'

He smiled ruefully. 'I'm not going to disagree.'

'The biggest question is what do I do when I find out who the enemy is? Can you tell me? Can't just steam in and finish him off, nor even tell the police. They're not going to babysit me. So where do I go from here?'

Mike shook his head. 'No idea, mate, absolutely no bloody idea.'

I drained the last of my drink. 'Just have to let it roll and return the volleys, only thing I can do.'

'Well, if you want some help just shout.'

'Thanks, but I'll take a rain check on your offer, Mike. Bad enough somebody's on my case – no sense in pointing them in your direction.'

'OK, just remember, when you get to the last fence, you're not on your own.'

I looked at him steadily. 'I'll remember.' It felt good to know I had a staunch friend and it was precisely because he *was* such a good friend that I didn't want to involve him. It was one thing to pick his brains, quite another to stand him in front of the firing squad.

We wandered out through the car park and drove off in convoy, Mike leading. As we parted at the Saxondale roundabout – Mike driving straight on, myself swinging right – the dark blue Peugeot that had been behind us from Gunthorpe also turned right. I flicked a glance in my rear-view mirror. A similar car had been a couple of cars behind me as I'd driven to Gunthorpe. Was it following me? Was somebody actually stalking me? Or was I simply getting neurotic? Only one way to find out.

Approaching the brow of Saxondale hill before it swooped down into Radcliffe-on-Trent, there was a staggered junction. To the left was Henson Lane, which had originally led through to the old Saxondale hospital but was now blocked off fifty yards in. Only local people would be aware of this rat-run. If I swung off the A52 into the cul-de-sac and the other car followed, it must be following me, because the lane led nowhere. Also, I didn't want to give away the location of my cottage.

Leading off the junction on the right-hand side of the road was Oatfield Lane, snaking narrowly away over a hump-backed railway bridge and running between fields for about three-quarters of a mile. It ended in a crossroads above Shelford. The road running west led straight down into Radcliffe village. I could cut across country and get back to the cottage unseen.

At the very last moment I swung the car to the left and into Henson Lane. I drove straight up to the barricade, braked and dropped into reverse gear ready for a speedy get away. Behind me I could see the A52 clearly through my rear-view mirror. A couple of cars, caught out by the stiff camber, swished past the end of the lane. I held my breath, heart beat getting faster. Any second now I'd see the blue Peugeot.

And there it was. Sailing past just like all the rest. Complete with a deep dent in the bonnet.

I let out a gusty sigh. That was another year I'd just knocked off my life. Get a grip, I told myself, did a rapid seven-point turn within the narrow lane, shot across the staggered junction and went home the scenic route.

I was congratulating myself on losing the possible tail when, a quarter of a mile from home, waiting for the traffic lights to change, the same blue car flew past heading back the way it had come.

The lights changed, I turned right and floored it back to the cottage.

This time, after double-locking the door, I poured a double whisky and took it upstairs to bed.

EIGHTEEN

I arose very early the next morning and by seven was hard at work.

Leo, having been on the prowl all night, was now gracing my desk, languorously stretched out on top of today's newspaper. I found his presence relaxing. I'd set a target of 2,000 words and was completely absorbed in the writing, the words flowing. A shaft of sunshine slanted through the window, falling across Leo's orange fur. Feeling the warmth, he stretched out a careless back leg and began to purr softly.

From this delightful fugue, the strident notes of my mobile jarred us both back harshly to the present.

'Yes?' Even to my own ears, my voice sounded abrupt, abrasive. Every day I was becoming more like a writer, hating to be interrupted when the words were going well. As for Leo, his ears flattened and he jumped from the desk in a huff.

'Mr Radcliffe, could you come over to the nursing home, please? Silvie has contracted an RTI. She's not very well, I'm afraid.'

I immediately felt guilty for my ill-humour. 'Thank you, Matron. Yes, of course, I'll come over straight away.' I saved the precious script and closed down the computer.

I was concerned about Silvie but we'd been here before, plenty of times. She was particularly vulnerable to infection. However, I knew that one day one of the infections was very likely to ravage her delicate body and she would lose the battle. Pray God, it wasn't going to be this time. I didn't want to lose her.

I headed the car east and ate up the intervening miles. Having turned off the Fosse, I was driving down a lane between fields when I glanced in my rear-view mirror – then did a double take. A dark blue Peugeot was following me, belting along at an alarming speed, dead centre of the lane and closing rapidly.

Automatically, I pulled to my left and floored the accelerator. I looked behind. He accelerated. The gap closed. If he intended running me off the road, it was more than a possibility he'd succeed. Holding that course, a smash was inevitable. He must be raving. At the speed we were doing, it would probably take him out, too.

No way could I pull any further to my left. The impenetrable hedge ran unendingly along the narrow grass verge. Not a gateway in sight. But up ahead there was a bend and immediately after I knew, from countless trips this way, there was a cattle grid fronting a dirt track off to the left. No gates flanked this grid and it was just possible I could swing off the lane and the momentum would carry my car over on to the track. Bloody dangerous, though – the car could flip over.

I risked a glance behind. He was closing very fast, bearing down on me like a maniac. Sweat ran down my face. If he hit me before we rounded the bend it was going to be a hell of a smash. I felt a sickening clutch of my guts knowing I didn't have a choice. Trying to outrun the Peugeot was not an option. It had to be the cattle grid. At least I stood a fifty-fifty chance of survival.

Desperately I increased my speed, knowing I could easily lose control going into the bend. But I had to be in front at that point. Gripping the wheel, hands aching with the effort, I expected the screech of metal on metal any moment. Then the bend was upon me.

I swung the steering wheel round, burning rubber, the tyres screaming. Then immediately wrenched it savagely to the left, felt the wheels spin and clatter deafeningly as the car bucked and plunged over and across the cattle grid, scattering a fog of flying dried mud particles all around as the tyres sought a grip. The car tipped at a crazy angle, bounced back and slewed from side to side. I braked hard, trying to keep it upright on the dirt track. Fighting for control, I finally ran it into the choking, tall grass at the side. As it came to a long, juddering halt, I slumped over the wheel, dripping with sweat.

My relief was short-lived as I remembered the maniac driving the other car. Was he still pursuing me? I jerked around, still held by the seat belt. The dirt track was empty, no vehicle in sight. I let out a shuddering breath. Putting the car into reverse, I extricated it from the clogging herbage, dropped into first and turned back, nosing it gently over the cattle grid and out on to the lane. I scanned both directions. Nothing. Not a car in sight.

Gingerly, heading for the nursing home, I drove at a steady pace, keeping a close eye on the road in front and also constantly checking my rear-view mirror. A driving examiner would have been proud of my rubber necking. But I didn't intend to be caught out again. Whoever had been driving that Peugeot had had only one thought in mind: to put me out of action, possibly temporarily, but more likely permanently. And I wasn't going to give him that satisfaction. It was my turn to take the reins.

Reaching the nursing home, I parked near the front door. I'd wasted enough valuable time getting here and I found myself urgently wanting to see Silvie, to reassure myself that this latest respiratory infection wasn't going to gain the upper hand.

A young nurse, who I'd seen before, let me in.

She smiled briefly. 'Mr Radcliffe, to see Silvie?'

I nodded.

'If you'd like to go on, you know where her rooms are, don't you?'

I nodded again.

'Good, and if you'll excuse me whilst I drop this note off in Matron's office, I'll follow you.'

'Busy this morning?'

'Frantic.' She flashed me a smile and was gone.

I made my way down the long corridor. At Silvie's door I tapped, walked in and stopped abruptly. The French doors were wide open, golden curtains billowing in the breeze – not conducive to a sick patient. As I made to go across and close them, two things happened. The emergency alarm beeped stridently and the inner door to Silvie's bedroom was flung open. Once again, despite my resolve, I was taken off-guard, wrong-footed.

A figure clad in dark clothes and wearing a balaclava erupted from the bedroom and plunged out through the open French doors. I hesitated fractionally, torn between wanting to see if

Silvie was all right and my instinctive reaction to chase after the man.

There was a rush of movement behind me as two nurses burst into the room, their eyes wary, accusing. 'What's happened, Mr Radcliffe? Have you touched any equipment?'

I shook my head forcibly. 'Check on Silvie. There's been an intruder.' Leaving them momentarily open-mouthed before professionalism quickly kicked in and sent them dashing through to the bedroom, I went after the man.

Cursing my indecision that had given him a two- or three-second head start, I sprinted across the lawns, headed for the only possible cover – the tall shrubbery. Pushing my way through to the fencing behind, I checked almost the whole of the boundary, drawing a total blank. With heaving lungs, I skidded to a halt. Beyond the fence I heard the unmistakable double click of a car door being opened and closed again. No mistake – the noise was followed by an engine being turned over and a gear grated.

I flung myself at the fence and scrabbled desperately up the wood panelling, rubbing patches of skin from my knees and knuckles, and finally clawed myself up to the top. A dark blue Peugeot was just driving off down the lane. It was too far away to get any indication of the registration number but I'd have bet Harlequin Cottage on it being the same car that had tried to finish me off.

As that thought struck me I let go of the fence and kicked myself off and away from it, landing on all fours. Silvie! What had the bastard done to Silvie?

Inside the nursing home, as I gasped my way in, the bleeper was now mercifully silent and two nurses were attending to Silvie.

'How is she? Has she been hurt?'

'Fortunately, there was little time lapse. She's OK.'

'Thank God.'

'So,' the senior nurse eyed me, 'what happened, Mr Radcliffe?'

'I don't know. I came into the sitting room and the French doors were wide open, curtains blowing. Before I could close them, Silvie's bleeper went mad and her bedroom door crashed open. A man in a balaclava ran off through the open doors.

'So you didn't touch Silvie?'

'Me? No, I still haven't seen her. I left you two nurses to look after her and I legged it after this man.'

'Did you catch him?'

I slumped against the doorframe. 'No, no, the bastard got away. He had a car waiting the other side of the fence. I just managed to see it as he drove off.'

I moved across the room into Silvie's bedroom. I needed to see her, make sure she wasn't harmed in any way. Her eyes, wide – afraid – searched for me and she gave a cry of distress. I was beside her instantly, holding her close. 'Everything's fine, Silvie, you're safe, darling.' I smoothed the damp hair back from her forehead and looked across at the nurse. 'Why did the bleeper go off?'

'The oxygen-feed tube had been dislodged.'

'If it hadn't been put right straight away could it have proved fatal?'

'Because she has an RTI, very possibly, yes.'

We stared at each other above the top of Silvie's head.

'Could she have dislodged it herself?'

'Oh, no,' the nurse said emphatically. 'The whole apparatus had been moved.'

So it was attempted murder, then. Not able to finish me, the bastard had tried to finish Silvie.

'I see,' I said.

And we stared at each other some more.

NINETEEN

An hour later, my statement taken by the police, I slid into the driving seat of the Mazda and drove away. Silvie had drifted off into a drug-assisted sleep in my arms. The comfort and reassurance she seemed to draw simply from my presence was humbling in the extreme. But there was so very little I could do. The nurses were angels. They took such good care of her that all her physical needs were met and they kept her spirits high with their cheerful, smiling faces.

For my part, I knew from years of experience that Silvie got enough stimulation from an hour's visit and then usually succumbed to a restoring nap. And today, the fact that she was more fragile than normal, the infection raging through her delicate frame, weakening and lowering her defences, was bad enough. Now, on top of that, the attempted murder had naturally terrified her. I could only guess at her state of mind and emotions when the balaclava-clad man had entered her bedroom and snatched away her breathing aid. The stress was going to knock her back, take what little feeble strength she had, strength that should be going towards fighting the virus in her lungs.

Just thinking of her ordeal made my hands clench white on the steering wheel. If I had managed to catch up with the man I would have inflicted a lot of damage.

Deliberately taking deep breaths and telling myself to calm down, I forced myself to concentrate on my driving. Having a smash and possibly injuring some other innocent motorist would certainly not help the situation.

The police had been very efficient, turning up only minutes after the matron's summoning call. They had questioned each of the nurses – even, extremely gently, assessed Silvie's recollections – and, of course, questioned me.

The only thing that annoyed me was their calm but firm reaction to my description of the dark blue Peugeot. 'But did you actually *see* the intruder climb the fence and drive off in the car, sir?' And, of course, I couldn't swear I had. So, no go. 'Sorry, sir, that's an assumption, not a fact.' As far as I was concerned it was a very fair assumption but they remained unimpressed.

And so I'd watched as the French doors had been secured and with nothing more I could contribute, I'd left Silvie in the capable hands of the nurses and made myself scarce. What I needed right now was a person I could talk to, bounce my theories off, someone less emotionally involved, to see if there was some fact I'd overlooked by being too close. That someone had to be Mike. His handling of crises was legendary. He'd had plenty of practice.

*   *   *

I drove into his stable yard forty minutes later. It was gone eleven; third lot was still out but a few of the horses that had been exercised in the first and second lots swung heads out over half-doors and followed my progress with large, liquid eyes. They say cats are curious but racehorses certainly are too.

I tried the back door of the main house but it was obvious Mike wasn't indoors. His truck was missing, which meant he was probably out on the gallops tracking the progress of his horses.

I walked back to the line of stables. Joe, Mike's head lad, was in the tack room. Hearing my footsteps approaching, he came out. The title 'lad' was incongruous. He was a stringy man the wrong side of fifty, grey at the temples and with a kindness in his blue eyes. I knew Mike thought a lot of him and left a good deal of the daily routine in his capable hands.

'Hi there, Harry. How're y'doin?'

'Getting there, thanks, Joe. His nibs out with the string?'

'Yeah, be about another ten minutes I should think.'

I nodded. 'Any racing today?'

'No, later in the week.'

'I'd like to collar him for a while. Would that cause any problems?'

'No, everything's running sweetly. No probs.'

'Right.' I nodded. I'd no wish to disrupt Mike's routine but I really needed to unburden myself to him. Get his take on the hateful business. My judgement was skewed by being emotionally involved. I needed his clear, analytical mind to look at it objectively and give me advice on what action, if any, I should take next. Joe and I chatted for a few minutes until the familiar clip-clop of many hooves sounded on the hard surface of the approach to the stables.

Joe straightened up and tugged his baseball cap firmly into place. 'OK, then?'

'Yes, you carry on, I'm fine.'

And he strode off to meet the incoming string of horses. Following on behind, Mike's truck was turning into the stable yard.

I went over and opened the door. 'Hi, Mike.'

'Can't keep away, y'see.'

Despite my shocking morning, I managed a brief grin. 'You're better than a whole bottle of tranquilizers.'

His eyes slid over me, assessing, forming opinions. 'Now, why would you be wanting those things?'

'I don't. But I do want your judgement, your take on what happened earlier today.'

He pursed his lips and jumped from the vehicle. 'Right. Come over to the house. We'll get some coffee and you can tell me what's up.'

His down-to-earth approach was just what I needed. I felt myself calm down. 'And after coffee, how about I treat us to a bite at The Horseshoes?'

'I'm not going to turn down an offer like that.' He chuckled. 'You're on.'

We repaired to his comfortable den, a cross between an office and a snug sitting room. I subsided into a leather recliner as Mike thrust a mug of coffee into my hand. He sprawled back in his own chair, took a long, appreciative slurp of his drink and fixed me with an intense stare. 'Come on, then, faze me out. What's happened?'

'Try attempted murder.'

He drew in a sharp breath, his brow wrinkling. 'You serious?'

'Yep.'

'*Who* tried to murder you?'

'Not me, Mike – Silvie.'

'My God!' He jerked forward, slopping coffee. 'Is she still with us?'

'Yes, thanks to the fast reaction of the nurses.'

He eased himself back in the chair. 'Give me the full S.P.'

So I filled him in on the whole sordid story, starting with the moment the night before when I'd realized a dark blue Peugeot was following me back home after leaving the pub at Gunthorpe. 'What I need from you, Mike, is an objective view on where I go from here. I'll be quite honest, I'm still reeling from what's happened.'

'It beggars belief,' Mike said. He shook his head. 'I can hardly take it in. I mean, poor, dear Silvie . . . the most innocent, vulnerable and inoffensive person. It's sickening. I'm not surprised you're in a mess. I'm not related to her and it's thrown me completely.'

We sat in silence for several minutes. The atmosphere in the room was heavy, brought down by the negative darkness of our depressing thoughts. I sighed, and added to it. 'My overriding concern now, of course, is when will the next attempt be made?'

'That thought,' Mike said, 'had already occurred to me.'

'You think it likely as well, then?'

'Unfortunately, Harry, I'm sure a further attack *will* be made, or attempted. But preventing it, well, that's something else. I mean, you can't stand guard over Silvie night and day waiting for it to happen.'

'So what do you reckon I should do?'

He rolled the coffee mug back and forth between his palms and shook his head. 'It's been said the best form of defence is . . .'

'Attack.' I finished his sentence.

'Hmmm.'

'That's feasible if you can see the enemy, but when you don't know who the enemy is . . .'

'Quite.'

'The start of all this was when I came off Gold Sovereign. All the aggro has happened since. And, let's be correct, since the results of the fall forced me to take on the job of writing Elspeth's biography.'

'So it has to be someone connected to her, or with her, however loosely. The answer must lie in the information you already have or what you will turn up during the writing.'

'My summing up exactly, but I might be looking right at it and not realize I am.'

'Very true. And I suppose there's any amount of contacts and casual acquaintances she's come across during a lifetime's work. Pretty hopeless to pinpoint any one person, I should think.'

'Yeah,' I agreed despondently.

'But you do know Elspeth's son is violently opposed to you writing this book.'

'Are you saying I should pack it up?'

'No-ooo,' he said slowly. 'Although, if you think it would take the heat away from Silvie I wouldn't try and dissuade you.'

'What are you saying, Mike?'

'I *think* I'm saying it's too late, mate. The cat's probably out of the bag already.'

'Meaning?'

'Whoever's behind this has probably already decided you have unearthed the hidden facts and what has been learned cannot be unlearned.'

'I see what you mean,' I said slowly. 'As in the only way now to shut me up is to blackmail me with Silvie's life or to finish me off altogether.'

He spread his hands. 'Basically, yes.'

'The irony of that is I haven't discovered any damning evidence.'

'You may not think so, but I'd lay good money that you have. OK, you've not yet recognized what its damaging potential is, but that's only a matter of time.'

I drained the now cold coffee. 'Well, as you say, what's learned cannot be unlearned. So it may be the way to minimize future risks is to plough on. Find out what it is that's hidden below the surface, then I should find out who's responsible and put a stop to the attacks.'

He jumped up, clapped me on the shoulder and relieved me of the empty mug. 'Lunch, yes?'

I nodded and stood up. 'My shout, though.'

'Whatever. We can work out a better campaign easier on a full stomach.'

I drove us over to The Horseshoes. It was packed, as usual, because the food was good and not overpriced. Surrounded by racing stables, it was a magnet to ravenous stable staff. Finding a table with difficulty, we waited to be served and deferred conversation until we had polished off jacket potatoes filled with tuna and sweetcorn.

'It's Leicester races on Thursday,' I said as, replete with food, we progressed to the washing it down stage.

'Oh, yes, you were going to grill that jockey, Carl Smith.'

'I still am. He's the one firm lead I've got.'

'If you need any more funds for greasing . . .'

I held up a hand. 'Stop right there, Mike. I'm not here to take handouts. I appreciate the offer but no, OK?'

'Fair enough. So, what are you going to ask this Carl Smith?'

'Dunno,' I said wryly, 'except find out if he's working on his own for the big cheese or just how many others there are.'

'He may not know.'

'True, but it's a question that needs asking. If he can point the finger at anyone else it gives me another lead to follow. And I want to know why he's involved. Is it just for the money? Or is it more personal?'

'You mean, does he have a grudge against you?'

'Yes, because if it's something I've inadvertently done maybe I can sort it, take away the need for getting even.'

'Good thinking. Get him on your side and you've got a mole, haven't you?'

I glanced around the crowded pub. 'Anyone here could be involved, you know. They're all in racing. Not a nice thought. I'm not going to be able to rest easy until I've found out who's pulling the strings.'

'Have you told Annabel . . . about Silvie?'

'No. And come to think about it, I haven't told Uncle George either.'

'Don't you think you should? They're family. If things hadn't turned out as they did today . . .'

'Yes, you're right again. See why I need your take?'

'I'm being logical.'

'Exactly. And I will let them know. As soon as I get back. I'll try to catch Annabel on her lunch break, then ring Uncle George.'

An hour later I was back at the cottage, having dropped Mike off at the yard on the way. I picked up the phone in the office, dialled and waited. Annabel picked up.

'Not disturbing you, am I? No clients waiting – or Jeffrey?' I felt the usual kick of jealousy in my guts at his name, even though it was me who had voiced it.

'Hello, Harry, darling. Yes, of course, there's a client in the waiting room. And thank God for it. But no, Jeffrey's not here and I still have a few minutes left of my lunch break.'

'I'm afraid I've some disquieting news. No way of softening this, either . . .'

'Harry,' she cut in, 'just tell me.'

'Yes, right.' So I told her.

Her gasp of outrage and shock came loudly down the phone.

'Steady on, girl. Silvie's all right.'

'Don't be stupid, Harry. How can she be all right? The fright alone would be enough to see her off. You know that. How could anyone *do* that?' Her voice had raised in pitch, which was unusual for Annabel. I knew she was finding it a shock herself, trying to cope with the reality that some bastard could actually take an oxygen tube away from someone with a lung infection.

'I'm truly sorry, Annabel. I hate upsetting you. But Mike said I should let you know what's happened. Uncle George, too.'

'No, no, you did right.' I could hear her sniffing back tears proceeded by a rustle of tissues as she blew her nose very hard. 'I'm glad you did. Please, promise me, Harry, you'll always keep me in the picture regarding Silvie. I still look on her as a sister-in-law – she *is* my sister-in-law. Just because we aren't together doesn't alter that.'

'Thank you,' I said humbly.

'Have to go.' She gave another teary sniff. 'A client . . . you know . . .'

'Of course. And I'm sorry to have upset you. Annabel . . .' I hesitated, 'You know . . . I love you.'

She gave a little choking sob and put the phone down.

Feeling almost as big a bastard as balaclava man, I pressed a finger on the phone rest, released it and dialled Uncle George's number. His shocked reaction was on a par with Annabel's except he didn't break down in tears, just swore violently instead. Funny, I'd never heard Uncle George curse before. I thought he was a quiet-tempered man. Until today. Now I was hearing expletives I'd never heard before. I held the phone away from my ear whilst he released all his rage.

'By God, if I get my hands on him . . .' He finished up.

'Stand in line, Uncle George.'

'What? Oh, yes, yes. You must be damned upset, too.'

'Believe it.'

'Is she being looked after now, you know, kept safe, in case the sod comes back?'

'The nursing staff are on red alert. I think it doubtful anyone can gain access after this.'

'Right, yes.' He calmed down. 'We still on for Friday, son? I think the sooner I tell you what I know the better.'

'Yes, I hadn't forgotten. Right now I need all the information I can get.'

'Quite. But not now, not down the phone. Friday.'

I found myself nodding. 'See you then, Uncle George.'

I limped through to the kitchen and made a strong coffee. My injured leg was displaying sympathy with the rest of my shattered nerves. My kneecap was hurting like hell. Best if I took a walking stick with me on Thursday to Leicester races. There'd be a fair bit of walking to do. But not the grotty hospital-issue one. My father had used a fine hickory stick occasionally because of arthritis. I'd dig it out of the dark hole under the stairs and use that. Didn't want the opposition to think I was still very weak on that leg – which I was. Dad's stick made a statement, had style. It was the type to be used even if you didn't need one.

I took a sip of the scalding black coffee and right then the landline rang. I hobbled back to the office. Placing the coffee down on the desk, I picked up the phone. 'Yes.'

A very soft, silky voice said, 'Harry Radcliffe?'

'Yes. Who is it?'

There was a low chuckle, mirthless. 'We won't waste time on questions like that. Just listen—'

'Now wait a minute—'

'No! You listen.' It was said in the same low tone that somehow achieved much more effect than a raised voice – the very opposite of Uncle George's diatribe. It was chilling. It reminded me of a snake slithering. Cold, dangerous.

'Your sister was lucky, very lucky, *this time.*'

'You bloody bastard.' I felt livid rage scour through me.

'I've been told that before. Now I'm telling you, Harry Radcliffe. Back off. Back off – or get broken.'

There was a click. And I was left holding a dead phone.

TWENTY

My searing-hot rage had gone, replaced now by icy determination. The telephone threat on Tuesday, far from staying my hand, increased my desire to hunt down Silvie's attacker and expose him for the evil bastard he was. My mind was totally focused. Nothing was going to stop me. I'd told no one about the phone call. No sense in distressing Annabel, nor causing anxiety for Mike. I knew where I stood now and it was up to me to act.

Rising early on Thursday morning I went downstairs, made a cup of tea and checked on Leo's whereabouts. His litter tray was still pristine, not so much as a paw print on the surface. I concluded he'd gone on one of his hunting jaunts – he'd not been in since Wednesday morning. Nothing to worry about there – a cat had to do what a cat had to do. Leo was his own man and the local pussies had better watch out.

All the same, I washed out and replaced his water bowl and refilled his dinner bowl with dry food. With the cat flap for access when he deigned to return home, his needs were met.

I took my mug of tea back upstairs and sat on the edge of the bed, drinking it and watching sparrows down in the garden taking dust baths in the rose bed. All was peaceful, uncomplicated. Why couldn't life stay that way? I sighed and made my way to the bathroom where I bathed, shaved and chose my clothes with care, aiming for the dressed-down look. It was important that I didn't come across as high on the social ladder, nor give off the subtle vibrations of being wealthy. True, I was going to offer Carl Smith a fair hand-out for his dubious allegiance, but my funds were far from being bottomless and he might try pushing for a lot more if he thought I could afford it.

Back downstairs, I dug around under the stairs and found Dad's hickory stick. Thick, heavy and gnarled, it was a substantial support for my left leg. It would do the job nicely. Stepping outside into the fresh morning air, I opened up the Mazda's boot and stowed it away.

There were a couple of hours to kill before setting off for Leicester racecourse so I went back indoors and phoned Silvie's nursing home to check on her welfare as I did twice every day now. There was no change, they said, no further alarms, no attempted entry. I thanked them and switched on my desktop computer. Two hours without interruption would push the biography along nicely.

At ten o'clock I called a halt, made some coffee and read through what I'd written. It was all holding very nicely on the clothesline. Satisfied, I closed down the computer and picked up the car keys. Time to go. What I'd say to Carl when I met him I hadn't a clue but some things were best not pre-planned. I had a feeling this was one of them.

Bumping over the grass in the car park as a visitor at the racecourse felt very odd. It was already fairly full and I'd been directed to park down the far end. I opened up the boot and took out the hickory stick. I was glad I'd brought it. Walking back over the field, I paid my entrance fee and was admitted through the turnstile. Buying a race card, I took it into the bar, bought a coffee and sat down to digest both.

According to the card, Carl's horse was in the first race. It was possible that he hadn't even arrived yet. Dougie the barman came across to collect stray, empty glasses. He stopped at my table.

'Hiya. Haven't seen you for a while, Harry.'

'Hi, Dougie. No, sidelined at the moment.'

'Reckon you will get back to riding?'

'I sure hope so. Takes time finding out.' Not to mention the sweat of effort doing physio three times every week.

He eyed the stick propped up by the table. 'Yeah, guess so. It was a bad 'un, that fall.'

'It was.' I smiled ruefully. 'Do me a favour, Dougie – if you see Carl Smith in here could you tell him I'm looking to have a word?'

''Course. Haven't seen him yet, mind, but the day's early.' It may have been, but the bar seemed to suddenly fill up. Dougie flipped a hand. 'Take care, mate.' He walked back behind the bar and began filling glasses.

A tall, angular man coming in behind the throng caught my eye. He slapped on a smile and made a beeline for me.

It took me a couple of seconds to place him. Nathaniel Willoughby, artist, specializing in horseracing and people intimately involved. He was one of the people on my list to have a few words with, hopefully get a few quotes and useable copy for the biography.

'You're Harry Radcliffe.' He thrust out a hand.

'That's right.' I shook it.

'Elspeth emailed me, said you'd be contacting me regarding her book.'

I had found a mention in her racing diary of Elspeth having had a portrait painted some fifteen or more years ago when one of her horses had won the Champion Hurdle. I recalled seeing it hung on the wall in her study. The artist had captured the essence of her character. Not only the public image of a good-looking, smart woman, but also one with the glint of steel in the eye, telling of a formidable personality. Not an easy accomplishment, but Willoughby hadn't reached his present state of top-level professional without years of dedication and graft. I admired his work and wished I could afford to buy one of his racing pictures. It would undoubtedly be a sound investment, but you'd need to take out a mortgage to buy one.

'What're you drinking?' He cocked an eyebrow at my coffee cup.

'I'm fine.'

'Oh, come now. Seeing as I'm here to soak up the atmosphere as well as the liquid,' he chortled, 'I can't drink on my own, can I?'

I didn't think it would influence him at all – he had a reputation as a hard drinker. I'd no intention of having a drink but he steamrollered me into agreeing to have a half.

He pushed up to the bar for the drinks and I covertly watched him. Everything he wore said top quality, top price, even down to his handmade leather shoes. His hair had been cut by a master and fell into place perfectly. Not a man to take second best. I'd have bet he was a man who could hold his own in most circumstances.

I wondered idly how he'd got on with Elspeth. That was one of the questions I intended to ask. As to what he would tell me that would provide interesting copy I'd have to wait and see, try to direct the conversation and hope he would let fall some gems. He bustled back with two foaming pints.

'Oh . . . a half, I think . . .'

He brushed aside my feeble protestation.

'One swallow and that would be gone.' He demonstrated by emptying his own glass by two-thirds in one massive gulp. 'If I've caught you at a disadvantage by pre-empting our meeting, I apologize. We can always arrange a further date if you like.'

He drew a small, unlined notepad from his inner pocket. 'How about I jot down the questions and then I can email my answers back to you tonight, eh?'

I nodded. 'That would be great, thanks.' He beamed, clicked a biro into service and proceeded to scribble down my email address.

'You here to work today?'

'Yes, make a few thumbnail sketches, catch the mood, the odd expression, facial reactions, the gestures, that sort of thing.' For a moment he looked almost embarrassed. I understood. For all his fame and professionalism, he still retained inside the childish joy of doing something that gave him personal satisfaction. I, too, felt that keen uprush of pure pleasure every time I swung into the saddle. The thought brought me sharply to the fact that I might never again be able to ride a horse or win a race. Looking at his smiling face, I felt a pang of jealousy. He would never experience a fall from a horse that would result in losing his chosen career. But hard on that thought came another. Maybe he wouldn't fall from a horse but the world was a hostile place, full of dangers. Who was to say he wouldn't suffer some accident that would have horrendous consequences? He might develop crippling arthritis in his hands, or worse, he could lose his sight.

I reproached myself for being such a self-pitying loser. Life dealt out the cards and it's up to each of us to play the hand we've been given. I gave my full concentration to asking questions of him that I thought might provoke original, amusing replies that would give colour to Elspeth's character. We sat for nearly an hour before, surprisingly, I quite reluctantly excused myself. 'I must find someone before it gets any later.'

'You carry on, Harry. Business is always priority, eh?'

'Yes,' I said. 'Look forward to seeing your emails later.'

'A refill before you go?'

I shook my head.

'Oh well, I'm not so strict with myself. Got to keep up my reputation.'

I left him heading back to the bar and made my way outside towards the pre-parade ring and the saddling boxes.

During the last hour, race-goers had flooded into the race-course all intent on having a good time, and now it was heaving with excited, happy people. There was a great atmosphere of relaxed goodwill.

I threaded a path through the throng. It felt strange, unsettling simply to be a visitor rather than a working jockey. Down by the pre-parade ring things were hotting up. Trainers were busy in the boxes tacking up, getting their horses ready to be walked round. I pushed through the crowd and leaned on the rail, watching it all with a hollow feeling in my stomach. The pull of racing was a physical thing. The only thing I wanted, hungered for. Coming here when I couldn't participate wasn't perhaps the smartest thing to do.

Then I thought of Silvie, helpless, in danger. I had to be here, had to find Carl. And undoubtedly he was here somewhere, working for Sampson, the trainer. The race card had Sampson's horse, Sandfly, down to run in the first race, which meant I stood a good chance of spotting him at this point.

I scanned the run of boxes. Horses were being led out, walked up ready for the parade ring itself. I knew several of the lads leading them round, got nods off two or three as they acknow-ledged me. I recognized John from Elspeth's yard approaching, leading a big bay with a white blaze. I leaned over the rail.

'Hi, John, seen anything of Carl Smith?'

He slowed and turned the horse in a tight circle. 'Sure, he's down there. Want me to send him over?'

'Be grateful if you could. Tell him it'll be worth it.'

He grinned slyly. 'Like that, is it? OK, I'll tell him.' Clucking to the horse, he led it forward on long, rangy strides.

I watched and waited. Saw him turn at the corner and walk past one of the doors, then slow and call out before walking on. A head stuck itself round the door jamb – Carl Smith. I raised my hand a couple of inches from where it rested on the rail then let it drop back. Carl gave a slight nod and disappeared back into the box.

Content to wait now I'd tracked him down, I watched the horses. They'd been sadly lacking in my life for the past few weeks; I gratefully drank them in like a man deprived of water.

A few minutes later Carl emerged and made his way over to me. 'Yeah, so what d'y'want?' he muttered, almost inaudibly.

I, in turn, deliberately kept my voice low. 'To offer you a proposition.'

'Like what?'

'Money for information.'

A cunning glint came into his eye. 'Too public here. Meet you in the gents, just before the off for the first race.' Wheeling away, he retreated.

I stayed where I was. The crowd around me shifted and moved constantly, restlessly, following the progress of the horses as they left the pre-parade and saddling boxes before entering the parade ring, where they could be seen at close quarters by all the hopeful punters.

In a few minutes' time the jockeys would stream from the changing room and meet up with their respective mounts, trainers and owners. The so familiar spectacle of brightly coloured silks atop chestnut coats, circling round emerald-green grass, was pure chocolate-box England.

Today was a flat meeting and the jockeys would canter their mounts out on to the course and down to the start where they would all, if the horses didn't disgrace themselves, enter the starting stalls. That would be my signal to slip across to the gents. Hopefully there would be no stray man with a waterworks problem in the toilets. The crowd would be crammed along the rails and in the stands. Presumably Carl thought it a quick bit of business. Ask what question and what amount of cash – bingo.

I knew it would take longer than he'd anticipated but whilst the race was running everybody's attention would be riveted on the racecourse. It gave us several minutes. I felt my pulse quicken. I was getting closer to knowing who had tried to kill Silvie. I couldn't wait to find out.

By now I was pretty much on my own looking over to the saddling boxes. Listening intently, I waited for the order to mount. At that point I had maybe six or seven minutes' grace. It would only take three minutes to walk to the toilets. The overall noise level was increasing as excitement rose but then, clearly, I heard the summons: 'Jockeys, please mount.' I checked my watch, counted down three minutes then pushed away from the rails and walked in the direction of the public conveniences.

I could hear the muted drumming of hooves cantering away down the course towards the start and smiled grimly. At this point there would be a hasty last-minute zipping up of flies before legging it to find a space by the rails to watch the race. Indeed, two older, grey-haired gentlemen came rushing out, puffing their red-faced way towards the scene of the action. Neither of them appeared to notice me. I was the only person heading in the opposite direction.

I entered the toilets, went through the square, tiled entrance lobby and pushed through the door into the main area. Predictably it was empty. I walked over, past the urinals, and came to the first cubicle. Water was oozing out over the tiles. Water tinged red. The door was ajar. Indeed, it couldn't have been closed.

Carl Smith lay sprawled on the toilet floor, arse in the air, legs grotesquely splayed. His ripped trousers were soaked in blood. From the back of his right leg, the femur bone was sticking out through white flesh. His head wasn't visible. It had been thrust down forcibly into the toilet bowl.

TWENTY-ONE

I stood transfixed with horror. And in the split second it took me to realize Carl was dead, all hell broke loose behind me in the entrance lobby. Racecourse security came in at the double, together with police, a St John's ambulance attendant plus the two red-faced, elderly gentlemen I'd seen leaving the toilets. Obvious now, of course, that they hadn't been going to watch the race. They'd been rushing to report finding the body.

The St John's first-aid attendant carried out a swift examination. Straightening up, he faced the policeman. 'Dead, sir, I'm afraid,' he confirmed. 'In addition to the broken femur, he's also sustained a bang to the front of his head. There's a big gash across his forehead.'

The policeman nodded, took out his radio and phoned for back-up and the police pathologist. 'I want all this area cordoned off. Nobody is to be allowed in.' He scanned the tiled room, assessing the possible effects on the general public of withdrawing essential services. 'Even in the *direst* circumstances, OK?' The security chaps nodded.

'You two gentlemen,' the policeman continued, nodding at each of the elderly men waiting by the door, 'will need to make a statement.' Swinging round, he eyed me with grim suspicion. 'And who might you be, sir?'

'Someone who came in at the wrong moment,' I replied.

His lips snapped shut. 'I shall need your full particulars – and a statement. I don't want anybody leaving the racecourse, all right?'

We all acquiesced meekly.

Things happened very quickly after that. The clerk of the course's office was taken over as an immediate incident room and the Leicestershire police arrived in strength, together with the pathologist. Myself, along with the other two men, were interviewed and made statements. In my case, I didn't deny I knew the man and identified him as being Carl Smith, jockey, working for Fred Sampson, who subsequently confirmed the identification. What I didn't enlighten the police about was the assignation I'd made with the deceased.

Instructions were broadcast from the commentator's box informing the bewildered race-goers that an incident had taken place and no one was to leave. There was no immediate danger – nobody was at risk. The public were asked to be patient whilst the police carried out inquiries.

It was a magnificent display of crowd control, defusing the potentially panicked situation. An ambulance had been driven over to the gents and Carl's body, after being photographed from every angle, leaving nothing to dignity, was driven away.

I was sitting things out, nursing a mug of tea, when I heard my name called; my presence was required. I took a long pull of tea and, very carefully, set down the mug. For the first time I felt a shiver of apprehension run through me.

I hadn't told the police I'd asked Carl to meet me; I'd just said I'd gone in for a leak. But it seemed one of their bright sparks had come across a hickory walking stick stowed down inside a waste bin. The stick was covered with blood and particles of body tissue.

Dougie, the bar man, had apparently confidently identified it as belonging to one Harry Radcliffe.

I was taken by police car to the main headquarters in Leicester. I spent a very taxing afternoon being questioned by stern-jawed detectives, changing my economical statement for the truth – the whole nothing-left-out-this-time truth, if you don't mind, sir – before being released under caution and ordered not to leave town. Or in other words, don't do a runner – or else. Which, of course, I had no intention of doing.

It had been Dougie, despite having been the one to put me on the spot in the first place, who passed on the vital information that led to my release. Apparently, after I'd left the bar, he had taken it upon himself to lean my stick up behind the bar for safekeeping. Later, a colleague had reported to Dougie that he'd seen a man lean over and retrieve the stick a short time after. He'd thought it funny that the man had got gloves on –

golfing gloves. And that man, he said emphatically, hadn't been yours truly.

I, minus Dad's hickory stick, which had gone to forensics, tottered back into Harlequin Cottage later that evening feeling I'd been trampled into the ground by a herd of wild horses. Most definitely it hadn't been the most enjoyable day I'd spent on a racecourse.

Pouring myself a large whisky, I slumped down on to the settee. Despite having had nothing to eat since breakfast, I'd no stomach for food. The vision of Carl Smith repeated itself in my mind's eye and was not conducive to providing an appetite. I took a gulp of whisky, felt the burn going down and was humbly grateful to be here, safely at home and not occupying a cell in Leicester nick.

For the first time I thought about the consequences of Carl's death in relation to Silvie's safety. Carl had been my only lead and, without doubt, he'd been silenced to stop him talking. But whoever had murdered him had obviously been watching me. Had seen my stick, stupidly forgotten, left behind leaned up against the table I'd occupied with Willoughby. It had been used specifically to tie me in with his murder. I didn't hold any hopes of fingerprints being found on it.

And that same someone had been close enough to overhear my conversation with Carl – must have been – and had then taken one almighty risk by following Carl into the gents.

The official view was that Carl had been facing the wall actually taking a leak when he'd been savagely hit across his lower thighs with the hickory stick. It was thick and heavy, and would have acted like a baseball bat – unbending. The stick had broken his right femur and pitched him forward and downwards. His forehead had connected with the urinal and it seemed likely he had been knocked unconscious. His assailant had then dragged him to the nearest cubicle and forced his head down the toilet. Because he wasn't conscious, there wouldn't have been a struggle. Death would have occurred very quickly. The murder hadn't been planned; the murderer had simply taken full advantage of the circumstances. A case of silencing Carl and putting me in the frame in one go.

Fruitlessly I bent my brain to think who had been close enough to hear us make the assignation. But it was useless. The crowd around me could have concealed an elephant. Virtually anybody could have listened in to our brief conversation. The police had already grilled me on this point. Then an idea struck me. Who knew I was intending to visit the racecourse today? And the answer to that followed straight after. I hadn't known myself until Monday night when I'd sat in the Unicorn at Gunthorpe with Mike and we'd gone through the *Racing Post*. That was where someone had learned of my proposed Thursday attendance at Leicester races. It didn't take any further working out. It was blindingly obvious: blue Peugeot man. Where he hadn't succeeded in killing Silvie, he had finished Carl. I took a deep, ragged breath and swallowed the rest of the whisky. I felt dirty, tainted by the whole sordid mess.

I put the glass down, went upstairs and stood under a very hot shower.

Emerging twenty minutes later, red, scoured and feeling considerably cleaner, I padded barefooted downstairs wearing just a towelling dressing gown. I raided the fridge, found half a pork pie and, munching it, went through into the office and switched on the computer. By now I hoped to find an email from Willoughby waiting for me.

I wasn't disappointed. There was a short message referring to our meeting earlier that day together with an attachment. I opened it up. Methodically, he had listed down chronologically all the questions I'd asked together with the corresponding answers. And they weren't monosyllabic ones either, but full, open ones running, in some cases, to several sentences. He must have put a lot of time and work into the email and I was very appreciative. A good deal of the content I could certainly use in the biography. It took me several minutes to read through them all. When I'd finished I reached for the telephone and dialled his number listed at the start of the email. It rang for a few moments then he picked up.

'Willoughby here.'

'Hello, it's Harry. Harry Radcliffe.'

'Oh, yes, dear chap. Did you get my email?'

'Certainly did. I must thank you; the answers will be a great help. It must have taken you some time and I really appreciate it.'

'No need to thank me, Harry. My pleasure.'

'Elspeth's a lucky lady to have had you paint her portrait. I thought it showed real insight to her character.'

'Elspeth's a very good subject, multi-faceted, as they say. It was a pleasure to paint her. And answering your questions is a way of saying thank you to her.'

'Oh? Surely it's the other way round? Shouldn't she be thanking you for doing such a good job?'

'My dear Harry,' Willoughby chuckled softly, 'indeed not. I consider myself a gentleman, my lips completely sealed . . . et cetera. But you do follow me?'

I was beginning to.

'Elspeth, the lovely Elspeth, didn't *pay* for her painting.'

'Oh, I see . . .'

'Thought you would. But I'm sure I don't have to remind you that you, too, are a gentleman.'

'Point taken, Nathanial. I shan't mention anything out of place in the biography.'

He chuckled happily. 'Knew I could rely on you. We must meet up for a drink sometime. Celebrate, perhaps, when the book comes out.'

'Fine by me. And thanks again.'

I put the receiver down and sat thinking about what he'd said, or rather, hadn't said. So, fifteen years ago or more, Willoughby and Elspeth had had an affair. How long it had been going on – or still was, perhaps – was an unknown. But I'd bet Victor Maudsley hadn't known anything about it. For a brief moment or two I wondered if this little nugget of information was what Marriot didn't want me to find out. Then I dismissed it. It was no sort of motive for the ghastly things that had been done to Silvie and to Carl Smith. No, there was something much larger at stake.

I spent a restless, mostly sleepless night. Bad dreams weren't the words to describe what happened on the occasions I did drop off. The sight of Carl Smith's bloodied body must have been indelibly inscribed on my subconscious to release the horrors I came up with whilst asleep. Finally, at around five o'clock, awaking with sweat-soaked sheets, I rolled out of bed and went in search of some strong tea. Whilst in the kitchen waiting for the kettle to boil, there was a bump and clatter behind me and, nerves rubbed red raw, I jumped and spun round ready to defend myself.

A big, ginger tom paced across the quarries and took a measured leap at me. Leo landed with a heavy thump on my shoulder. He began rubbing his head against my jaw, purring like a buzz saw.

'Hi to you, too. Had a good result?' He purred louder. Our neighbourhood was littered, no pun intended, with his distinctive ginger offspring. At least one of us had spent a good night. But it wasn't just yesterday's murder causing me to lose sleep. Today, Friday, I was due to meet Uncle George at the Royal Oak. What form his disclosures would take I couldn't begin to guess. But since they would obviously affect Silvie as well as myself, conjecture on the outcome, without the murder, was enough to cause insomnia.

Leo had already polished off a dish of chicken chunks in jelly and put up the 'Do Not Disturb' notice above his basket, while I was only partway through a bowl of cereal when my mobile rang. For a second, cravenly, I hoped it was Uncle George ringing to cancel today's meeting. Instead it was Elspeth enquiring on progress being made with the biography.

'Going well, and thanks for paving the way with Nathanial Willoughby.'

'You've seen him already?'

'Yes, well, he happened to be at Leicester racecourse yesterday, as I was, and he found me.'

'Er . . . did he give you some *useable* copy?'

I tried not to smile as I answered her. I didn't want the amusement travelling down the line.

'Yes, yes, he did.'

'You won't forget what I said, Harry? Not too revealing?'

'Trust me, Elspeth. Your reputation will be . . . almost . . .'

'OK!' She was smiling, I could tell. 'Try to keep your exposé tantalizing, not explicit.'

'Right. The merest hint you do have a *private* life.'

'Exactly.' She was openly laughing now. 'And talking of

having a life other than work, I'd like you to come to a family bash on Saturday night. You are free, aren't you?'

I took a deep breath. 'Will, er, Marriot be there?'

'Silly boy – of course he will.'

Talk about going into the lion's den. But it wasn't so much an invitation as a command.

'Now don't start thinking up an excuse, Harry.' The tiniest edge of cold steel could just be discerned. And I didn't want to antagonize her. Not before I'd found out what Uncle George needed to tell me. Silvie's future was insecure enough right now. I needed to keep Elspeth sweet because I needed the money from her biography to help pay for Silvie's ongoing care.

'I'll be there, Elspeth.'

'Good.' The word was said with satisfaction. 'See you at eight o'clock on Saturday. Oh, and press on with the book. I want it finished now, asap.' She disconnected before I had a chance to comment.

Gratefully, I went back to chewing my soggy cereal.

At a quarter to eleven, I started the car and drove down to the village. Parking at the side of the Royal Oak's impressive car park, I sat and waited for Uncle George's car to turn up. I was a bit early but I needed to know what the bombshell would be. A few minutes later he drove in. I locked the Mazda and walked across.

'Hello, Uncle George. You all right?'

'Hello, Harry, not bad.' Grunting, he extricated himself from the vehicle, put two hands in the small of his back and stretched. 'Getting old, son, a bit bent.' He smiled ruefully. 'Come to think of it, that's what we're here for, isn't it? So I can unbend and take a weight off my shoulders.'

'Since I'm totally in the dark . . .' I began.

'Come on,' he patted my arm, 'let's go inside and have a drink.'

I followed him.

'Now,' he said as we sat down with our beers, 'are we here for lunch as well?'

'Up to you. I'm free.'

'Shall we say yes, then? But if you want to walk out at anytime, do so.'

'Will I want to?'

'Yes.'

My stomach knotted. If it was going to be that bad, maybe lunch was not such a good idea. Following on from my non-eating day yesterday, I thought irrelevantly, it would do wonders for my riding weight. Until cold reality poured over me. I wasn't riding – not now, perhaps not ever.

'Uncle George, I just want the facts, OK?'

He nodded and polished off his pint. 'You shall have them, without garnish.'

'Would you rather go back to my cottage and, you know, talk in private?'

'No. I'd never have the bottle. Better it's here. That way either of us can run for the hills. Just remember, Harry, I don't want to upset you . . .' He stopped, flicked a twenty-pound note across the table at me. 'Look, be a good chap and order me the sausage and mash.'

I didn't argue, just took the money and ordered double bangers and mash with onion gravy.

When the food arrived it smelled wonderful and tasted even better. The phrase 'the condemned man ate a hearty breakfast' came to mind but as the aroma titillated my olfactory nerves my body decided enough of starvation, it wanted nourishment. Uncle George was of a similar mind and we dug in. Mentally I was poised on a cliff edge to hear what he wanted to say. However, I could see it wasn't going to be easy for him. I had to let him take all the time he needed.

About halfway through the meal he turned to me. 'I know you think I'm hard-hearted because I refused to go and visit Silvie. But I'm not.'

To cover my confusion, I cut into my second juicy sausage.

'I never thought that. Even I find it difficult to visit her at times. It's not easy for an outsider, I can see that.' As soon as I'd said the words, I regretted them. 'Sorry, really, I'm sorry . . .'

He shook his head. 'Don't be, Harry. You're quite right. I am an outsider.'

'I didn't mean it like that.'

'But I do.'

'What do you mean?'

He laid down his knife and fork. 'Best I tell you straight out. I loved your mother. I'd loved her since my late teens. But she didn't want me, see, she fell for John, my brother. They got married. I stood aside, it was the only thing to do, and made a life for myself, went out with other girls, but none of them meant anything to me. Then I met Rachel. We seemed to get on, so,' he spread out his hands helplessly, 'we got married. Probably the wrong thing to do . . . I don't know.' He lowered his voice. 'Even though Elizabeth was married to your father, I was still in love with her.' He sighed. 'Always will be.'

He glanced swiftly at me then down at his plate, picked up his cutlery and tackled the last of his meal. He waved his fork at me, indicating I should continue. To save him embarrassment, I resumed eating.

'I've tried to be a good husband to Rachel. Treated her as well and as fairly as I possibly could.' It was taking an effort for him to unburden himself.

'I'm quite sure you have,' I put in gently.

'Yes, well, if John hadn't had the accident and died, nothing would have happened. I respected Elizabeth's choice just as I respected John.' He finished his meal, then dabbed his lips with the paper napkin. 'But he did get shot and he did die. And, as you know well enough, Elizabeth turned to me for comfort and help. I couldn't deny her my support, Harry. It isn't in my nature to be a hard, uncaring man.'

'Uncle George, I know you're not. And I know she needed more help at that time than I could give her. I'm not blaming you at all for what happened.'

'But that's it, son. *Nothing happened.*'

'What?' I said incredulously. 'Now, come on, Uncle George . . .'

He hung his head and I had to bend over the table to catch his whispered words. 'Yes, OK. Elizabeth and I, we . . . comforted each other . . . And yes, we made love . . . but that's all.' He swallowed hard. 'I'm telling you the honest truth, Harry.' He looked at me despairingly. '*I'm not Silvie's father.*'

TWENTY-TWO

I felt my jaw drop. I gaped at him, couldn't take it in. Then the shockwave hit my body and knocked me for six.

'Not . . . *not* . . . Silvie's father?'

'No.' He shook his head sadly. 'I'm sorry, Harry. Should have told you a long time ago, when Elizabeth died.' He closed his eyes briefly. 'But I didn't.'

'Why?' I forced the word out.

'Why is easy to explain. I'd never have said anything whilst Elizabeth was alive, never. But even after she died, I still found myself wanting to protect her reputation.'

We stared at each other, my awareness of what he meant becoming clear. My hands clenched into fists on top of the table.

'Are you saying my mother was promiscuous? Are you, Uncle George?' Anger and hurt made my voice rise.

'Shush.' He glanced round nervously to make sure nobody had heard my outburst, but the pub was more than half-empty and, in our corner alcove, our conversation went unheard.

'No, of course I'm not saying such an untruth.'

'Then just what *are* you saying?' I deliberately tried to unclench my fingers but found it difficult.

'Your dear mother was beside herself with grief when your father died so unexpectedly. She adored him, had never looked at another man during their marriage. Don't you see?' He pushed his face close to mine. 'That's why I married Rachel. I knew there was no chance for me. Elizabeth was deeply in love with John.'

I took a shuddering breath, tried to calm down. I was finding this conversation unpleasant but I realized the truth needed to be known. Uncle George's revelation had been like the opening of Pandora's box and couldn't now be undone.

'Then how come she got pregnant? Whose baby was it if it wasn't your—'

'I blame myself,' he blurted out, not meeting my eyes. Red suffused his face, turning it to beetroot colour. 'I do, I blame myself. In the fragile state she was in, I should never have left her that day . . . But Rachel had rung, said she needed me. So what else could I do?' He looked at me imploringly. 'I'm *married* to Rachel.'

'Uncle George,' I said very slowly and carefully, 'you're not making any sense.'

He took out a large handkerchief and mopped his face. His breath was now coming in sawing gasps. I looked at him, saw an elderly man in a highly distressed state and made a decision.

'Come on.' I stood up. 'We're both going back to my cottage.' He started to protest. 'No, please don't argue. You won't need any more bottle. You've done the hardest part – at least, I think you have. And neither of us feels too good right now. Let's drive home before we feel any worse, OK?'

He nodded, slumping in his seat.

'You're right, son. I can't speak for you but it's taken it out of me.'

'Come on, then.' I slid a hand beneath his elbow. 'Let's head home.'

Back at my cottage I sat him down on the settee and poured us both a small brandy.

'I'm driving . . .'

'Medicinal. And you've had a good meal.'

He reached for the tumbler gratefully, knocked off the tot and leaned back against the cushions, closing his eyes. His high colour had drained away now, leaving him looking pale and worn. I was feeling pretty shattered myself. It had been an almighty shock to learn he was not Silvie's father after eighteen years of assuming he was. Even his wife, my Aunt Rachel, hadn't known. She, too, thought he was Silvie's father. And had made his life a living hell because of it. He'd never said a word to the contrary. He must have been totally besotted with my mother. The whole situation beggared belief. But equally devastating was the question the disclosure threw up: if Uncle George wasn't responsible, who was Silvie's father?

I realized at that moment why Nigel, the solicitor, had been so insistent on keeping the name of Silvie's trust fund benefactor a secret. It hadn't been Uncle George at all but her real father who had signed the document. So, who was he?

I'd have to let Uncle George tell me in his own time. He wasn't a young man and no way did I want to pre-empt a heart attack or stroke. His high colour in the pub suggested it wasn't an unlikely possibility.

Over on the desk my mobile rang, the shrill sound making Uncle George jump and open his eyes.

'It's OK, I'll take the call outside.'

He closed his eyes wearily and I took the phone into the kitchen.

'Harry Radcliffe.'

'Harry, darling, it's Annabel.'

My fingers tightened around the phone and my heart leapt as it always did at the sound of her voice. Oh, how I wished she was here right now, wished I could hold her, share the shattering news. See her reaction, listen to what she had to say. Her presence was always balancing and soothing. And, by God, I needed a bit of balance right now.

'Harry? You still there?'

'Yes, yes, I'm here.'

'Are you all right? You certainly don't sound it.'

'No, not really. But I will be soon.'

'Why, what's happened?'

'Had a bit of a shock, that's all.' Bit of a shock! What a bloody understatement.

'Darling, I'm so sorry. Can you handle some more pressure?' She carried on before I could reply. 'It's the nursing home. They've been trying to ring you for the past couple of hours but had no joy. So, they rang me to see if I could get hold of you.'

'Annabel, nothing would give me greater pleasure right now than to have you hold me, believe me, but what do they want? Is something amiss with Silvie?' The recollection of the attack on her life hit me. 'Is she OK . . . Not been hurt . . .?'

'Whoa, slow down, Harry. Nothing like that. But she is poorly. Apparently her temperature's gone up and she's very restless.

They want to know if you could go over and calm her down.
She always seems to find your visits calming, reassuring.'

'Yes, of course.'

'Are you sure you're OK, because you really don't sound it.'

'Sure I am, don't worry. I'll go over in a few minutes.'

'They said straight away, if you could, please, Harry. And
that was an hour ago – more.'

'Yes, I will, but I've got Uncle George here. I'll have to see
him safely off home first.'

'Oh, right, I see.'

'Thanks for calling me. Er, Annabel, I . . . I really need to
talk to you, later, if it's possible . . .'

'If it's important come round to the house tonight. I should
be back from work around five or just after.'

'Thanks, I will. Bye, my love.'

I pushed the mobile back into my pocket and went to see
how Uncle George was going on.

The brandy had brought a healthy colour to his face and he
looked much better. On seeing me he scrambled to his feet.
Before he could say anything I told him the gist of the phone
message. 'So I have to go over to the nursing home.'

''Course you do. I quite see that. And I'm off home.'

'Will you be OK driving? I could nip you over.'

'No, I'm fine. We'll speak another time, son, eh?'

'Yes. It's kept for eighteen years – another few days won't
make any difference.'

Except his disclosure had already made a difference, and we
both knew it. My perspective had shifted from thinking of him
primarily as Silvie's father to the more unsavoury one of simply
my mother's lover. At least I knew the truth about Uncle
George's role. The other fact, establishing just who was Silvie's
natural father, would eventually become clear in any case as
soon as she reached her eighteenth birthday, which was only
a couple of weeks away. I had to admit feeling relief that
her trust fund was obviously now going to be paid over and her
financial future, from being seriously questionable, now looked
secure.

I was approaching seventy thousand words already completed
on Elspeth's biography and, if I plugged away, could possibly

finish it by then. The book would net me a substantial sum – enough to run my personal ship until I received the hospital verdict as to whether or not I'd ever be able to ride again. But if I'd still had to support Silvie, the future would certainly have been grim – for both of us.

I saw Uncle George safely into his car and waved him off. I was sure that he, like myself, sighed with relief that the upsetting and difficult meeting was over, at least for now.

And with the time at only one thirty I had three and a half hours free to drive over to comfort Silvie before I could meet up with Annabel and give her the facts.

In the event, Silvie responded, as she always did, to my reassurance, and after only half an hour at her bedside her temperature had returned to normal and she had calmed down and drifted off into an untroubled sleep.

I managed over two hours' work on the book, punctuated by several mugs of tea, took a quick shower and set off for Leicestershire.

Annabel had said not to come to her office in Melton Mowbray but to her home instead. It was a delicate situation, visiting my own wife in the home she shared with another man. But I really needed to see her, to tell her about Uncle George's disclaimer and get her rational point of view.

The irony of it struck me as I slowed down and drew up at the entrance to her long, curving drive. I'd been over to soothe Silvie and now found myself in a similar situation of being in need of calming down. I checked my watch. She'd said she'd be home after five and it was about twenty past now. Engaging first gear, I turned in through the open gates and slowly drove all the way down to the house.

Parking up, I rang the bell. The sound ebbed away and a couple of minutes later the door opened.

'Why, Harry . . .' There was surprise in Sir Jeffrey's voice as he stood in the doorway.

My heart sank. He was the last person I wanted to see. I'd hoped for a quiet chat alone with Annabel. It didn't look like I'd get one now. He collected himself first.

'Do come in . . . I take it you want Annabel?'

What a damn fool question to ask me. He knew the answer,

knew the choice between us was down to Annabel herself. Suddenly, unexpectedly, I saw a flicker of uncertainty in his eyes and recognized myself. For all his wealth and status, he was still a man, prey to insecurity like the rest of us. And right now his emotional insecurity was showing.

'Hello, Sir Jeffrey.'

He held up a hand instantly. 'No, please, Harry, Jeffrey is fine, just fine.'

I nodded. 'Afraid I need to speak to Annabel . . .'

'You all right?'

'Well, yes . . . and no.'

He became the perfect host. 'Come on inside, do have a glass, something cheering.' He waved me through to the lounge. It was a massively proportioned room done very cleverly in toning russets and warm colours. The open fireplace was screened by a beautifully worked tapestry and flanked on either side of the hearth by tall stone jugs holding dried grasses. He poured us both a whisky from the decanter on the walnut sideboard and thrust one into my hand.

'Can I help?'

The query was genuine, as was the look of concern in his grey eyes. I could see why Annabel had described him as a good man.

I took a sip of whisky. 'To be frank, er, Jeffrey, I don't think there's anything anyone can do. It's just me, I'm afraid. I'm reeling a bit at the moment.'

'I'm sure Annabel can balance you up. Have to say she's good at that.'

I smiled briefly. 'My thoughts exactly, which is why I've come, to be honest. I've had an almighty shock, silly really, but it does seem to have knocked me for six.'

'Do you want to tell me, or perhaps you'd prefer to wait and tell Annabel?'

I was about to opt for the latter but, strangely, found myself giving him the facts instead. He sat quietly and listened, didn't interrupt and waited until I'd finished. I took another sip of whisky. I hadn't meant to tell him. But, catching a glimpse of the vulnerable inner man, somehow my view of him had changed and our relationship seemed to have moved on. I didn't think we could ever be friends, but I had warmed a little towards him.

'My word, it's a facer, isn't it? Not surprised it's thrown you. As you said, there's nothing anyone can do, just have to accept it. But I know how fond Annabel is of Silvie. You certainly did the right thing in coming.' He stopped speaking.

Footsteps were coming down the hall towards the lounge. The door opened and Annabel came in, stopping abruptly when she saw Sir Jeffrey talking to me.

'My dear.' Jeffrey rose and, going across, gave her a welcoming kiss.

I sat and stared at the contents of my glass.

'Is there a problem?' She turned a wide-eyed look at us.

'Not a problem, no,' Sir Jeffrey reassured her. 'But Harry's had some rather disquieting news.'

'Oh?'

'To do with Silvie,' I said.

'You were going to visit her . . . Is she worse?'

I shook my head. 'No, she was sleeping peacefully when I came away. But today Uncle George disclosed something which came as a hell of a shock.'

'You've already told Jeffrey?'

'Yes.'

'Can you tell me?'

So I did.

She sat down, her brow furrowed, stunned by the unexpected news. Sir Jeffrey hastily poured her a whisky and placed the glass in her hands.

'What a bombshell,' she whispered and sipped the spirit gratefully. 'All these years . . . and George wasn't to blame.'

I knew instantly that she was thinking of the emotional abuse he'd suffered from Aunt Rachel. And not simply emotional – he'd been banned from the marriage bed as well. Apparently it hadn't occurred to Aunt Rachel that she was punishing herself at the same time. They were two unhappy people caught by circumstances and their own moral codes.

'Why *did* he keep quiet?'

'To protect my mother's reputation.'

'A tragedy.' Annabel shook her head.

I understood but Sir Jeffrey was looking confused.

'Well, we don't *know* it's one, I mean, until we discover the father's identity . . .'

Annabel caught his hand. 'Darling, you're so sweet. I wasn't referring to Silvie, because for one thing, I don't think it will have any effect at all on her. I was thinking of Uncle George's wasted life.' She turned to me. 'Harry, would it be possible to sort it out with George's wife, do you think?'

I thought of the ingrained bitterness of eighteen years and shook my head. 'I don't know. You'd be better at guessing than I would.'

'Unless your Aunt Rachel asked me for help, there's really nothing I can do.'

'Hmm,' I agreed ruefully, 'I do see that. But then Uncle George needs to tell her himself and I can't see him having the courage.'

Sir Jeffrey cleared his throat. 'Does Uncle George know who the father is?'

'He knows.' I drained my glass. 'But confessing left him in a bit of a state, so we agreed he'd tell me about how it happened – and who it was – later, in a few days.' I didn't add probably next Friday when Aunt Rachel wasn't on the radar.

'I would say,' Annabel said thoughtfully, 'it's most likely a male friend of Uncle George's and a married man.'

The simple logic of her words had us nodding agreement.

'He did start to say he blamed himself for leaving my mother but it was my fault I cut him short at that point. He was pretty upset, red-faced, gasping. I thought it best to get him out of the pub and back home to the cottage.'

'Absolutely right,' Annabel agreed. 'His stress level would have been incredibly high.'

'And in a couple of weeks or so it's Silvie's eighteenth birthday. The man, whoever he is, who set up the trust fund may have to sign its release. I don't really know but certainly the solicitor does.'

'A possibility, of course.' Sir Jeffrey nodded. 'The man might do the decent thing and admit his paternity.'

Annabel looked at her watch, tutted reprovingly and stood up. 'Time I was attending to dinner. You will stay and join us, Harry?'

'Another time, possibly, thanks,' I said. 'It's very boring of me but I have work to do on Elspeth's biography. She's begun cracking the whip.'

Annabel giggled. 'And she certainly knows how to.'

'Yes.' I smiled back, thinking of her illustrious earlier days as a jockey.

'Tomorrow evening, then?' Sir Jeffrey added his support to Annabel's suggestion.

'No, sorry. Elspeth has me booked for her family party tomorrow night.'

'Never mind.' Annabel, sensing my lack of enthusiasm, squeezed my arm. 'When you've finished the book we'll fix a date.'

'Sure,' I said, 'and thanks.'

'What for?'

'Your sane common sense.'

'Haven't done anything.'

'Well, I feel better anyway.'

I took my leave and motored back to the cottage.

Opening the fridge door I scanned the near-empty shelves, the hunk of cheddar cheese going hard, and wished myself back at Annabel's table. She was a fabulous cook. Come to think of it, she was a fabulous woman full stop. And she'd chosen Sir Jeffrey for her lover. And, damn the situation to all hell, I was actually beginning to like the man.

TWENTY-THREE

'**M**urder!' The Land Rover lurched sharply to the left as Mike jerked round in his seat to stare at me.

We were driving along watching his string of race-horses on the gallops. It was six thirty on Saturday morning and first lot was out doing their stuff. The riders were dressed in drab jackets concealing body protectors but jauntily topped with defiantly bright-coloured silk quarters over crash caps. It was a glorious morning, the sun already up and a sky so incredibly blue and wide it seemed to stretch to infinity. A morning to give thanks for being alive. Except Carl Smith wasn't, as I'd just told Mike.

'Yep. Murder in the first. Totally unsuspecting, unarmed, unzipped—'

'*What?*'

'The police established he was facing the urinal, taking a leak because his urine was all over the floor and down his trousers. He couldn't have known who his attacker was. The blow came from behind, aimed at mid-thigh level. Broke his right femur, pitched him headfirst and his forehead connected with the porcelain. They think he was knocked out cold.'

'Bloody hell!'

'But that wasn't what killed him.'

'No? What then?'

'His attacker apparently dragged him into the nearest cubicle, thrust his head down the lavatory pan and held him there.'

Mike slammed both feet out and the vehicle stopped suddenly, tossing us against the seatbelts. He twisted round to face me. 'My good God! It could have been you, Harry.' His face had blanched to the colour of chalk.

'I don't think so. Carl was set to sell information. He was stopped before he could tell any tales. I'm still no wiser. If he had divulged who he was working for then yes, I'd agree no firm would offer me life insurance.'

'How can you take it so lightly? A man's been murdered.'

'Believe me, Mike, I'm not dismissing Carl's death. I feel partly responsible, if you must know.'

'Now you're just being bloody silly.'

'Am I? It was because of me going to Leicester races and arranging a liaison with Carl that he was killed. Killed using my walking stick, too.'

'Now, wait a minute,' Mike ran a hand through his thatch of hair in agitation, 'are you saying you were the patsy?'

I nodded. 'Looks like it from where I'm standing.'

'And the police? What's their take?'

'They grilled me like a rasher of smoked back but in the end someone else was seen handling the walking stick so they said I was free to go. But not to go too far, as in "do not leave town".'

'Phew . . .' Mike blew out his cheeks. 'If anybody's to blame, it's me.'

I almost laughed but he was serious. 'How did you come up with that idea?'

'Look, Harry, it was me who sent the racing paper over with Annabel. The one with the article about Elspeth's retiring and needing a ghost-writer. That's what started all this.'

'Rub that idea out. If you're looking for the start it was because I was riding Gold Sovereign and came off. Without that accident, none of what followed would have happened. OK?'

Grudgingly, he agreed. 'But you – and Silvie,' he waved a finger, 'don't forget Silvie, are targets.'

'I won't forget Silvie, Mike,' I said soberly. 'And since you've brought her into the conversation, you ought to know what I was told yesterday by Uncle George.'

He listened in silence, shaking his head in disbelief. 'Do you think all these things could be somehow connected?'

I stared at him. 'How do you mean?'

'Well, she's going to be eighteen very soon, isn't she? I mean, this trust fund money, is it a substantial amount? What happens if, God forbid, anything happens to Silvie before her birthday? Who's likely to benefit, eh? Have you thought about that?'

'No,' I said slowly, 'it's never occurred to me until now that everything might all connect up.'

'I think it's possible, like events are all playing out to the end, whatever that may be.'

'Perhaps I've been linear thinking and it's time to alter my approach. You know, start at the end and work back.'

He nodded. 'I reckon that's a good idea. And whilst you're on the trail, keep your head down. I've only one dark suit and I don't get time to go shopping.'

'What?'

'You know, dark suits, funerals.'

'Not mine, Mike. Well, in another forty years maybe but not just yet. I've got to keep batting. I'm all Silvie's got.' I pursed my lips. 'Well, until we find out the name of her father.'

The racehorses, having finished their morning canters, were

being circled round at a walking pace. The stable lads were
obviously at a loss as to why their trainer hadn't taken an active
and verbal part as usual.

Mike started the engine, drove to within shouting distance
and issued the order to head back to the stables. He set off in
a wide arc around the last of the string and then pointed the
vehicle downhill. At the last moment before we drove over
the brow, the whole of the stable yard and Mike's house and
grounds were laid out like a tapestry.

To one side at the rear of the stables was a parking area
partially filled with cars belonging to his staff. In one corner I
spotted a dark blue familiar-shaped car. Maybe it was just
coincidence – there were lots of them about – but I pointed
through the windscreen.

'See that car, Mike, the one in the corner, dark blue. Do you
know who it belongs to?'

He leaned forward over the wheel and screwed his eyes up.
'The Peugeot, do you mean?'

'Hmm.'

'Reckon it's Ciggie's.'

'*Who?*'

'Tony Lonsbury. Everybody calls him Ciggie because he
smokes a lot. To excess, really. And not just the legit sort.'

'Aaah.'

'He's a user as well. 'Course, I can't prove it but he's treading
a thin line. If he turns up for work high he'll be down the road.'

'Right.' An idea had just come to me and a wriggle of excitement squirmed through my solar plexus. 'When you get back,
Mike, I'd like to take a quick butcher's at the car, is that OK?'

'Sure, doesn't matter to me. Any reason why?'

'I'll tell you over breakfast when I've had a look.'

We drove on down the hill.

I left Mike in the stable yard and as unobtrusively as possible
made my way round behind the stables. I'd left my own vehicle
parked alongside the others and I went over, unlocked it and
slid behind the wheel. To make it look good I flipped open the
dash and pretended to search for something. If anybody was
keeping tabs on me, it would appear completely natural. To
complete the authenticity, I took out a biro and made a note on

my writing pad. And under cover of writing, I scanned the car park, but it was completely empty.

I gave it five minutes then walked over to the Peugeot. I didn't touch it, didn't even go all the way round, didn't need to. I simply stood in front and looked at it. In the centre of the bonnet was a dent – a dent with a deep, distinctive cleft.

'You're saying it was Ciggie who tailed you back from Gunthorpe?' We were sitting in Mike's kitchen making up for not eating earlier.

'And followed me at a stupid, suicidal speed when I was on my way to visit Silvie. I tried to catch a glimpse of his face but, just like the previous time, he was wearing a baseball cap pulled low over his eyes. I did see that much.'

He took a bite of sausage sandwich, chewed thoughtfully.

'But he's only a kid. He wouldn't tamper with Silvie's oxygen supply. I can't buy that, Harry. Oh, I know the evidence is plain. It's definitely the same car; what I'm saying is I don't think he's capable of attempted murder. Car chasing, yes – young lads, speed and all that, but . . .' He left the words hanging.

'I fully agree, Mike.' I nodded. 'At the time I thought it strange that he didn't come after me when I escaped over the cattle grid. I certainly expected him to. But now, with all these additional bits of information falling into place, I'm pretty sure. It explains things.'

Thoroughly confused now, he shook his head in bewilderment and reached for the bottle of brown sauce. I passed it over without him asking. I'd just added a lovely dollop to my own banger. Last night's dinner had been sparse and I was now making up for it.

'Just what are you saying?'

'I'm saying, for my money, he was hired to drive the car – full stop. And it didn't really matter if I saw the car. In fact, I think I was supposed to. I'm saying I think Ciggie was also set up. There was a second person, a man, wearing a black bala-clava, who tried to finish Silvie and who actually did finish Carl. Ciggie was just the stool pigeon. Whilst he was taking my attention, someone else, the real man behind it, was doing the deeds.'

Mike chewed and thought. 'You know something, Harry, I reckon you're right on the button. Ciggie's . . . *habits*, shall we say, must cost him – a lot. More than he could possibly afford on a stable lad's wage. And if he is an addict, he'll do *anything* to get the necessary money to fuel it.'

'Exactly. That crossed my mind when you told me his name earlier.'

'Talking about motivation, did you know Carl wore dentures?'

'No, not until the police found them down the toilet.'

'Hmm, thought not. Well, don't go on a guilt trip, Harry, but when you landed on top of Carl at Huntingdon races, you, er . . . well, your elbow connected with Carl's front teeth, his *own* teeth.'

'You're saying it was my fault Carl wore false teeth?'

He inclined his head. 'I'm only telling you because I can see now he probably held it against you. A bit of personal revenge as well as being paid, possibly, I don't know.'

'I'm sorry it happened, Mike, but no, I'm not going on a guilt trip.'

Mike blew out his cheeks. 'Thank goodness.'

'It was an accident, not done intentionally. You race ride, you accept the risks.'

'True enough. Anyway, it adds to the jigsaw, doesn't it?'

'Absolutely.' I finished the last of my sandwich and stood up. 'Sorry, Mike, work calls at my end. Much rather stay and play, but . . .' I spread my hands and smiled.

'Huh,' he grunted, 'just remember what I said.' He delivered a parting shot at me as I opened the door: 'You keep your head down.'

I threw him a smart salute and left.

TWENTY-FOUR

Leo had returned from an all-night foraging expedition and, rejecting his basket, had settled down on yesterday's *Racing Post* where it lay on the floor in the conservatory. Morning sunshine flooded through the glass and it was jungle hot – with all the perennial pot plants providing an abundance of leafy green, it even looked like a jungle.

I joined him, after pouring a coffee, and settled back in a wicker recliner to assemble thoughts and facts.

One downed cup of coffee later I halted the spool of spiralling assessments, partially satisfied where they'd led to, and closed my eyes. It was all speculation, of course, but it might just happen to be true. The warmth in the conservatory coupled with the comfort of the plush padded recliner was seductive.

Almost an hour later, I was awoken by the shrilling of 'The Great Escape' tune. Disoriented, I stumbled through to the office where my mobile lay reproachfully on the desk.

'Harry?'

'Hello, Elspeth. What can I do you for?'

'Cheeky young sod,' she said good-humouredly. 'I've just remembered – you know there were two or three people we agreed you could approach for copy for the book?'

'Yes.'

'Well, I thought you should know that my old friend, and Marriot's old headmaster, Walter Bexon, will be at the party tonight. No sense in running over to his place, you can interview him here. You can bring your tape recorder and whatever, can't you? It will save messing about any more. I agree with Marriot – you've had time enough to produce the book.' Her good humour melted away.

Messing about. After all the scores of hours beavering away, very often until early morning, missing sleep, missing social occasions, putting my own life on hold. Marriot had a bloody nerve. He'd obviously been working on his mother. I bit back an acid comment.

'Sounds sensible. And instead of running over to Mr Malton's stables, I'll just give him a ring, shall I? Cut it short, just get his personal opinion?'

'Yes, yes. That'll surely do. I really don't want it dragging on much longer.'

Charming.

'Very well, Elspeth. I'll do that.'

She hung up.

I booted up and kicked on – no dragging of heels in sight.

Around one o'clock I broke off to make a mug of soup and sat sipping minestrone and tapping away at the keyboard. Hitting a block in the writing some time later, I saved the work, rose and stretched. Took my mobile into the conservatory with a builder's strength mug of tea.

I drank the scalding, reviving brew and tickled Leo's ginger tummy, exposed to the last bit of sunshine edging its way round the corner of the cottage wall on the way west. The purring was deep with satisfaction. I sighed and thought about Annabel. If she was truly lost to me it would be best to make the break clean, leave the way open for her to marry Sir Jeffrey.

It would also allow me to start looking for a new lady in my life. But even the thought of surrendering rankled. How the hell could I fall in love with another woman, even supposing I could find her, when, God help me, I was still hopelessly, helplessly in love with Annabel and wanted no other female? Far from moving on, being parted from her only made me crave her, love her more.

I took a deep breath, tried to put her out of my mind and dialled Mr Malton's number. He was out doing evening stables but was generous enough to spend a few minutes fully answering each of my carefully selected questions. If Elspeth wanted a prune down, she would certainly get one. But Thomas Malton was obviously a close buddy, or appeared to be, and insisted I wrote down and quoted back to him what he'd said.

By the time he'd finished extolling qualities it sounded like a glowing reference for a job application. One given to ensure the person got the other job perhaps? Underneath the rich cream a sour base layer showing? Possibly pleased that the competition was, or would shortly be, out of commission and leaving the field clear?

Still, I thanked him for his time and looked over my notes. Undoubtedly I could polish them up and use them in the book, but I knew there was precious little bite. Maybe tonight's sortie with Walter Bexon would produce a little spice.

Then, quite quickly, the sunny room was shrouded in shade, the temperature already starting to drop. The sun had moved on along its journey and gone behind the corner brickwork.

'That's your lot today, Tiger,' I said to Leo, who, knowing

perfectly well this would happen, was already stretching his long back legs and preparing to stalk out as he followed the sun. I knew where he was heading for – sunny climes in the spare bedroom, which would now be receiving its share of warm basking time. I shook my head. Next time, I reckoned, what with unlimited food, willing females and building up strength for both by sleeping in the sun all day, I was definitely coming back as a cat.

Taking the mobile back into the office, I typed up my notes. Time had marched on and I hastened to finish the work before dashing upstairs to shower and change.

Elspeth was a lady you didn't argue with, and if she'd said eight o'clock it was cut in stone.

I was only late by a short margin and was admitted by the lady herself, who looked like she'd been dragged away by the doorbell during an engaging conversation with another dowager. They were still at it as Elspeth opened the door.

'Harry,' she practically purred. 'Do come on in. Have you met Daphne before? No? Her husband runs Broadman's the estate agency. They allow me to train one of their horses, Scarlet Salvia.'

I nodded. Bloody Sal's owners.

She turned to Daphne. 'Harry is helping me with my biography, you know, the technical details.' We both nodded to cement relations and I was led away and force-fed with introductions and much bonhomie to other partygoers.

Finally, drink in hand, I was washed up on the shore and left to make small talk with one David Feltham, another poor sod who Elspeth had deemed the right recipient for my favours of conversation. One who I did know by sight, if not by name, as an owner of one of her racehorses, and a regular in the parade ring at the local racecourses.

He grinned sheepishly. 'Strong lady, Elspeth, wouldn't you agree?'

I grinned back. 'Definitely.'

He emptied his glass and a passing waitress immediately whipped it out of his hand, replacing it with a full one. 'Do help yourselves to the buffet, gentlemen.' She smiled, showing lots of whiter than white perfect teeth.

We took her advice and ambled over to a fully stocked table in danger of collapsing from the weight of all the delectable goodies up for grabs. Heaping our paper plates and catching up napkins, we made ourselves scarce in a corner that boasted a shoulder-high shelf, where we promptly stashed our glasses. Munching away companionably, we chatted all things racing and got on just fine. It crossed my mind that Elspeth wasn't daft at giving successful parties. She'd obviously earmarked Feltham and myself from the off.

Music was playing through hidden speakers vying with gusts of laughter and there was a definite air of happy punters. From where we were standing, I scanned the large room but saw no sign of Marriot's presence anywhere. I found myself beginning to relax and enjoy myself. Buried in the dreaded biography and beset by the recent accidents and traumas, I'd just about forgotten what it felt like to go out and have a good time.

One or two other people that both David and I knew drifted over and added in new topics of conversation. I had to remember to take my cue from how Elspeth had introduced me to the redoubtable Daphne.

'Haven't seen you riding for a while. Not retired yourself, I take it?' The question was put by a large, fleshy man who had wandered into our orbit and introduced himself as Eric.

'Grounded, I'm afraid.'

'So, how're you filling your time? Just writing for the newspaper?'

'Well, yes,' I answered cautiously, 'and helping Elspeth out with the technical aspects of her biography.'

'Ha, yes, heard she was writing one. Not just a hands-on horsewoman, got a brain, too. I like that in a woman. Can't be doing with dim bimbos. Amazing woman, isn't she?'

'Oh, yes.' David and I exchanged glances, our lips twitching. I was pretty sure he'd sussed out the true state of Elspeth's claims to be writing the book herself but we both kept up the pretence.

A pretty girl came up to me, one I seemed to recognize but for a moment I couldn't place or name her.

'Harry – it is Harry, isn't it?'

'Yes.'

'Joanne. I'm a friend of Annabel's, your *estranged* wife.'

'Oh, right.' The jigsaw clicked into place. Joanne Manchester, daughter of the much-respected John Manchester, owner of at least twenty racehorses around the Midlands.

'Sorry you had such bad luck and got grounded. I do hope you'll be back riding soon.'

'Thank you.' I smiled at her. 'I certainly hope so, too.'

There was a speculative look in her big blue eyes, not quite a come-on nor an invitation but certainly an opening for me to pursue should I want to try. David gave a discreet cough, trying to hide his amusement and, chivalrously, I filled the gap.

'Maybe we'll meet again.'

'Yes,' her smile widened, 'indeed we may.' And she floated away in a froth of pale cream towards the next little bunch of people.

'Think you're in there.' David chortled into his glass.

I inclined my head. 'Could well be.' But even as I agreed, I knew I wouldn't. And the depressing knowledge that although Joanne was a good-looking woman who should have been bringing me to life, the necessary spark hadn't ignited.

Elspeth came across with a man in tow and introduced him as Walter Bexon, a very old friend and Marriot's former head-master. 'David Feltham, Harry Radcliffe, Walter,' she said. 'I rather think Harry wants to ask you some questions to help me with my biography.'

'Yes, that's right,' I answered obediently.

David excused himself, saying he had to find one of the other owners to talk shop, and Walter and I were left to talk on our own.

'By, she's going to miss her work, y'know. Those stables are her life.'

'Yes, I'm afraid she will.'

'I've known Elspeth for years, since the days she rode as a jockey, and then through her married life with Victor. Well, I've been a friend to both – still am.'

I nodded and took out a discreet hand-held recorder. 'Do you mind?' I indicated the machine.

'Not at all, Harry, not at all. Happy to help in any way.'

'Probably better if we disappear to the kitchen for a few minutes.'

He nodded agreement and we removed ourselves from the fray.

'That's better, much quieter in here.' I clicked the recorder into life. 'If you could just chat about where you first met, any momentous times you had, big events in her life, also any sorrows.'

'Sorrows?' He frowned.

'Please, if you could. The readers like to know what makes the person tick. Not just the glory days but the little bits of sadness, too. It makes them more rounded and real. The reader needs to identify with the storyteller – it makes all the difference.'

He pursed his lips. 'Do my best. Stop me if it's no use. Don't want to bore you.'

'You won't,' I assured him. 'I'll fish out what's relevant later.'

So he did, drawing on old memories, feelings, meetings and weaving a unique, intimate pattern of Elspeth's life. Hearing it for the first time, it was fascinating. Even before he'd started to run down, I knew it provided all the script I needed. Although I hadn't been looking forward to this press gang party, I had actually enjoyed myself and, regarding copy, it had been invaluable.

Elspeth had, obviously, been keeping an eye out for our return to the lounge, and she materialized beside us, keen to introduce me to more people.

'No Paula here?' I inquired.

She was Victor's much adored first-born daughter. Elspeth's adoration was exclusively for Marriot. Victor, I'd heard, didn't get on with his son, hadn't much time for him. He thought Marriot should have been as keen on racing as he was and saw him as a traitor to the cause of 'following in father's footsteps'. As parents, they were the perfect stereotype: the mother bonded to the son and the father besotted with his daughter.

'No, Nigel's too busy down in London to come tonight so Paula's stayed down there with him and the three G-forces.' Elspeth laughed.

I knew she saw Paula's marriage to Nigel, an ambitious junior minister, as a social plus factor. And I could appreciate her description of the three grandsons. From the little I knew of them, they were hell-on-skateboards.

Elspeth deftly drew Walter away, but not before she'd introduced me to someone else.

'Harry, I want you to meet another member of my family. This is Samuel Simpson. Samuel is Marriot's father-in-law.'

'Very pleased to meet you.' His smile was wide and genuine. I shook hands with relief. At least Marriot hadn't poisoned his mind against me.

'It's mutual.'

'Know my daughter's husband, do you?' Looking across the room, he added, 'Seems he's just arrived.'

I swivelled round and had my eyes met by Marriot's hostile, hot gaze. There was an exceptionally pretty young woman hanging on to his arm who, when she spotted Samuel, peeled herself away from Marriot and tripped over to us.

'Daddy, so sorry we're late.' She rose on tiptoes and kissed his smooth, immaculately shaved cheek. He beamed down at her, his chest swelling with pride. As well he might. She was a first-class, well-turned-out filly, a real eye-catcher. Her off-the-shoulder wine-coloured dress was figure hugging, leaving nothing to guesswork, and showed off her creamy shoulders and glossy raven hair. Even in my state of malaise over Annabel, looking at her was raising my spirits. But, God help her, she'd married Marriot. What a bloody waste of gorgeous womanhood.

'Harry,' Samuel said, 'I'd like to present my daughter, Chloe. Tonight's party is to celebrate her birthday. I won't embarrass her by telling you her age . . .'

'Oh, Daddy, don't be so stuffy.' She punched his arm playfully, smiling at me. 'I'm thirty – a milestone, wouldn't you agree?'

'I would.'

'The very prime of a woman's life,' her father said dotingly. 'And high time to think about giving me a grandson.' She tinkled a laugh and looked across the room to where Marriot was holding court with a tumbler of whisky and chatting to his mother.

'Perhaps you'd better have a word with my male.'

'He shouldn't need one, my darling.' His voice had hardened slightly. 'He's a very lucky man, having you for his wife.' He directed a cold glance towards her husband.

Interesting. Could it be Samuel shared my opinion of Marriot? It seemed likely. If so, I might have an ally in the enemy camp.

Chloe wiggled fingers at us. 'Better mingle.'

Samuel watched her slender figure walk away and said, 'It's all about family, isn't it?'

'Er . . .?'

He looked me full in the face. 'Life, lad, life. Like Elspeth's book.'

I inclined my head.

'Oh, I know who's writing it, don't you worry.' He chuckled. 'Marriot's made his feelings very clear, but I can't see his objection, to be honest. Anyway, I make it a rule not to let other people make *my* mind up.'

'I'd say that was a pretty good rule.'

'I reckon since Elspeth chose you to do the work, you'll make a good job. She's a very shrewd lady, a businesswoman.'

'I'll certainly do my best.'

''Course you will, lad. She's made a success of her life. Always got her hands on the reins, eh?' He laughed out loud at his own joke and I smiled because it was expected.

'Not that she doesn't trust her staff, don't get me wrong. I'm sure she trusts you. But she's always at the cutting edge, attends all the race meetings, and that takes a lot of energy and commitment. Never lets anything get in the way.'

His words reminded me of the one time she hadn't attended a major race meeting. But it wouldn't be any good asking Samuel, although I was sure he'd tell me if he knew, as it had all happened before his time. Maybe, though, Walter Bexon could provide the answer. He'd been a close friend as well as being in charge of Marriot's education.

Across the room, Walter was approaching the buffet table for a refill. It would be easy to intercept him.

'Would you mind, Samuel? I need to have a word with the gentleman over there.'

'Go right ahead, Harry. Business is all about networking, I understand that.'

I caught up with Walter as he was choosing between a piece of Melton Mowbray pork pie and a triangle of quiche. 'Can I butt in, Walter? I've remembered a question you may be able to answer.'

'Fire away.' He chose the pie and dropped it on to his plate.

'You were Marriot's headmaster. Do you recall, when he was about twelve, he was away from school, ill? In the May, I think. A long shot, I know, but I thought I'd just ask. What was it that made Elspeth miss her runner that day?'

'Oh, I can tell you that, Harry. It was Yorkshire Cup day. As you know, nothing keeps Elspeth away from the racecourse but she did miss that particular big race. She chose to stay home with Marriot. He'd contracted one of the childhood illnesses – measles or something like that – but then on top of that he got glandular fever. Particularly nasty, you know. He was running a high fever at the time. Touch and go whether he needed hospitalization. In the end Elspeth engaged a private nurse. He didn't have to go into hospital. Good job, too. He's got a phobia about hospitals, you see.'

'No, I didn't know.'

'Hmm, well, that's why she missed seeing her horse win. And it was one of the biggest races of her career.'

'Thanks, Walter, you've been a great help.'

He frowned. 'Look, I don't think you should put it in the biography – about Marriot's phobia, I mean. I think he'd be a bit touchy about that. See it as a weakness and wouldn't want the world to know.'

'Don't worry, Walter. I'll be very discreet.'

His face cleared. 'I'm sure you will, and good luck with the rest of the writing.'

'Very kind of you.'

We were suddenly interrupted by Elspeth. 'Harry, there you are. Thought you were talking to Samuel. A telephone call's just come through for you. If you'd like to follow me you can take it in the office.'

'Of course.'

She led me down the hall and opened the office door. Looked with disgust at a partially smoked cigarette lying in a glass ashtray and wrinkled her nose. 'Sorry about the smell. It's

Marriot's cigarette. He's the only person who smokes. I do apologise.'

'Don't worry about it.'

She nodded and walked out, closing the door. I fished in my pocket, came up with a clean tissue and dropped it over the stubbed-out cigarette. Wrapping it, I put the offending object in my pocket. It could prove to be very useful.

I picked up the telephone receiver. 'Hello. Harry Radcliffe here.'

There was an incoherent, distressed voice at the other end. It was Aunt Rachel. Uncle George had suffered a heart attack the previous day. The hospital had kept him sedated for the first twenty-four hours but he was awake now.

And he was asking to see me – urgently.

TWENTY-FIVE

It was the smell, always the smell that got me. A mixture of food cooking and antiseptic. And after that, you had to be in good physical shape to traverse the seemingly endless miles of corridors. Covering a massive footfall, interior maps of the hospital were handed out to visitors to ensure they found their way out again. And without a map you didn't stand a chance of finding the right ward.

I received mine gratefully from the reception desk and set off in the general direction. But I hadn't gone more than twenty yards before a woman came rushing after me.

'Wait, Harry . . . please . . . *please* . . .' I stopped and she practically threw herself at me. 'Oh, thank you, thank you for coming. I've been such a bitch . . .' She clutched my arm as tears ran down her cheeks.

'Aunt Rachel, steady on.' I sought to deflect her from beating herself up. 'Can you tell me how Uncle George is?'

She gulped and dashed away tears. 'He's conscious now, not in pain, thank God. He's on massive medication, mind.'

'Only to be expected.'

'Yes, yes.' She nodded vigorously. 'And he's talking to me
. . . which is wonderful. I don't deserve it.' She caught back a
sob. 'Go on, Harry, go and talk to George, he's been asking for
you. He wants to tell you something, I know he does. It must
be important. He won't tell me, but can't seem to rest till he's
seen you.'

'Don't stress, Aunt Rachel. I'm here now.'

We made our way to the intensive care cardiac unit and
found Uncle George. Whey-faced, wired up to monitors, he
looked half the man he'd been. It was a shocking deterioration.
I tried to hide my dismay but Aunt Rachel ignored me.

She went down on her knees at the side of his bed, leaned
over and kissed his cheek. If I hadn't seen her do it, I wouldn't
have believed it. George must have thought he'd died and gone
to heaven. He hadn't been kissed for the last eighteen years.
But looking at his frail form, the idea of him dying was certainly
no joke. The prospect was unpleasantly real.

'George, I've brought Harry. You asked for him . . .'

His eyelids flickered and opened. I moved closer. 'Hello,
Uncle George. Sorry to see you in here.'

'Be home soon.' His voice was weak but quite audible. 'All
I want's back there.'

Aunt Rachel gave a little sob.

'Don't take on, me duck . . .'

'Tell Harry what you wanted to say, George. I'll wait outside,
give you some privacy.' She gave him another kiss and left us
alone.

'I'm glad things are better between you and Aunt Rachel.
But we've only a few minutes, Uncle George. The nurse said
I mustn't wear you out.'

His eyelids closed briefly and I knew there had been a lot of
bravado for Aunt Rachel's benefit. The man was totally
exhausted.

'OK, if you've something you need to say, say it now and
you can sleep easy.'

'It's my fault, Harry, entirely my fault your mother became
pregnant. I got blotto – in the nineteenth hole at the golf club.
I was playing golf with my buddy and we'd gone round eighteen
holes. We ended in the clubhouse. First time ever I'd beaten

him. Got drinking, had too many. Left my car there and he drove me home.

'Trouble was I'd already arranged to pick up your mother from the breast-screening clinic. Couldn't go. Couldn't leave her waiting – no mobile phones then. So after he'd dropped me off, my buddy picked up Elizabeth. The clinic weren't satisfied with her screening result. She was frightened, upset, needed comforting. He took her home, consoled her . . .' His face contorted.

I thought he was in pain – he was, but the pain wasn't physical. His buddy had betrayed him *with my mother.* The door opened and a nurse stuck her head round. 'Time's up. He needs to rest.'

'Sure, sure,' I said, rising.

'No!' Uncle George's voice sounded weak but agitated. 'Please . . .'

Shaking her head, the nurse wagged a finger. 'One minute.'

I turned back to Uncle George. 'His name, you want me to know his name?'

'Yes.'

He told me.

I was still reeling when I parked up at Harlequin Cottage. Aunt Rachel had refused a lift home. She intended to stay at the hospital, had been there for George since his admittance yesterday. I just hoped to God he'd pull through. It had taken a heart attack to bring Aunt Rachel to her senses. It would be a cruel, ironic tragedy if they were parted now.

I went up to the bathroom, stripped off my shirt and repeatedly splashed my face and neck with cold water. I needed to calm down and clear my head. I felt like I'd been given a physical pasting.

But, undoubtedly, it had helped Uncle George. As soon as he'd told me the man's name, the tension in his grey face had drained away, the lines smoothed and his body had relaxed. He lay limply in the hospital bed, at peace at last.

'Don't worry, Harry,' he murmured, on the edge of healing sleep, 'I've everything waiting at home. I'll get there.'

I knew he wanted this second chance with Aunt Rachel and I

marvelled at the resilience of human love. I came away feeling somehow humbled and privileged by the experience. At the same time, I was aware that what Uncle George had told me would need to be dealt with.

I buried my head in a thick towel and dried off. Thought it was a great pity I couldn't just bury my head full stop. I wished I could totally forget what I'd been told. But knowledge once learned couldn't be unlearned.

It was late but I needed to boot up my computer and do a spot of digging on family trees and relations. Leo came padding into the office, jumped up on to the desk and cosied up to me. I found his presence soothing. I had a dilemma now whether to keep the man's name to myself and wait for Silvie's birthday to come round or whether to make a journey and confront the man. Tell him I knew.

First, though, I needed to check out my new theory in the light of Uncle George's revelation, and with a smidgen of luck the computer would come up with the goods. It didn't take too long. I had to allow that centuries ago ancestors didn't use the same words and names to describe ailments and disabilities. But it didn't need much imagination to translate long-ago non-specific expressions into present-day clarity.

My findings triggered a memory of the doctor's words when Silvie was born. 'Medical knowledge has taken great strides forward but, for all that, we can't give you answers why one child is born severely disabled and another isn't. Genetics is still largely a mystery. It's an imprecise science.'

I sat and stared at the screen in front of me. What I read on it translated not into cold clinical facts, but instead into tragedy, fading hopes, gut-wrenching grief and pain of the worst kind. The world may have changed, evolved beyond recognition since those long-ago days, but people hadn't. Their emotions and priorities were still the same.

Samuel was right: it was all about family.

I sat and thought for a long time before eventually closing down the computer and dragging myself off to bed. I lay there sleepless for hours, stupidly arguing with myself. Did I wait for Silvie's birthday and hope to see the man, or did I go and find him? If he was the one pulling the strings, it wouldn't be a smart move. Despite cribbing about my left leg and my thrice-weekly physio visits, I still valued my overall health and working order. Being carted off to the hospital again – or worse – was not an enticing prospect. And as the debate raged on inside my head, at some point I must have abdicated and fallen asleep.

But now, this morning, I was still undecided. It was not a comfortable state to be in. What made it worse was the man wasn't a stranger. I knew him. What I didn't know was his address. But I knew a man who could tell me.

I shoved aside my half-eaten bowl of breakfast cereal and flipped open my mobile. Mike answered and filled me in with the required information. Thanking heaven for the efficiency of Mike's bush telegraph, I wrote down the address. Like the good mate he is he didn't ask why I wanted the address and I didn't tell him.

I was surprised that the location was really predictable. When they retire, an awful lot of people in Nottinghamshire head east, only stopping when the land runs out and they reach the coast. A little bungalow by the sea seems to be the perennial dream of landlocked Midlanders.

It took me an hour and a half to hit the coast at Skegness, and a further ten minutes to find the property. But a little bungalow it wasn't. 'Saddler's Rest' was a large house built on the edge of the sands with a massive inland front garden sloping down to St Andrew's Drive, an upmarket part of Skegness, with a magnificent golf course bordered by the beach only minutes away and stretching north to the village of Winthorpe.

I parked at the kerb. Thoughts of possible violence directed towards me dwindled and dissolved. Peace pervaded the place. There was a holiday atmosphere, a civilized and relaxed feel to the whole area. The only disharmony came from two mewling seagulls squabbling over a scrap of food. They disappeared from sight over the rooftops and total silence wrapped itself around everything. Maybe the communal, perennial dream of a retreat by the sea wasn't far wrong. Maybe when I was seventy-five and retired it would be tempting. And with a shock I realized that the man I was about to come face-to-face with must be about that age. No way would he be swinging a baseball bat about or knee-capping anybody.

I walked up the long drive and rang the bell. I'd no precon-
ceived idea of what to say, but at least I had the advantage of
surprise. As far as he was aware, nobody had the slightest
suspicion that Uncle George wasn't Silvie's father. He'd lived
eighteen years in a bubble of protective silence. Known Uncle
George was an honourable man who would never willingly
disclose the truth. I was about to burst that bubble.

The door opened. A man stood in front of me. I'd worked
for him years ago. He was my old boss: Victor Maudsley.

I watched a mixture of emotions chase across his face as we
stood there staring at each other. I didn't need to say anything;
he read my face.

'You know,' he said flatly. It wasn't even a question.

'I know.'

'You'd better come in, Harry.' He opened the door wide. 'I've
been expecting you for the last three years, ever since Elizabeth
died.'

'And her death released Uncle George? I take it he gave you
his word of honour to keep quiet for her sake.'

'Yes, yes, he did.'

'He's a man of honour to his fingertips.'

'A good friend.'

'Who you betrayed.'

He looked at the floor, shaking his head. 'I've no excuse,
Harry, none.' He lifted his gaze to my face. 'Well, except for
a very personal one.' He chewed his inner lip. 'Your mother
was so beautiful, and so in need of comfort . . . in need of love.
And I'd been denied sexual relations for many years with
Elspeth.'

'Are you asking for my forgiveness, Victor?'

'No, I'm not. I'm just telling you how it was. I don't expect
forgiveness. I'm just giving you the straight facts.'

'The facts are you were responsible for my mother getting
pregnant, giving birth to my half-sister, Silvie.'

Pain shot across his face. He passed a trembling hand over
his eyes. 'I promised Elizabeth,' he said brokenly. 'I promised
I'd never try to see Silvie. She's my daughter . . . and all
Elizabeth would let me do was set up a trust for the baby, to
mature when she reached eighteen.'

I swallowed hard. His emotion was for real, his pain revealed in all its bloody rawness.

'And when Elspeth found out, as she did – God only knows how, but believe me, son, wives always do – she divorced me. But I'll say one thing: Elspeth never let on, not to anybody. Not even to Marriot or Paula.'

'They don't *know*?' I could hardly believe it.

Victor shook his head. 'The only people who knew, apart from Elizabeth, obviously, were your uncle George and Elspeth.'

'And the solicitor who drew up the trust fund document?'

'Oh, yes, and the solicitor.'

We were both silent for several minutes.

'Look,' Victor roused himself, 'we've both had to face some tough truths. What do you say to a coffee with a snifter of whisky?'

'Sounds good.' I nodded.

He took me along the hall to a long sunny conservatory at the back of the house. It overlooked the beach. He flung both the double patio doors open and the salty tang of the sea filled the room.

'Won't be a moment.' He left me. And I sat watching the breakers running up the sand in creamy, clinging fingers while I pondered over what he'd disclosed.

So much for my self-battering fear over whether to risk confronting him. He hadn't attempted to lie, nor deny his paternity. And I was totally convinced he wasn't behind the attacks. It was doubtful if he was even aware of them.

What I did feel was sadness for all the lives that had been wrecked through his one act of making love to my mother. An act that I was sure hadn't been wholly selfish on his part. I actually felt sorry for him. In his own way, he was cut from the same cloth as Uncle George. He'd tried to do the best he could for Silvie without ever seeing her. Setting up the trust fund had been all he could do to try and shoulder his responsibilities.

Victor returned with a tray of coffee and a whisky decanter.

'Here we go, help yourself, Harry.' He set the tray down on a cream ironwork table. We sat and drank the reviving, hot, laced coffee.

I tossed him a question. 'How do you get on with Marriot?'

'Oh, well, don't see much of him. You know, he's married now.'

'Yes, I know. I went to Chloe's birthday party last night. She seems a nice girl.'

'Too true she is. A really lovely girl, well, woman. She's thirty now.'

'Yes.'

'Don't know why she's waiting so long before she starts a family. Not like she's got a career. Still, it's their business . . . but . . .'

'You'd like a grandchild?'

He dropped his gaze and swirled the dregs of his coffee around and around. 'I'd love it if they had a little girl.' His voice had a catch in it.

'A second chance . . . for yourself . . .?'

'Something like that.'

'But you and Marriot,' I prompted. 'You two get on?'

'Not well, no. Just go golfing sometimes.' He jerked a thumb. 'North Shore golf course just up the road is wonderful. We were supposed to go for a round but he rang up at the last minute, said he'd double booked himself and was playing with Samuel, Chloe's father. Said he'd take a rain-check on our game.'

My pulse rate increased as a spasm of excitement ran through me. The nugget of information might just be the one I needed. All I needed to do was ring Samuel and check if Marriot did in fact spend that afternoon on the golf course.

'All right with you if I say you're good friends in the biography?'

'Fine by me. I hope the book goes well for Elspeth. She's mellowed towards me lately and I don't hold her divorcing me against her. It was all my fault because she stayed faithful to me through all her married life.'

I nodded and rose to go. No way would I disillusion him about Elspeth's extra-marital frolics with Nathanial. And maybe, just maybe, that affair started after her divorce. For his sake, I truly hoped it had. I was also not about to add to his guilt by telling him that Uncle George had had a heart attack. I looked at his downcast face.

'Victor, do you want to see Silvie?' I don't know what prompted me to ask. Silvie had only two weeks more as a juvenile, as his child, before she came of age as an adult. I saw the wild hope flare up, the emotional struggle in his face. Knew he wanted very much to see her. Then he shook his head regretfully but firmly.

'No, no, Harry. I appreciate your offer, I can't tell you how much, but I gave my word to Elizabeth.' He straightened his shoulders rigidly. 'And I'm keeping my promise.'

It had been a hard decision to make and I certainly wasn't going to try to persuade him otherwise. I nodded.

'Yes, I understand.' And I did.

He showed me out and we said goodbye as friends.

TWENTY-SIX

As I drove home from Skegness there was no doubt in my mind that Marriot had been at Leicester races. But I needed to ring Samuel, check he hadn't been playing golf with his son-in-law. On its own that didn't prove conclusively that Marriot had been at the races, but I'd have bet Harlequin Cottage he had.

Sitting inside my dashboard compartment was a small plastic bag with a tissue containing one partially smoked cigarette, the one I'd picked up at last night's party. It could, possibly, be called evidence and should be handed over to the police to help their inquiries.

I'd read the ongoing reports of the murder in this morning's newspaper. Information had been released to the press that in a waste bin – not the same one where the supposed murder weapon, the hickory stick, had been discovered – a pair of all-weather golfing gloves had also been found. The gloves had been sent for DNA testing. But unless Marriot had previous convictions, which was doubtful, the results of the DNA wouldn't get the police very far. However, if the cigarette checked out, it would at least prove the gloves did belong to Marriot.

It was a chargeable offence to withhold evidence in any form. After being on the receiving end of yesterday's grilling, I didn't fancy upsetting the police again. And as the car ate up the miles back from the coast, I reluctantly decided I'd have to detour, call at Leicester police station before going home.

'What is it in connection with, sir?' enquired the constable on the desk, making a note of my name and address.

'The murder at Leicester races.'

His eyebrows raised.

'I believe you've discovered a pair of golfing gloves, in addition to the hickory walking stick.'

'Yes, sir.'

'Well, you see, the hickory stick belongs to me. I was helping your fellow officers most of that afternoon. The stick has been sent for DNA testing and now you've found the gloves, according to today's newspaper, they are also undergoing tests.'

He nodded stolidly, giving nothing away.

'What I have here,' I handed over the plastic bag, 'is a partially smoked cigarette. I think it *could* prove a DNA match to the gloves.'

'I see, sir. Well, I shall pass on your . . . er . . . exhibit, and comments to the correct department.' He unbent and gave me a smile. 'Thank you very much, sir. Wish more members of the public were as helpful. We'll be in touch if we need you.'

I closed the door of the police station behind me and took a long, deep breath of cool air. Even when you are totally innocent, being inside on their patch is distinctly unnerving.

Twenty minutes later I drove in through the gate of Harlequin Cottage. I had to pull up sharply because there was already a car parked. A very familiar one. My heart lifted immediately and I couldn't wait to open the door. The kettle on top of the Rayburn was singing away, coming to the boil.

'Smelled the tea, Harry?' Annabel was sitting in the easy chair cradling Leo in her arms. The daft animal was reaching up to her face with his paw, patting at her cheek. His purr was deafening.

'I wouldn't say no. I've just driven back from Skegness, via Leicester, of course.'

'Oh, of course.' She smiled and the world was a beautiful

place. 'Here, hold my gorgeous boy, I'll fix the tea.' She dropped Leo into my arms but he wasn't having any of it and removed himself straightaway to sit on my shoulder.

'I've something to tell you, Harry.'

'I've something to tell you, too. Two things actually.'

She laughed. 'You first.'

'About Silvie's father's identity. I've discovered who he is.'

'Really!' She deposited the used teabags in the waste bin and handed me a steaming mug. Taking her own through to the sitting room, she sank down on to the settee and patted the cushion. 'Sit with me, Harry.'

I didn't need persuading. 'I found out last night—'

'How?'

'That's the second piece of information, but I'd rather tell you about Silvie's natural father first.'

She nodded and took a sip of tea. 'Sorry, go on.' Leo slid down from his perch on my shoulder and draped himself across our knees – exactly as he used to do in the days when Annabel was living with me and life was wonderful. It was a poignant, bitter-sweet reminder. The cat hadn't forgotten, and neither had I.

'I found out the name first and then, this morning, I traced his home address.'

'At Skegness?'

'Yes.'

'Do I know him?'

'Uh-huh, we both do. I used to ride for him when he was a trainer. Retired now, of course, and enjoying living by the sea – and golfing.'

'Harry,' she clutched my arm, 'is he the person? You know, the police have found a pair of golfing gloves, it was in the paper.'

'No, no.' I shook my head. 'Nothing to do with all that.'

'So, who is he?'

'Victor Maudsley.'

'Good heavens!'

'Exactly. I'd never have guessed.'

'Does Elspeth know?'

'That's why she divorced him. But according to Victor, she's kept it secret all these years.'

'And all their lives ruined.' Annabel shook her head with regret.

'I was prepared to go in, guns blazing, but do you know, my love, when I came out, all I felt was sympathy for Victor.'

'Did he set up Silvie's trust fund?'

'Yes, poor bugger. He's never ever been allowed to see Silvie – not from the moment she was born till now.'

'And you gave him a choice?' Annabel was no dumb blonde.

'I did, yes. But he's like Uncle George – both of them all kept in a straitjacket by their sense of honour. Said he'd promised my mother he would never see Silvie nor try to contact her in any way. The trust fund was the only thing Mother would let him do, apparently.'

'But thank God for that provision, Harry.'

'Oh, yes, I am grateful, believe me. It's taken a big worry off my shoulders. Especially as my riding days may already be over.' We looked at each other. Neither of us said anything, but I knew we were both thinking the same thing.

'There's still something else I have to tell you, Annabel, and it's not pleasant.'

'Oh?'

'About Uncle George. Aunt Rachel telephoned whilst I was at Elspeth's party last night. I cut it short and went over to the hospital. Uncle George had a heart attack on Friday.'

'Oh, no.' Her hands flew up to her face. 'So that's why she rang me to see where she could contact you. I told her you were at Elspeth's, gave her the number. But she didn't tell me about Uncle George.'

'I did wonder how she knew but it wasn't the time to mess about asking. We don't know how it will go – he looked very poorly in intensive care. The thing is Aunt Rachel is with him. Everything between them is OK now. Talk about irony. At the point she almost lost him on Friday, she rediscovered she very much wanted him. And vice versa. Uncle George says everything he wants is now waiting for him and he's determined to get over the heart attack and go home to her.'

'Well good for him. Poor man, he deserves all the happiness he can get now.'

'I think he may recover. Telling me all the details took a lot

out of him – no doubt brought on the attack – but now he's
come clean on who Silvie's father is, it's all over. He can relax
and start to heal.'

'I really hope so.' She set down her empty mug and leaned
forward caressing Leo.

The closeness of her was both unbearable and exquisite. I
let my left arm slide across and rest on her slender shoulders.
There was a silence between us but it was a waiting silence.

'Harry,' she paused. 'I have something to tell you.'

'Will I like it?'

'I hope you'll be pleased.'

'Go on then, tell me.' My left hand was now gently moulding
the soft flesh at the top of her arm. And she wasn't objecting.

'I'm going to have a baby.'

It stopped me for dead. I felt like I'd walked into a brick
wall.

'A . . . a baby?'

'Hmmm.'

'Jeffrey's?' I said foolishly, floundering in an amalgam sea
of disbelief, jealousy and incredible pain. She smiled and gently
removed my arm.

'Darling Harry, it wasn't the milkman.'

'No . . . no, stupid of me . . .'

'Be happy for me.' There was a hint of pleading in her soft
voice.

I looked at her much-loved face and saw the inner glow
illuminating her and shining out through her eyes.

'Annabel,' I said huskily, 'your happiness is all I want.' The
words were true, and the feeling behind them, but the intense
heartbreak I felt was equally true. I heard the clang of the steel
door closing on any lingering hope that we might yet get back
together.

'We didn't plan for this to happen; it's taken both of us
unawares . . .'

I took her hand and stroked my forefinger across it. 'Do you
love him, Annabel?'

'He's good to me, good for me. I feel secure, happy. And I
know he loves me. My future's with him, it has to be.'

'But do you *love* Jeffrey?'

'Harry, I'm having his baby. It's the child that matters. He . . . she, is my first concern, has to be. Please, you do see that, don't you?'

I nodded. 'Of course. And you'll make a marvellous mother.'

'I didn't want to tell you in front of Jeffrey. That's why I came over today.'

'But he knows?'

'Oh, yes, he knows. He's ecstatic with happiness.'

He would be. Bloody hell, I would be. Only I wasn't, because the baby wasn't mine. It was his. But despite that I was happy for *her*.

She leaned into me, gave me a soft kiss. 'Life isn't easy, is it?' she whispered, her eyes large and soulful. Right then I knew that she, too, had heard the clang of the same steel door. My arms went round her very tightly and just for a few precious seconds we clung to each other.

She pulled away first. 'Must be getting back.'

'Yes.' I scooped Leo up and walked her to the door.

Outside the sun was shining. It would be shining all the way for her. I waved goodbye, went back inside the cottage and closed the door.

For the rest of the day I buried myself in work and, by bedtime, bog-eyed from staring at the computer screen for too long, had finished the penultimate chapter. I said goodnight to Leo and climbed the stairs wearily.

I slid between cool sheets and all the thoughts I'd kept at bay during the day washed in like a flood tide. I hadn't wept for years. Not since the horror of Silvie's birth, not even when Mother died. I was gutted losing her, yes, but pleased for her release from suffering. Tears weren't appropriate then. They certainly weren't appropriate now.

But they flowed.

TWENTY-SEVEN

Monday morning. Yesterday's sun was a memory; today it was stair-rodding down. Four things vied for my attention. I wanted to ring Samuel and check on Marriot's whereabouts. Make a start on the last chapter of the book. Visit Mike's stables and talk to Ciggie, offer him an incentive to tell me who was the mystery man behind it all. And lastly, I wanted to take Silvie some flowers. No, not wanted to, needed to.

No contest – I drove to the flower shop.

She was a beautiful woman, Janine, who owned the shop. I walked through the glass door that tinkled my arrival and found her serene and smiling, surrounded by beautiful blooms. I'd bought Silvie flowers from Janine for many years.

After countless tries to guess her favourite I'd discovered the right one and I now only bought freesias, white freesias.

Silvie's pleasure on seeing them was out of all proportion to the cost of the simple flowers. Undoubtedly it was the exquisite perfume that she adored. But the happiness a bunch gave her couldn't be bought with money.

Janine didn't bother to ask, just selected two dozen of the most perfect blooms and wrapped them skilfully into a bouquet.

I laid them carefully on the back seat and their delightful scent filled my car. There was so very little I could do for Silvie but this one thing, I knew, would bring her joy.

It was still pouring when I reached the nursing home. I held the bouquet close to my chest to protect it, dashed from the car to the shelter of the porch and rang the bell.

A nurse opened the door, recognized me and smiled sympathetically. I felt a twinge of unease.

'Silvie?'

'Not too well, I'm afraid, Mr Radcliffe.'

Now I was afraid. 'Can I see her, please?'

'Certainly.'

I followed her and went into Silvie's suite. We crossed the sitting room and walked into the bedroom. The curtains were partially closed, cutting out any strong daylight that might disturb her.

She lay fast asleep, one hand resting on the pillow alongside her cheek. If you didn't know her age, you'd have guessed her to be twelve years old. A vulnerable child. It was very quiet in the room – peaceful. The monitor flickered away unalarmed, showing a steady level of progress.

I tiptoed to the side of her bed, was tempted to take her hand. Like I had taken Annabel's yesterday – a reassuring gesture. Today it would have had the opposite effect. The nurse must have picked up on what I wanted to do.

'Best not to disturb her, Mr Radcliffe,' she whispered.

I nodded.

'She's in a very deep sleep.'

I looked down at her familiar loved face. She was so far away from this bed, the room, the here and now. I felt the clutch of fear freezing my guts. I looked up at the nurse.

'Is she in a coma?'

'Well,' she raised her eyebrows, 'it's a natural sleep, but very deep.'

'That's healing, though, surely?'

'Yes,' she agreed, 'but it depends. Silvie is still fighting the virus.'

'But she's not on oxygen.'

'No, she doesn't need it right now. She's breathing adequately for her needs on her own.'

'She looks at peace . . .' I swallowed.

'Yes.' The nurse smiled sympathetically again. Only I didn't find any comfort in it.

Very gently, I laid the bouquet of white freesias on the bedside table. Perhaps she would be able to smell the perfume even if she couldn't see their pure perfection. I badly wanted to kiss her cheek but held myself back.

'Very thoughtful,' the nurse murmured. 'I'll find a vase for them.' She leaned over and took a sniff. 'Aren't they gorgeous.'

'Is it true she'll be able to smell them even if she's not awake?'

'It's one of our five senses. Certainly people in comas are thought to be able to hear, yes. So why not the sense of smell?'

I nodded and drew away from the bedside. 'I'll leave you to look after her – I know you all go the extra mile.'

'Our job, Mr Radcliffe. Our pleasure, too.'

'I'm so very grateful.' I shook her hand. 'Let me know if I can do anything, even the smallest thing, to help.'

'We will. Don't worry about Silvie, we're doing everything we can. If we need you we will certainly give you a ring.'

'Any time, day, night . . .'

'Of course.'

I took a last look at Silvie's dear face resting on the white pillow close to the white flowers and said a silent prayer.

I drove home in a sombre mood. I'd virtually lost Annabel and, dear God, I hoped I wasn't going to lose Silvie as well.

Once home at Harlequin Cottage I prowled around, poured a stiff drink, downed it in one and eventually went through to the office. Work. That's what I needed to keep unwelcome thoughts from taking charge.

I collated all the final shoeboxes of cuttings, photographs and miscellanea, stacking them in chronological order. The job was very nearly done. All I retained was the tape recording made on Saturday night. The personal memories of Walter Bexon were just what I needed to balance the necessary facts and data of Elspeth's working life. I intended to end the book by showing her as a fully rounded personality, not just an incredibly successful trainer but also a caring woman.

I thought about Victor's rosy view of her as a faithful, loyal wife and gritted my teeth. Tempted to expose the more accurate version, I knew it would achieve no good. In fact, it would cause grief to him as his sustaining illusion shattered into pieces. It was because I genuinely liked the man and felt sorry for the way his life had panned out that I'd purposely remained silent about the long-ago facts I'd discovered on the computer about his family.

Had Victor blustered and taken the stand of denying being Silvie's father, then yes, probably I would have used my knowledge as ammunition to back Uncle George's revelation. Would have told Victor that history was repeating itself. That his pain at Silvie's condition – and as her father it must be ghastly for him; no one living could not feel compassion – had been felt before. Twice over, in fact. Three generations ago in his family line there had been twins born with distressing disabilities akin to my half-sister's shocking physical state. Both had died in their early teens. But I'd kept quiet. Despite his wealth, Victor was an unhappy, lonely man. It would have been utterly callous to have kicked him further down the dark road of depression.

So I worked on, using the page-turning material provided by Walter until Leo's profound yowls reminded me it was getting late. And it certainly was. Hours had passed whilst I'd been glued to the computer. Extremely productive hours, but now I realized I was ravenously hungry. And judging by Leo's decibel level, so was he.

I banged a ready-made lasagne into the oven and opened a tin of cat food. Whilst the food was cooking I made a mug of strong tea and tore off a sizeable chunk from a breadstick, lathered it in butter and chewed away along with the cat. Washing down the crumbs, I reached for my mobile and dialled Samuel's number. He answered straight away.

'Hi, Samuel, it's Harry Radcliffe. We met at Elspeth's party.'

'Hello, Harry, nice to hear from you. How's the book going?'

'Going well, thanks. Very close to finishing it.'

'Glad to hear it. So, what can I do for you?'

'I've a question to ask. It's about you and Marriot playing golf.'

'Oh, yes?'

'Last Thursday afternoon, did you play golf together?'

'Now, let me think. Chloe and my wife took off into town for a spending spree. Well, that's what I call it; they call it "retail therapy". Amounts to the same thing.' He gave a deep bass chuckle. 'Basically, it means spending my money.'

I laughed with him. 'Doesn't seem to bother you much.'

'No, I love my girls. Nothing's too good for them. They light up my life. You married, Harry?'

I wasn't laughing now. 'Living apart, Samuel.'

'No chance of a reunion?'

'None, I'm afraid.'

'Too bad. Like I said to you before, it's all about family.'

'Sure you're right – only wish I'd got one.'

'Elspeth told me you had a half-sister. Sorry about her situation . . . tough on you.'

'Hmmm.' I didn't want to talk about Silvie, had managed to put the anxiety aside whilst I'd been working. I directed the conversation back to my original question.

'You were telling me about the retail therapy for the girls, but what about you? Did you play golf with Chloe's husband?'

'No, no, I remember now, he rang. Said he was double booked, did I mind, he was playing with his father. Well, what can you say? Told him to go right ahead, we'd play another time.' His chuckle vibrated down the line. 'I had the house to myself for a change, had a lovely snooze. Until the girls came back loaded down with bags of shopping.'

'You wouldn't be without them.'

'Too right. Hey, we must get together for a drink sometime.'

'It'll have to be after I finish the book.'

'Oh, sure, business and all that.'

'These next few days should see it done.'

'Great. Looking forward to reading it. Anyway, let me know, eh? We'll fix a date. Got to go. Bye, Harry.'

I put down the mobile and breathed a sigh of relief. I'd found out what I needed to know and he hadn't even queried why I needed the information. But the all-important fact was that Marriot had lied to both Victor and Samuel.

TWENTY-EIGHT

Six o'clock the following morning found me sitting in Mike's office drinking strong, honey-laced coffee. Outside, his stable yard was buzzing with activity.

'You see my dilemma, Mike? Carl was about to name names, and now he's dead.'

'Indeed I do. And I'm with you. We don't want any more deaths. But unless you ask Ciggie, what other leads have you?'

'None.'

'Quite. Which means you *have* to ask him. At the same time, make it immediate and in private. That way nobody else knows you've propositioned him. It's just between the two of you.'

I nodded. 'Makes sense. So what do you suggest?'

He chewed a lip and thought. 'I'll keep him back from the ride out, find some extra job that needs doing. Get all the others out in the string. That way you can move in on him safely. It will look a bit odd but the other lads know what a state he can get into taking drugs. He's headed down the road for sure if he doesn't pack it up. They'll probably think I'm just playing safe. Just make sure you're back in the office before first lot all get back for breakfast.'

'Will do. I'll make dead sure, don't worry. If he won't tell me, well, that's it, but if he does give me a name, maybe I can crack this business.'

'You reckon it's this chap Marriot?'

'Yes. When we get in the same room, the hate that pours from him – well, it's practically tangible. I've never felt anything like that from anyone else, ever.'

'But all you've done is write his mother's biography.'

I shrugged. 'I've turned up one thing he won't like other people knowing but it's pretty trivial . . . just a matter of pride really. Nothing damning as far as I can see.'

'Obviously he sees it differently.' Mike refilled our coffee mugs. 'At least you've about cracked the book. You doubted yourself on that, but I knew you could handle it, so did Annabel.'

'Haaa, Annabel . . .'

'What about Annabel?' He slurped coffee and looked at me over the rim of his mug.

'She came to see me, yesterday. Told me she was expecting Jeffrey's baby.'

'She's pregnant! That's great news. Hard on you, mate, but great news for her.'

'Yes, I know. And I am pleased – for her.'

'Life's all about change, moving forward. You can't hang on to the past, you've got to let go.'

'That's rich, Mike. You've always played it from the view we'd get back together – only a matter of patience. Now you're saying the opposite.'

'I am, Harry, because things aren't the same. You *can't* get

back together; it's no longer just you and her. It's now you, her
– *and Jeffrey's baby.*'

'Yeah, yeah . . . you're right. But I'm still trying to get my
head round it.'

''Course you are, because it wasn't just me who thought it
was possible. You thought it was possible, too. Admit it.'

'OK.' I held up a hand. 'Yes, I did think so, hoped so . . .'

'Let go, Harry. You have to now.'

I drank the last of my coffee. 'Go and organize your troops;
fix it so Ciggie gets left behind.'

He stood up, clapped me on the shoulder and walked out
across the yard. I watched him go. My best friend, longstanding.
He was absolutely right – as always.

I waited and watched the lads mount up, pull out and disappear up the lane towards the gallops. Saw Ciggie, scowling,
take a bucket and yard brush and march off. Slipping out of
the office door, I followed him.

I could hear the noise of water flowing into the bucket and
followed the sound. I came up behind him.

'Short of cash?'

He froze. I walked round in front of him. Taking the wad of
money originally intended for Carl from my pocket, I brushed
my thumb across the edge, riffling the notes. His eyes greedily
followed the movement.

'Like the look of this?'

He glanced quickly at me.

'Are you short of cash?'

He ran a nervous tongue over his lips. 'Isn't everybody?'

'I'm talking about you.' I flicked a nail against the notes.
'Want to earn this little lot?'

He glowered at me under his eyelids. 'How? Why?'

'Why doesn't matter. But the money does. You've got three
seconds . . . then I withdraw my offer.'

'What yer want?'

'A name.'

'What name?'

'The name of the man who hired you.'

He scoffed and spat on the yard. 'Go to hell. He'd kill me,
he would.'

'Who's going to tell him? Are you? I'm certainly not. He won't get to know.'

Ciggie eyed the money. Need and want played a tug-of-war with fear. And the lad was afraid. It showed in his body language, the sweat standing out on his forehead.

'You don't know what he's like. He's a right vicious bastard. Do anything for money, he would.'

'Kill?'

He looked down at his boots and jerked his head. 'Has done.'

I felt a rise of excitement. If he had been convicted his fingerprints would be on record. I asked casually, 'Any pre-cons? Been inside?'

'Did three years for GBH.'

I held back from punching the air. 'Where do you meet? In a pub?'

'Naw, nowhere public. He's not stupid.'

'So?'

'In my car. Safe, y'see, just the two of us, no witnesses. We have a few beers, talk business. I don't do no violence, see, I'm just the decoy car driver.'

'There are no witnesses here, Ciggie. Just tell me his name and you can have this money. Just think how much crack this would buy.'

He cast a furtive glance all around; nobody in sight. 'Give us it.' He made a snatch at the wad but I held on.

'His name, Ciggie.'

'Frank Dunston.' He tugged at the cash.

Despite the jolt of surprise, I held firm. Not Marriot himself, then. A paid piece of muscle. 'From?'

'Christ, give it 'ere, will yer.'

'Tell me,' I said urgently, 'before the string comes back in.'

He shot a fearful glance behind him. 'Grantham, Forge Street.' He tugged the notes violently and I let go. The information was cheap at the price. The money disappeared instantly into his pocket.

Leaving him to his scrubbing, I hastily made for the car park and the last spot I'd seen the dark blue Peugeot. It was still parked up in the same place. I tried the driver's door. My luck was still good. It was unlocked. And inside there were several empty cans of beer. With even more luck, they'd have fingerprints all over them. I whipped my shirt loose at the front to make an improvised sling and, hooking a finger through the hole in the top of each can, I dropped the lot one by one into it.

I hoofed it back to the office and was safely inside when the string came clattering back. But no one had seen me, thank goodness, which meant hopefully Ciggie's life wasn't in danger, and the cans could prove vital evidence.

I found a plastic carrier bag in Mike's kitchen drawer and transferred all the cans into it. Then I went out through a side door to where I'd left my own car parked up out of sight. Unlocking the boot, I put the carrier bag inside, tossing an old jacket on top.

By the time Mike had driven back into the yard after the string, I'd made myself scarce and was back in his kitchen. For Ciggie's sake I needed to keep out of sight. My sense of fair play dictated that because he had given me the information I'd asked for, I needed to keep my part of the bargain and protect *him*.

I filled the kettle and pushed it on to the hot plate of the Aga just as Mike breezed in.

'All OK?'

'Very much so.'

'Was it Marriot?'

'No. It was a Frank Dunston, from Grantham.'

'That figures.'

'You know this guy?'

'We're not close friends but I have heard of him. And not in any complimentary way.'

'Carry on.'

Mike took four slices of wholemeal from the bread bin, stowed them in the toaster and switched it on.

'Firstly, he's a drug pusher. Supplies Ciggie – and relieves him of his wages. Secondly, Dunston's violent . . . bashes first, thinks after.'

'Yeah, Ciggie told me he'd done time for GBH.'

'He's available muscle, for a price.'

'That's what I figured.'

'So it could still be Marriot pulling the strings.'

'Indeed it could.'

The toast jumped up and we each buttered a couple of slices and munched companionably.

'Where does it leave you now, Harry?'

'Pushing on to finish the book. Then I take the manuscript over to Elspeth. Wait for the results from DNA.'

'But the DNA won't match Marriot's.'

'That's true, but if the DNA from the gloves match this Frank Dunston's . . . Don't forget, he's already served time so they'll have his on record.'

'Hmmm . . .' Mike chewed and nodded. 'We can't do the police's job for them but my guess is they'll pull him in for questioning.'

'And he's going to sing loud and clear. He won't go down without incriminating Marriot.'

'Let's hope so. I need to get the book over to Elspeth before the shit hits the fan about Marriot. And another thing – Silvie will be eighteen in a few days' time. That means she'll have the money from the trust fund. Her financial future will be secure, irrespective of my circumstances and ability to pay her care bills.'

Mike nodded. 'Talking of your circumstances, when are you expecting the verdict from the hospital?' He grinned. 'I've horses that need riding. And you're the one I want riding them.'

I looked at him steadily. 'However much you want me riding, Mike, believe me, I want it a thousand times more. I've maybe a couple of physio sessions left to go. After that . . .' I shrugged. 'After that, it's a lap-of-the-Gods job.'

I drove home thinking over the whole affair. It made sense that Marriot had hired a hitman in order to keep his own hands clean. What was not so clear was the reason why.

When I got inside the cottage I found a message on the answerphone. Victor Maudsley had rung the landline earlier this morning.

'Harry, don't know if it's of any interest at all but you know we were talking about playing golf? Well, strange thing is, my all-weather golfing gloves have disappeared. I put them back in the cloakroom drawer last Tuesday, no question. Now, they've gone.'

My heart lurched with misgiving. An idea that had been simmering at the back of my mind began to take on substance. On their own, the individual pieces of information didn't add up, but put together in sequence, a picture formed. Not a pleasant one – and distinctly unwelcome from my own point of view. I needed to get hold of Victor straight away. Ask him for all the facts. I rang his number.

'Hello, Harry, take it you got my message. Funny business.'

'Certainly is. You sure you've not just misplaced them?'

'One hundred per cent sure. They didn't walk on their own. Someone's taken them. Question is, why? They're not worth anything.'

'Is there any evidence of a break-in, Victor?'

'No.'

'Have you had any visitors, people in the house?'

'Yes. But they're all friends. I had a drinks party on Wednesday evening.'

'Can you tell me their names?'

'Well, for a start, all the family members were here—'

'Could you list them for me?'

'OK. Elspeth, Samuel, Marriot and his wife Chloe, and Samuel's wife. Several members of the golf club, Dave and Jack, Larry – oh, yes, and Graham, along with their wags.' He chuckled. 'The current ones . . . don't know some of their names. And then Dan and Gavin, barmen and reception desk staff from North Shore Hotel, good friends of mine. They make me very welcome at the hotel and I always make them welcome here. We all sort of flowed in and out of the downstairs reception rooms, talking, laughing, having drinks. You know the sort of thing.'

'Anything else disappeared, any object of value?'

'No, nothing.'

'Right. Thanks for letting me know. But if the gloves turn up, could you ring me?'

'I certainly will.'

I replaced the receiver and sat thinking about what he'd told me. The answer had to be staring me in the face. Each new fact added to the previous ones and, like a jigsaw, with just one more piece to fit into place, the picture would become clear.

However, it was that one elusive piece that I needed. And it was all to do with motive.

Shaking my head, I decided to stop thrashing my brain and get back to work on the book. It was imperative I cracked on, got it finished and handed over to Elspeth.

I logged on, transcribed the rest of the taped interview with Walter Bexon. I couldn't believe how easy it was. He'd done me a great favour with his recollections, anecdotes and personal reminiscences. I typed away, editing as I went, and the last half chapter all but wrote itself. Stopping only to grab a sandwich and a mug of builders' tea at lunchtime, I forged on. By nightfall, tired yet exhilarated, I typed the last paragraph, emphasizing that at the very top of her professional career, Elspeth proved she was her own woman, had her priorities firmly in the right order – choosing to be at the bedside of her sick child rather than at York races watching her horse Purplesilk win the Yorkshire Cup.

I finished typing, pressed save and sat back, rubbing my aching eyes. It was finished. There had been times I doubted it ever would be, but now it was in the bag and I had a good feeling about it. A warm glow spread through my insides. I was satisfied with the work.

And as I sat reading over the last pages, the final elusive piece of jigsaw slid effortlessly into place. I knew beyond doubt what the motive was, saw the whole picture in Technicolor. Knew the police were wasting their time, could have told them they were looking at it back to front.

And that was my fault. I'd sent them in totally the wrong direction.

TWENTY-NINE

My mobile rang at three fourteen a.m. Struggling up from the deepest depths of sleep, I reached across to the bedside table.

'Yes?'

'Matron speaking, Mr Radcliffe, from the nursing home.'

My heart felt like it had been punched. I knew what was coming. I was instantly awake, felt icy cold . . . and sick, very sick.

'Could you come straight away?'

'On my way, Matron. Thank you for contacting me.'

I lurched into the bathroom, threw up violently, splashed cold water over my face and neck. Back in the bedroom I dragged on trousers, a shirt, snatched up my mobile and ran downstairs.

I drove like a man out of his mind, and maybe I was. I didn't know if I would be in time or whether Silvie was already dead. Hospitals had a habit of ringing in the early hours and asking you to step on it. The impression they gave was if you raced fast enough you'd make it in time.

What they didn't say was the truth. That however fast you ran, it was already too late. I knew how the system worked. I'd been here before, firstly with my father and, far more recently, with my mother.

I screamed the tread off the tyres. And prayed. Perhaps this time the system had failed and I could reach her in time. Spun the car off the A52, floored it down back lanes with black running rivers of hedge on either side penning me in. No other cars on the move, only me. And coming along just for the ride was the shadow of death. However fast I drove, I couldn't shake it off. I turned down the last lane, the nursing home a sombre dark shape at the end of the drive.

I screeched to a stop outside, flung myself out of the car and hammered on the front door. A light came on and Matron herself let me in.

'Am I in time . . . is Silvie still . . .?'

She was gently shaking her head. 'I'm very sorry. She died a short time ago.'

I slumped against the wall. My panic-stricken driving hadn't been needed. It had already been too late. The system, of course. This was how it worked. And I'd known. Of course I'd known. Had still hoped with every vestige of my being that this time there might be a chance of at least saying goodbye to her. But she hadn't waited for me. And now she was gone.

'I want to see her, please.'

Matron nodded. 'Of course.' She led the way down the familiar hallway to the suite and drew up a chair beside the bed.

Silvie lay in very much the same position as I'd seen her last. One hand still on the pillow, the white freesias perfuming the room. The monitor was silent. Its job done. Silvie's face was serene, her spirit gone to where it should be.

I sat down heavily on the chair.

'I'll leave you with her. Take all the time you want. If you need me, just press the bleeper.'

I nodded mutely. She left me in peace to my memories and my grief. A picture of Silvie's birth flashed through my mind. The full horror of her condition was instantly apparent. My immediate reaction then was it would be a blessing if she died. It was a view my mother didn't share. She had loved Silvie absolutely and unconditionally. And as the days and weeks passed, my feelings towards Silvie reversed. She might never go to school nor have a job, yet she still contributed to life simply by being herself.

She brought light and love into our little family and, since Father's death, those two things had been sadly lacking. Carrying her cross without complaint, she never knew she was disabled, and was certainly never a burden. Now she was gone, her cross lifted from her. And I couldn't wish her back to pick it up again.

But I was going to miss her terribly. The gap she'd left in my life felt like a chasm. I leaned over and kissed her dear face – she was still softly warm. My tears were warm too as, unashamedly and unchecked, they ran down my face and dripped on to her cheek. Tenderly, I stroked them away, sat numbly by her bedside and held her hand. Time didn't matter and I had no idea how long I'd been there.

But something penetrated my cocoon of silent communion. A slight sound and a movement of air behind me had me turning my head. The blow landed on the side of my face and not, as intended, on the back of my skull. It knocked me from the chair, had me sprawling on the floor. The blow was sufficiently hard and heavy enough to draw blood. I was dazed, my head ringing. Had it landed on the intended spot, it would have rendered me unconscious.

In a black balaclava, my attacker was now lunging towards Silvie as she lay on her death bed, his arm upraised, a monkey wrench already arcing downwards aimed at her face. I slammed an elbow against the bleeper and grabbed his knee joint with my right hand. Throwing my weight against his leg, I bent the knee backwards. Heard him scream out with pain and felt the swish of air as the steel wrench came down, missed Silvie and connected with my shoulder.

All I'd had time to put on was a shirt, no jersey, no jacket. The force of the impact ripped open the soft material and the even softer flesh beneath. Blood spurted up as I dropped back to the floor. The pain was agonizing, shooting up through my spinal cord nerves right to the top of my head. The whole of my nervous system screamed in silent protest. I bellowed aloud. As a jockey, I was well used to absorbing the pain of falls, but this pain was centred on a small area. Before I could struggle to my feet he was on me, raining blows indiscriminately. My entire body was on fire, blood flowing from a dozen wounds.

Still on my knees, I jabbed my elbow backwards, felt it connect with something soft, heard him whistle for breath, knew I'd winded him. Pivoted round and followed the blow with a double barrel kick from both feet powered by white-hot rage coupled with grief.

'You're too late, you bastard!' I yelled. 'She's already gone home.'

He flew backwards. The wrench left his hand and skittered away across the floor. Before he could rise I landed another blow to his solar plexus that had him doubled up, gasping, retching. Snatching a handful of hair at the back of his head, I forced his neck back just short of the snapping point and whipped off his black balaclava. I didn't recognize him, but I would never forget his face. At that moment the door of Silvie's room burst open and two men followed by the matron erupted into the room.

Taking in the scene, the burly security man threw one arm around the man's throat, bending him backwards. Ignoring the shrieks of pain, he grabbed the intruder's right wrist, forced it round behind his back and held him in an arm-lock impossible to break. The second man, with lightning reaction, slid his leather belt from around his waist and hobbled the man's knees together.

'Get him out of this room! Now!' Matron's face was contorted; she was barely able to contain her anger.

They half carried, half dragged him out and down the hallway.

'Are you all right, Mr Radcliffe?' The anger in Matron's eyes died and they filled with concern.

'I'm OK, I think. Nothing broken.'

'Let me see the damage.'

You didn't argue with Matron and I allowed her to gently push me down in the chair and explore my shoulder with experienced fingers.

'Hmmm, nothing broken, certainly, but you'll need two or three stitches in the top of your arm. There's a jagged tear.' She explored further. 'And a couple more above your cheekbone. Most of the other injuries are minor. They'll heal. The doctor's still here; we called him in for Silvie and he's treating another patient as well. I'll ask him to stitch you up when he's free.' She looked down at me with a tiny smile, 'You do attract the heavy mob, don't you?'

'He was here to kill Silvie.'

Her face blanched with shock. 'My God!'

'He didn't expect to meet me.'

'Obviously not. Thank goodness you managed to set off the alarm. It could have been much worse for you.'

'Hmm . . . I was quite glad your own heavies came to the rescue.'

'Do you know who the man is?'

'He's the same one who broke in before. I reckon it could be Frank Dunston. He's got a reputation for paid violence.'

Outside we could hear the wail of a police siren as the car came scorching down the drive.

'Here come the cavalry,' Matron said. She leaned over the bed, her face softening, and smoothed the bed sheet that didn't need smoothing. But I recognized the gesture of love.

I looked across at Silvie, still serene, unaffected in any way by the recent trauma. Lost to me now forever, but gone in her own and God's right time, not dictated by someone else.

Suddenly, I felt very tired.

*   *   *

A couple of hours later, stitched up like a mailbag, I parked the Mazda and unlocked the cottage door. Whatever painkillers they'd pumped into me were working but they made everything seem very unreal. It felt like my feet were stepping on feathers, not connecting with the ground at all.

I made a slow, weaving assent up the stairs and, pausing only to drop my clothes in a heap, I crawled between blessed cool sheets.

The painkillers must have been good at knocking out too, as when I finally surfaced it was almost dusk. I tottered to the bathroom, feeling like hell, washed down a couple more of the pills to blot everything out, and went back to bed.

THIRTY

Everything is supposed to look better in the morning. But I couldn't subscribe to that. I'd had very nearly twenty-four hours continuous sleep and whilst I physically felt much better and on the mend, it hadn't altered the fact that Silvie was dead. My emotions were still red raw. It was going to take more than sleep to heal them.

However, I took comfort from the knowledge that Frank Dunston was now languishing in a cell. He could be facing the double charges of the attempted murder of Silvie and the actual murder of Carl Smith.

What I needed to do now was to get myself over to Elspeth's and deliver the biography. But before that, I needed to notify everyone of Silvie's death.

I checked the time on my mobile. It was just gone seven, barely a respectable time to ring anyone, but I wanted to get the ordeal over because, for me, talking about Silvie's death was emotionally agonizing – and there were four people who needed to know, five if I counted the solicitor. But since his office didn't open for another two hours, I relegated him for later. Victor was the obvious choice to begin with; he was officially the next of kin, but before I could dial, the mobile shrilled. It was Aunt Rachel. Bubbling over with good news.

'I know it's dreadfully early, Harry, but I felt sure you'd want to know about George. The hospital gave him the all clear last night, totally out of danger. They've even moved him out of intensive care. Isn't that wonderful?'

'It's great news, Aunt Rachel. I'm very pleased for you both.'

'He should be home next week. Then we can re-start our lives. We were thinking of a cruise later in the year.'

'Sounds like a marvellous idea, getting away from it all, relaxing, yes, a great idea.'

'Harry . . .' She hesitated. 'Is anything wrong? You sound . . . oh, I don't know, strained, somehow.'

'I was going to ring you later, Aunt Rachel, and tell you what's happened, ask you to let Uncle George know when he's strong enough.'

'What are you saying?'

'I've some very bad news. I'm afraid it might upset Uncle George and that's the last thing I'd want right now.'

'Tell me, Harry. I'll use my judgement when I break whatever the news is.'

'It's Silvie . . . She died . . . yesterday.'

'Oh, no, how awful.'

'Yes.'

'George will be upset, even though he wasn't her . . .'

'Yes, exactly, it's OK, Aunt Rachel. I'll leave it to you to tell him, when he's stronger. Better go, I have to let her father know.'

'Of course. And I'm so sorry. Let me know when the funeral's fixed.'

'I will.' She rang off. I dialled Victor's number. His response was predictably more emotional.

'So young,' he moaned, 'so bloody tragic. It must be dreadful for you—'

'Please, Victor, no sympathy. I can't handle it.'

'Of course, I understand. It's knocked me over. And I never ever saw the poor child.' He choked back a sob. 'Keep me informed, you know, when all the formalities are fixed. I'll see you at the funeral.'

'Will do.'

'And Harry, don't worry about the solicitor, I'll go and see him. One less job for you to do.'

'Very thoughtful, Victor. Much appreciated.'

'Least I can do.'

'On a different subject, I've finished Elspeth's biography. I'm going over to Unicorn Stables later this morning to give it to her.'

'That's good news, anyway. Hope she likes it.'

'Yes, so do I. Bye, Victor. I'll be in touch.'

Mike was truly shocked by the news, as I knew he would be.

'Do you want to come over to the stables, mate? Take your mind off it a bit.'

'Thanks, but no. I can't, Mike. I'd like to, believe me – your place represents sanity and I could do with a large dose, but there's something I have to do. I've finished the biography and I'm taking it over to Elspeth's this morning.'

'Pleased you've finished it, but then, I never doubted you could do the job.'

'What I'd like to ask is if I give you a ring when I get to Unicorn Stables, could you provide back-up if things turn rough?'

'Sure thing. I told you I'm here for you when you need help. So, what do you want me to do?'

'Could you meet me outside the stables and park up out of sight? Give me, say, half an hour to speak with Elspeth, and then if I haven't come back out, steam on in.'

'Sure, no problem. Tell me what time I need to meet you.'

'How about ten o'clock? That suit you?'

'Do fine, yes.'

'Oh, and Mike, don't let it throw you, but my left arm's in a sling, better in a few days. It's one of the reasons why I could use reserve muscle.'

'Sounds like it. See you there, Harry.'

And that left just one more person to ring.

'Annabel Radcliffe, can I help you?'

'Hello, Annabel.'

'Harry, darling. Lovely to hear from you.'

'Hmmm . . . perhaps it may not be, my love.'

'Why ever not?'

'Bad news. I can't wrap it up and soften it or I would, Annabel. Silvie's died.'

'Oh my God! I thought she was getting better.'

'We all did. I was called out to the nursing home the night before last. But you know hospitals. They'd rather tell you the bad news face-to-face instead of down a phone.'

'Did you say the night before last? Why didn't you tell me straight away?' There was annoyance as well as grief in her voice.

'Because that bastard in the balaclava arrived a while after I'd got there. I was sitting beside Silvie, just holding her hand—'

'Was she still alive then?'

'No. I wanted time with her, Annabel, just a little bit of time . . . you understand?'

'Yes, I do, Harry, of course I do. I'm so, so sorry. I wish I could be beside you now, hold you . . .'

I sighed. 'You and me both. Anyway, that man came in through the window, all but laid me out with a monkey wrench and then took a swing at Silvie.'

'No! Harry, I can't bear it.' She began to sob.

'Steady on, girl, steady. I clouted him before the wrench hit Silvie; it connected with my left shoulder instead.'

'How badly are you injured, Harry? Tell me the truth.'

'Not badly injured. Had a few stitches put in and the doctor says I have to wear a sling for a few days to support my shoulder whilst it heals, but nothing more serious.'

'Oh, thank heavens. What about that evil swine?' It was rare that Annabel used strong language or spoke ill of anyone and it was a good yardstick to her depth of feelings.

'He's been carted away by the boys in blue. He's in a cell as we speak. I think his name's Frank Dunston and that he was responsible for Carl Smith's murder.'

'Really?'

'Hmm, but we can leave all that to the police.'

'Yes.' Her voice dropped to a whisper. 'When's Silvie's funeral?'

'Don't know yet, my love. Have to arrange all that with the undertaker. I've told Victor and he's sorting things with the solicitor to help me out. As soon as I get a date fixed, I'll ring you.'

'Will it be at the local church?'

'Oh, yes. Mother would have wanted that, plus I'd like her buried close to Mother's grave. Seems fitting, don't you think?'

'I do, Harry. I do, my darling.'

'Have to go now, Annabel. I've finished my work on Elspeth's biography and I'm going over this morning to hand it to her.'

'Well done. Always knew you'd do a good job.'

Her voice had started to quaver and I knew she was trying to finish the call before dissolving into tears. Coward that I am, I didn't want to hear her break down, or I would be joining her.

'Must go. Ring you tonight.'

'Bless you, darling. Bye bye . . .' She was clearly weeping as she put down the phone.

I walked stiffly and painfully through to the kitchen and made a very strong coffee. On cue, Leo pushed his way through the cat flap and stalked over to me, demanding breakfast. I fed us both before going up for a long shower. The hot water helped enormously with loosening up my battered body and I began to feel a great deal better. I needed to. I had to face Elspeth – and possibly, Marriot – in a short while. And it was going to be potentially very nasty.

I dressed in my best dark suit. Very smart, very James Bond – except putting my arm in the sling rather spoilt the effect, but there it was.

I made sure my mobile was charged and carefully put it into my right-hand pocket. I would need it when I got to Unicorn Stables. Picking up the precious hard copy of the manuscript, I locked the cottage door and crunched over the gravel to the Mazda. The postman arrived at the gate.

'One letter for you, Harry. Hope it's good news.'

'Thanks, Phil. I could use some.' I stuffed it in my inside breast pocket. I'd read it later.

Half a mile from Unicorn Stables, I pulled into the side of the lane and dialled Mike's number. We agreed to meet fifty yards from the entrance gates, leave him sitting in his car whilst I went on up to Elspeth's house.

'Good luck, mate.' He gave me a cool, scrutinizing stare. 'Sure you're up for this on your own, especially with that?' He nodded towards the sling.

'Yes, Mike,' I said. 'I've worked out what the motive is. It was staring me in the face. It's taken a long time because there are two interwoven threads, not just one, but I've finally unravelled it. Now I have to put it all to bed.'

He gave me a short nod. 'Watch yourself. Half an hour and I'm coming in after you.'

I drove away, through the gate, up the drive to the big house. I'd phoned Elspeth a little earlier, made sure she knew I was coming. Was quite sure she in turn would make sure Marriot knew. Parking up near the front door, I took out my mobile and dialled. Spoke very shortly to the man who answered then quickly ended the call. Done. Now I was committed, couldn't back off.

I reached up and knocked on the door.

THIRTY-ONE

'Harry. Welcome, do come on in.' Elspeth smiled and held the door wide.

It reminded me of what the spider said to the fly.

'Elspeth.' I stepped inside.

'Have you brought my book?'

'I have.' I set down the last of the shoeboxes on her hall table and fished awkwardly in my briefcase for the manuscript.

'So what happened to your arm?'

'Accident. Nothing serious.'

She nodded, her thoughts already focused on the biography. 'Come through to the office. Coffee's waiting in there.' She led the way, hugging the block of printed foolscap to her breast. 'Help yourself, Harry. Cream, honey.' She tinkled a laugh. 'I remembered, you see. Pour one for me whilst you're about it. Oh, and take off your jacket, make yourself at home.' I humoured her and did as she asked.

She sank down on the swivel chair by the desk, moved the heavy glass ashtray, now empty of cigarette butts, out of the way and placed the paper on top of the desk. Flicking through the first few pages, she lifted her head and smiled. 'I think I picked the right man for the job.'

'Do you, Elspeth?' I handed her a cup of coffee.

'Hmmm.' She took a sip. 'Sure do.'

'Well, I've made it as factually correct as I could, whilst maintaining your reputation.'

'Which is what I wanted you to do.'

'I have to say your party on Saturday helped enormously. Especially the input from Walter Bexon.'

'Good.'

I drank some of the excellent coffee whilst surreptitiously checking my watch. Ten minutes gone – twenty to go, possibly.

'I have some bad news, Elspeth.'

'Oh.'

'My half-sister, Silvie . . .'

She lifted her gaze from the book. 'Yes?'

'She's died.'

'Before she reached her birthday.' It was said very quietly.

'That's right.'

Elspeth released a long sigh. She added a dash of cream to her cup and stirred.

'Victor was her father, wasn't he?'

'Yes, but then you knew that, didn't you?'

'Not to start with, no.'

'How much *do* you know, Harry?' She continued to drink her coffee, watching me.

'I know Marriot didn't want me to write this book.'

'True.' She nodded.

'So I had to ask myself the question, why? What does he have to hide?'

'And have you found out?'

'I believe so.'

The office door closed very quietly but we both heard it and looked up. Marriot was standing just inside the room, leaning back against the door.

'Talking about me, Radcliffe?' His eyes, cold as a snake, were fixed on mine. I felt the adrenaline kick in and my heartbeat increase.

'Admit it, Marriot, you didn't want me turning up your little secret, did you? So you tried to scare me off, arranged the horse-box road block with Carl Smith. And when that didn't work, you arranged a little spot of arson, again using Carl – which also failed.' His jaw jerked and locked. He didn't deny it. 'I figured whatever secret you were trying to hide, it must be pretty important. And it took me a long time to unravel the trail. But I did, in the end.'

'Shut up.' He raised a fist in my face.

'I had to decide what was the most important thing in your life – once I'd done that, the other bits of jigsaw pieces started to fall into place.'

'Shut your mouth or I'll shut it for you.'

'Marriot!' Elspeth rapped out. 'Don't be so stupid.'

'At first I thought it was because you had a phobia about hospitals.' He drew in a sharp breath. 'You know, a guy wouldn't want that made public, make him look a wimp. But it wasn't that, no, it lacked clout. Wasn't important enough. There had to be something else, something *vital*.'

'I'm warning you, shut your mouth.' His hands clenched and unclenched.

'Control yourself, Marriot,' Elspeth screeched. 'Do you want an assault charge?'

'The only thing I didn't know, Marriot, was why you lied to Victor and Samuel.'

He laughed harshly. 'Got you. You think I'm going to tell *you*, asshole?'

'No. I'll tell *you*. Aunt Rachel and her niece were at the hospital. At the fertility clinic. They saw you coming out, face down in your boots.' He froze. 'Couldn't reverse the effects or help you, could they?'

'Bullshit!'

'What you didn't tell Chloe when you married her was that when you were twelve you had the mumps at the same time as you contracted glandular fever. Walter Bexon let it slip when I was taping his reminiscences. It left you infertile. And nothing means more to Samuel than family. Both he and Chloe are waiting for you to give them an heir to the Simpson business. And it's not going to happen. So how long will your marriage last – and your posh house and your lucrative job – when they know?'

With a roar of rage, he took me by surprise and flung himself at me. Fury lent him strength and I found myself on the floor. His boot lashed out and he deliberately kicked my injured shoulder. The pain was something else. I gagged and gasped for breath, dragged myself on to my knees, saw him coming at me again. I grabbed a corner of the desk to pull myself up. Waves of red-hot pain swamped me. I was not going to withstand a long session of fighting. He would be bound to win.

My fingers knocked against the ashtray. I picked it up as Marriot leant over to put the boot into my shoulder again. As he drew back his leg for maximum power, I slammed the heavy glass down on to his head. The impact laid him out cold. Whilst I gasped for breath, riding out the raging agony ripping through me, he lay unconscious on the floor.

Elspeth, white-faced, held herself rigid against the desk.

'And you didn't know, to begin with, did you, Elspeth,' I gasped, 'that Marriot ordered those attacks on me?' She slowly shook her head. 'You didn't know because you were busy organizing Frank Dunston to kill Silvie.' Her mouth dropped open. 'Oh, yes, there were two threads to this vendetta. Firstly, Marriot, in his selfishness, trying to protect his future easy life. And then, secondly, there was you.'

'What about me, Harry?' Her voice was low, venomous.

'You couldn't bear to see Silvie turn eighteen and lay claim to her trust fund. A fund set up by Victor. You thought the money rightly belonged to Marriot as Victor's legitimate son. So you set about trying to eliminate Silvie. And had Carl Smith killed to shut his mouth before he could blow the whistle on Marriot. You were all set to pin the murders on Victor, weren't you, Elspeth? That's why you stole his golfing gloves, gave them to Dunston to use at Leicester races. 'Course, they had to be worn over rubber gloves because of DNA, but they were supposed to be discovered with the traces of Carl's blood on them.'

She leaned back against the desk, a twisted smile on her face. 'Anything else?'

'You really should have passed your audition for RADA, Elspeth; you're a superb actress. All that stuff about being friends with Victor after Marriot's marriage, playing happy families – it was all a smoke screen for Samuel's benefit. You never forgave Victor, did you?'

'What a busy little boy.' Her face contorted. 'Yes, it was me. A mother will do *anything* for her child, didn't you know that?'

'I've just found out.'

Her hand snaked round; she was holding a gun. 'I keep this little beauty in my desk drawer for emergencies. You never know when you'll get an intruder.' She was laughing, hideously high-pitched, eyes wild.

Bringing the gun up, she pointed it at my chest. 'Do you know why I wanted *you* to do the biography?'

I shook my head, playing along with her, playing for time, silently praying Mike would come. The twenty minutes must surely be up now.

'Because it had a kind of irony to it. Painting me in glowing colours, showing what a great woman I am.' She paused for breath, panting heavily, waving the gun up and down. 'And all the time, I was the woman who was going to destroy your sister.'

My guts twisted with revulsion. She was obviously raving mad.

Come on, Mike, come on . . . I prayed desperately.

She laughed hysterically. 'But I can't let you destroy Marriot, you do see that, don't you, Harry?' Then she fired.

The bullet struck me, the impact spinning me round, my injured shoulder pumping blood.

'Couldn't hit a barn door,' she sang out, still laughing crazily. And then she deliberately took aim a second time.

Out of the corner of my eye, I saw the door opening. Elspeth, facing me, was unaware of it. In two strides, Mike came up behind her and threw both arms around her in a pincer move-ment, forcing the gun upwards. She screamed and the gun went off, plaster showering down as the bullet buried itself in the ceiling.

For a few seconds Mike struggled to hold her, then managed to fling her down on the floor beside Marriot. We both fell on top of her, pinning her down.

Outside in the hallway, there was the sound of running feet and three policemen burst into the room.

EPILOGUE

Rain had fallen during the night. The old flagstones leading from the lychgate to the church door were gleaming wetly in the weak sunlight struggling to break through the clouds.

I felt Annabel squeeze my right elbow reassuringly as we led the rest of the mourners into the church. Mozart's twenty-first was playing – my choice. Silvie was all love, through and through. She was the nearest thing to a sinless human being I'd ever met, which was why I'd chosen a white coffin for her. On the top of it lay a spray of white freesias.

It was a beautiful service, with a simple hymn, 'All Things Bright and Beautiful'. And a perfect poem, 'Miss me, but let me go', simple words but oh so true.

We laid her to rest in the cemetery close to Mother's grave.

Then Annabel, Sir Jeffrey, Aunt Rachel and I took ourselves off to Mike's house for a wake that wasn't. It ended more like an intimate family party with memories and jokes, anecdotes and laughter, and yes, salted here and there with tiny grains of grief. But it left us all lifted, accepting and lightened the day.

'How did you puzzle everything out, Harry?' Sir Jeffrey held out his cup for a refill of tea.

'I didn't know Elspeth wanted me out of the picture – I was sure it was Marriot. Which, of course, it was to begin with. He was running scared for his own future, his marriage and job. Don't forget he was dependent upon Samuel for his financial security. But Samuel most definitely wanted a grandchild. He told me so himself. It was going to come out eventually if I completed the biography. But Elspeth wanted me to finish the book. She was putting pressure on me to hurry up and finish it. Only in the last few days did she want me gone. She'd just found out Marriot had paid Carl, so would be facing charges if it came out. As a mother, she couldn't allow that. So she had Carl Smith murdered. And set out to frame Victor – stole his golfing gloves. Paid Frank Dunston to use them.

'Dunston was keeping an eye on me at the races, saw his chance, took it upon himself to use my dad's hickory stick to try and set me up – insurance for himself, I think. And my quick phone call to the police before I went in to confront Elspeth was my own additional bit of insurance.'

'Didn't trust me, you see.' Mike grinned.

'But how did all this affect Silvie?' Annabel nibbled on a salmon sandwich.

'Elspeth never forgave Victor, although she pretended to after Marriot married into the Simpson family. She wanted the trust fund money to go to Marriot. If Silvie reached her eighteenth birthday, it would be lost to him.'

'I still don't see how you figured it all out,' Mike said, shaking his head and smiling. 'You could set up as a private eye.'

'It helped when Aunt Rachel told me she'd seen Marriot at the fertility clinic. And it was Annabel that gave me the clue that sent me off down the right road.'

'I did? What did I say?'

I smiled across at her and Sir Jeffrey. 'Your baby is what matters most . . . It made me realize how a woman's personality changes when she has a child.'

'Oh my dear, it's wonderful you're pregnant.' Aunt Rachel beamed at Annabel.

'Yes, it's fabulous.' Sunshine and pure happiness flooded her face.

'The very best thing that could happen to you.' There was a wistfulness behind her words.

Annabel and I exchanged a swift glance.

'He, or she, will need a godmother,' Annabel murmured. 'It's a little premature, Rachel, but do you think you could do the honours? And George as godfather, maybe?'

Now happiness spread across Aunt Rachel's face. 'Oh, yes, please.'

I stretched across to refill her drink, felt a stiffness in my jacket inside pocket. I set down the teapot, fished in my pocket and took out the letter the postman had given me.

'It's from the hospital. I'd forgotten all about it.'

An expectant silence fell.

'Kick on, Harry,' Annabel urged. 'Open it.'

I slit open the envelope, took out the letter. Read it quickly. Then looked up to find them all looking at me, waiting.

I felt a silly grin spreading across my face.

'Better saddle me a horse, Mike. I'll be riding out first lot tomorrow.'

CPSIA information can be obtained at www.ICGtesting.com
Printed in the USA
BVOW02*1051051115

424636BV00001B/4/P